BLIND
TONGUES

Also by Sterling Watson

WEEP NO MORE MY BROTHER
THE CALLING

BLIND
TONGUES

STERLING WATSON

**DELTA
FICTION**

For my mother, Polyana Watson

Published by
Dell Publishing
a division of
Bantam Doubleday Dell Publishing Group, Inc.
666 Fifth Avenue
New York, New York 10103

LIBRARY OF CONGRESS CATALOGING IN PUBLICATION DATA

Watson, Sterling.
Blind tongues / Sterling Watson.
p. cm.
ISBN 0-440-55007-6
I. Title.
PS3573.A858B56   1989   88-23730
813'.54—dc19   CIP

Printed in the United States of America

February 1989

10 9 8 7 6 5 4 3 2 1

The author wishes to thank the State of Florida and the Virginia Center for the Creative Arts for generous assistance during the writing of this book.

One

Behind her eyes, Merelene Durham was searching for something. The rain stuttered in Bedlam's voices on the camellia leaves in the yard. The dawn jiggled at her bedroom windows like the frantic light of silent films. She was waking, so she held to sleep.

She hoped to find this thing soon for she had been seeking it all night, in all the nights. Her sleep was a swim underwater. The river surface above was a distorted lens. The cold dim deeps below were the place of dreams. Through the surface she could see the bent shapes of the new day she must take into her hands. Then in her hands, dry in the logic of dreams, she held an official document. She read from it.

You have got to get up and go now. Your preparations are made. You know what you have to do. Take your son from his sleep. Open the door of this day to him quickly and keep things moving along.

In anger, she raised the hand holding the paper and broke the surface of the water.

She lay awake composing a letter to her departed husband, knowing she would never send it.

Dear Mayfield: I have just received in the mail an official order from the State of Florida. For years I have been afraid of it, and now it has come. I don't know what to do. Let me tell you about it, Mayfield.

Oh, I know you don't want to hear from me. That I am forgotten in you like the war and before the war, things you told me you had to forget. But I remember our life and now comes this summons in the mail, and I have to send one of my own to you.

In the letter, a man orders me to take Roland three hundred miles south to the Sunshine State Training Center. The State has judged it this way against me because he runs away, and because he made his one mistake. It is a week since the letter came and I do nothing about it. I don't want the boy to leave this place in a social worker's car. I get up in the morning and the letter is here on the night table and when I go to bed at night, it's the same.

I go to work and I come home and the letter is here like a shame. It is not like me to let it sit. So I am writing to the long-lost or the carefully hidden Mayfield. I feel you out there, sometimes as close as when you were the scoundrel hero of this town, these woods, these waters. I feel your fingers on the strings of my nerves and know you are still somewhere, hiding yourself like Howard Hughes.

It is a weekend. I have done all the chores. Not so many anymore. We don't make work by the way we live. Time on my hands. I go in circles. Inside me too, things go round, and each turn I come to this letter.

I tell you frankly, I have had to reach a long way back to start the words coming. I have had to remember you as you were to me early, or else my pride stops this pen. It is what we were to each other that begins this letter like the sun melts ice. And now I am started, am I not?

I remember how it was when you first came to my town. You were tall and lean and serious, above everything serious. That's what we said, the girls. Our mothers said it too but meant a different thing and we knew what they meant.

Your eyes were beautiful eyes, maybe your prettiest trait. Do you mind that word for a man's face? It applies. Your arms were long and sunbrown and always ready to do something. But it's your eyes I think about, still, late at night. Before I take that long slide down my pillow into the warm river of my sleep, it's your eyes I see. They never look at me. They look inside at you. And if I look at them, look closely in my sleep, for now I have slid and I am swimming, I think I see him, the Mayfield you hid so well. And always, just when I am close enough, and peering in, the dream breaks against the rocky bank, and I lose him. Again.

She could not keep it going. Something in her stopped it. What was left, what he had been to her, she could not write in any letter. There were things she hadn't said to him in the best of times. These were not the best of times.

She lay in her warm bed knowing the letter, when she wrote it, would be formal. She would make it a business communication because she could not bring herself to make it anything else.

And what if it never reached him, or he did not reply, because he wasn't able to reply or didn't want to? There was always the chance he had really disappeared.

In a drawer beside the bed, she kept the clipping. It was from the Jacksonville *Times-Union*, and dated a year ago. Someone had cut it and sent it to her without a note, or return address. The postmark was Atlanta.

Millionaire Recluse Calls Himself Successful

Mason Field, dubbed "the Redneck Tycoon" by *Fortune* magazine, was in Jacksonville today, promoting his perfume and powder empire, Kismet-Tique Enterprises.

Critics have called Kismet-Tique the scam of the decade while admirers call it creative corporate structuring.

In a rare public appearance, the affable, eccentric Field, always with his entourage of aides and entrepreneurs-in-training, visited shopping malls in the Jacksonville area, lecturing in a rambling style on "the self-made self," and the virtues of franchising. The graying but still handsome Field, whose suits are from Savile Row, told listeners that his "just folks" character was formed on the native soil and his money was made the hard way. Field, who has been called "charismatic," spoke softly but passionately to the obvious delight of crowds at the Oak Ridge and University malls before making a surprise exit by helicopter from the parking lot of the Countryside Sears, Roebuck Department Store.

Watching the helicopter ascend, Sears store manager, Ernest Barselm, remarked that cosmetic sales would rise with it.

Could this Mason Field be her own lost Mayfield? She had watched the papers for a photograph, but Mason Field had dropped out of sight. The reporters called it his mysterious disappearance. If it was him, it was his second disappearance, and the mystery was that a man who had walked away from this dusty coastline of mullet boats and tourist restaurants, taking only what he could carry, had walked until the smell of the Hudson Paper Company pulpwood mill was gone from his nostrils, until the last image and odor and familiar word was behind him, had somehow arrived at perfume and powder and helicopters. Like a singer or an actor, like Elvis the King, her old husband was a name in the public mind.
"Mudder?"
Slightly bowlegged and ridiculous in one of the lawyer's

cast-off nightshirts, the boy Roland stood at her bedroom door. She rose in the white cloud of her gown, and they were like two ghosts in this dark house with the thunder and rain dying away on the Gulf of Mexico. It was time to get him ready. He stood watching her, aware only of placing his feet into the beginning of another day.

He was tall and thin and raven-haired and had his father's lantern jaw. His eyes were large and dark and steady. Her own father had once gazed at little Roland and said, "Mayfield might have made that child himself, for all of you he seems to own." It was true of Roland's looks, but it had been spoken before the raging fevers of encephalitis had taken Roland's mind, before they knew how much or how little there would be of her in him. No one knew him as she did, and she knew he was more than his father's comeliness, the beautiful hair and eyes, the strong jaw of a matinee idol. Now he was a man, in his way, and she, not Mayfield, had made him one.

Because she feared she would cry for all he did not know, she turned him by the shoulder without looking into his eyes and aimed him at the shower. She must not let herself think of all the last things, last times this day promised them both. But a little, when he had turned the corner, and just before the rush and patter of the shower, a little, she knew the void this house would hold when she returned this afternoon.

With Roland on the seat beside her, and between them a stack of his picture books, she left the little town of Swinford. Shaking off the white powder of its crushed oystershell roads, her tires found the singing pavement of U.S. 27, and she aimed them from this backward county, from the lap of placid Gulf water toward the shores of Okeechobee, from one remoteness to another—the place where the State of Florida in its wisdom chose to sanctuary citizens like Roland Durham.

As the road straightened and her speed increased, the land was green and smelling of its break from winter. The driving drugged her, but even in this sleep of speed, she sensed a difference in Roland, and glancing over, saw him put down a picture book and thoughtfully touch his chin. With the force of nausea it struck her that she had forgotten to shave him. He stroked his new stubble and worry drew over him, and she could feel it swarm around them in the car. Her foot left the gas pedal. He turned to her, and almost, she was ready to give up. Let them come and take him. Try.

But he touched his cheek again, and made the face he made when she shaved him. *"Mmmm,"* she'd say, mugging her lips, and he would mug his own up or down, her face his mirror, making the contours she needed to get the whiskers.

She reached out and touched his cheek. "Sorry, baby."

He said, "I got my pitcher, Mudder."

He fumbled for his wallet. He'd rubbed and mussed the picture so, she'd finally had it covered in clear plastic. He held it up and she saw the two of them standing just above his thumb, the front porch behind them, the gray asbestos shingles, the dog of indifferent breed watching, the house cut off below its window sashes.

The land flattened below Port St. Jude. They were past the rolling orange groves of the north-central plateau and now there were only miles of scrub oak land, trash land, hot and wild and good for getting through. She drove faster. Tall grass grew to the highway's edge. She looked into the mirror at the dusty waves her slipstream made in it. She rode in a sea of green. Behind her, far back, was a silvery intersection where the waving grass healed over the asphalt, and far ahead was the same thing. In the mirror, she saw her face. "I was pretty," she murmured. "I once had a light."

"Pity," Roland hummed, pointing his finger at a page in his picture book. His voice was like the burr of her tires on the broken back of this road.

Emerging from a corridor of oaks into pasture land, she saw the Sunshine Center. Nearing, turning in, she knew it for the last place, the city of exiles. The entranceway, lined with oak saplings, wound through sun-hammered fields toward a low cluster of buildings; featureless, faded pastel shapes on a flat green table, they might have been a child's blocks. Merelene pulled off and sat in the soft vibration of the engine trying to collect herself.

From the nearest building, low like a factory, men came walking. They were child men, she could see it even at this distance. Shambling and shuffling and coming mechanically, some of them marching to music in their minds, they came like all the parade of Bedlam, a long line across the grass and spreading out, gaps among them, the missing teeth in the smiling afternoon. She forced her eyes to the inside of the car, to Roland, who was watching the parade with an honest curiosity. She removed the paper from her purse. There were instructions. Go first to the infirmary, they said.

She presented herself to the starched-white women in the polished corridors of the hospital. Business as usual to them, she felt their threat. They ruled this world of medicines and instruments. She gave them the boy's medical records. Roland went to stand on the scales. *Toledo. Fair weight. No springs.* Maybe he recognized them from the drugstore. "Come here, honey," she said. He stayed on the scales. "It's all right," said the nurse, writing.

At the cottage, a man met her car. When she got out and started in with Roland, he stopped her. He was short and portly and sloe-eyed, and said, "It just makes it harder, Missus. And we got the other ones to think about. One of them crying sets all of them off and pretty soon we got a riot on our hands." He held his fat hands out to her in proof, standing there like a picture of Jesus Christ, wearing a mournful face.

Us. We. Our hands. One of them. The others. She wanted to seize Roland back but a hand had taken his now. She wanted to make a getaway. But even as she saw it happening, she knew it would not happen. It couldn't. There was no one, nothing and no place. They had come to the end. Exile.

Suddenly, she hated. Mayfield for leaving. Her first son, Bull, for not helping somehow. The town for thinking she was better off. She hated God, most of all. He, who had made them, who wound the clocks of this world. Who allowed this.

As Roland walked away, she got back into the car so they would not see her cry. He had said, "Bye, Mudder," thinking, probably, that he was handed over for an afternoon. Halfway down the walk, the man stopped, put down the satchel, slapped him hard on the back and pointed to it. She did not hear the words they exchanged. She saw Roland lift the satchel and go in his slope-shouldered, shambling way through the double doors into the future, and she sat in the car and cried.

Two

She drove fast, blotting her eyes with her sleeve. She told herself she had better slow down or she would fly off this road. All she needed right now was to have to pay a traffic ticket. She told herself, anyway, that she would see him a lot. She repeated to herself all the things the social worker had told her months before—things like the new swimming pool the Center was putting in. She couldn't take the boy swimming, could she? No, she had told him. She couldn't take the boy swimming, his Momma couldn't. Thinking, I don't need any snot-nosed college graduate counselor to tell me about swimming pools. Who's going to keep him from swallowing water when he has a seizure with one hundred other boys like him in your damned swimming pool? Tell me that?

Then she saw the boy biting his tongue and the blood flowing out of him into the blue water of the pool, saw all of them, their arms and legs thrashing and stirring the water to red, the boy sinking down, rigid as a sash weight, looking up at all those humming limbs, and nobody seeing the blood because of all the arms and legs. She closed her eyes and then the truck was coming up big and greasy-faced from behind. She saw the driver's lips moving with wild curses and his hand reaching up to pull the cord, heard the booming of his horn, and then she was bumping across the shoulder and the weeds were lashing underneath, and she was hanging to the wheel as though lying on a whirling table and she saw the ditch coming, muddy water glistening in the sun, then watched the rear end of her own car go by just as her head was whipped around to see the front end fly away behind her.

A man stopped and opened her door.

"You all right?" The look on his face said he would like to do as little as possible.

Could he help her? What could he do? His face saying, please, Missus, as little as possible. She said, "Would you call me a wrecker?" *You're a wrecker*. They both laughed and she felt her hands unclutch from the steering wheel, her fingers keeping the shape of claws.

He drove off. It would not be long, he said. The next place was about eleven miles. But it was Sunday. That's all right. He knew a guy that did it anyway. He'd have them down here for her inside of nothing flat. Don't worry.

She sat looking back up the road at the slick, rubber-looking tracks her tires had made, crossing and recrossing each other along the ditch, writing her black progress from the highway to this spot. It was amazing how far she had slid. It must be two hundred feet.

She would see this place again. She got out and stood in sucking mud among the small roadside wreckage, slung treads, broken belts and bolts, and thought: I will pass this way time and time, coming to see Roland, and say, this is where I lost control.

Down the road, she could see the yellow blinking light of the wrecker. The driver passed her in the southbound lane, slowing, then U-turned and, slewing mud, pulled up behind her. A tall, lean man, in a brown gabardine work-shirt, he was chewing as he walked up to her.

"You got American Express?"

"No."

"Triple A?"

"I got a little cash and my checkbook. That's all."

He looked at her Alligood County tag. "That'll be an out-of-town check." He shook his head, looking back up the road in the direction from which he had come. She looked back up there too. What wouldn't be an out-of-town check up that way?

"How much to pull me back up to the hardroad? Just up that far?" She pointed toward where, once you were there, you could get out of here. Then she looked into his face. It reminded her of Mayfield's face. In his eyes, it seemed a long way.

"Same as to take you to town. One price. Soon as I hook up, you owe me twenty-five cash. No check."

She turned her back on him and opened her handbag. She could feel the sweat moving between her shoulder blades and she felt naked under his possum-faced gaze. She had nineteen dollars and silver. She turned and held it out to him.

He took it, counted it.

"I don't know."

"You can pull me up to the road for that much." It was not a question. She looked at him with the set of face she reserved for all the race of cheaters she had met when Mayfield left her, all the men who thought a woman without a man was easy.

He stared at her a moment longer. Then he shrugged, spat.

He was pulling the chain from the winch in the rear of the truck. She stood watching him, her arms folded. The sweat between her shoulder blades had pooled at her belt and she knew a dark stain was beginning to form on the back of her dress. She stood in muddy water over her shoe tops and her toes writhed in her stockings. Watching the man work, she said to herself, Merelene, you won another one. He would have done it for a couple of haw-haws if you were a man.

"Rot in hell," she muttered.

"S'at, ma'am?"

"Nothing. I didn't say anything."

The man stood up, clapping mud from his hands. He had attached his hook underneath.

She spoke to a piece of blue sky between the collar of his shirt and his pale earlobe. *Get me out of here.* She would not let herself think there might be serious damage. She did not even have money for gas unless she could cash a check somewhere.

The car shuddered, rocked and then started rolling up out of the sucking mud. The tall man spat, patted the money he had stuffed into his shirt pocket, unhooked the chain and drove off. She didn't look at him. Another man.

Three

She lifted the hem of her nightgown and carefully stepped
across a low place in the wire fence. On her right hand
was the cornfield that had been in the lawyer's family
since a time lost to local record. The Sawyers, people said,
had owned the last Florida tract which had touched the
Atlantic and the Gulf. Now, there were only scattered
holdings. He put a few acres under cultivation every year,
but set no store by the results. A little gentleman farming
was useful in a business way.

She did not know why she was going to him tonight.
Maybe she could not be alone with that other man, her
grief. Maybe it was what he owned that brought her.
Proximity to the security of his wealth, his unassailable
position in this town, might comfort the woman who had
lost her son to the State. Somehow, when her old Plymouth, shimmying and stinking of mud, had calmed itself in
her yard, her first thought had been for this midnight trip.
This habit.

The moon was a scythe above the cornfield. She held up
first her left and then her right hand. It lay white as butter
in the curve of her right thumb and forefinger, a waxing

moon. She moved along the fence line in the dew, a chill coming over her, a hint, she thought, at what it must be like, the change. They said you got chills, and fevers, unaccountable vapors. Not yet, she said to herself, not yet. She could see the glow of the light from his second-floor bedroom.

When she stood on the back stoop, her hand raised to knock, she heard his key in the lock. Then the warm, linseed-smelling air broke from under the door across her ankles. He held the door out for her with his right arm, bowing as she brushed past. She liked his courtly gestures.

Days, they worked together, performing that brand of law Swinford could afford—tax preparations, land sales and divorce—they were often like strangers. She was the hand that made the coffee, the toe that tapped while the typewriter sang. Nights were different, had been now for four years. The lawyer had wanted her long before she had given herself. But she had waited until the job was no longer a charity, until she was the best legal secretary in three counties and he knew it. And until Bull was gone to the army and the memory of Mayfield had no heat. And when her house had been, so to speak, swept by the works of hands and days, she had given herself.

She said, "Hello, sweet," as she walked past the man who held the door for her, and heard him say in his low, musical tone, "Good evening, ma'am." For this was their habit.

She walked straight to the landing and, lifting her hem again, started up the stairs. Behind her, she heard him step back into his study. Then, from his bedroom window, she watched the splash of light from the study disappear from the grape arbor. She heard the lawyer laboring his way up the stairs and she stood at the window for a last glimpse of the moonlight on the broken stalks of corn. She smelled whiskey before she felt the touch of his hand on her shoulder.

He placed a kiss, sweet and careful, on the back of her neck, lifting her hair to do it. "You taking up astronomy?"

"Just watching the moon," she said. The same moon that watches Roland tonight in a strange bed. She turned from the window and looked at the lawyer's parched face. She wanted to say to him: they took Roland today, but the truth was she had taken him herself, and the truth was he knew it.

"Come to the window," he said, in his courtroom baritone, "sweet is the night air, only from the long line of spray where the sea meets the moon-blanched land, listen, you hear the grating roar of pebbles which the waves draw back and fling at their return up the high strand, begin and cease and then again begin, the tremulous cadence slow, and bring the eternal note of sadness in . . ."

"What's that?" she asked him, but she had no curiosity tonight and no wish to hear the voice of his Yale college education.

"It's Matthew Arnold," he said. "Do you like him?"

"I like him just fine, only the night air smells like a swamp cabbage fart because the tide is out, and you know as well as I do the water's in the other direction."

She walked to the bed. "That part about sadness is right." Her eyes were dry. She had used her tears on that roadside by the State's little city.

The lawyer was there, where she had stood at the window, admiring the moon. "I *know* that part is right," he said. She heard in his voice what she wanted to hear—the help he would give her if she had to ask.

They lay together some nights for hours only warming each other, not saying anything. This, she knew from his whiskey visit to the study, would be one of those nights. He would want her to move to him and fit the curves of her thighs and breasts to his wounded back, to warm him.

Their first time together, he had said it was a miracle she could look at him, touch him in this room which had not known the nakedness of woman for thirty years. He did not understand miracles. Men never did.

She had loved the lawyer's mind for years before she had ever touched his body, and that had been enough to carry her at least experimentally to his flesh. He did not believe she could fit this curve of herself to that one of him without revulsion, let alone with love. So he drank whiskey in his study. To come up the stairs believing.

Sometimes they lay and talked: by a strange consent knowing whose it was to talk and whose to listen. The lawyer's were wild, rambling monologues she could only half understand, about lost things, things as they had been when he was a boy living on this place in its glory, among horses, dogs, old black men in livery. He had lived a life from movies and books.

Her own. The things she said. She did not know what they were. They came when she was half asleep. She only knew that she felt, in the mornings after she had rambled to him, a great purgation and some embarrassment as well. The lawyer told her she was a poet. Perhaps she talked from the curve, not from the mind. Maybe she said private things. She truly did not know. Nor did she care. What mattered was that they had found this way of having each other.

On the nights when he wanted to wed his flesh to hers, they did that too, but these were the rarer times. She would take his war-crippled body upon her, making herself pliant to his stiffness. She thought of herself, holding him, as a mirror. If he lay above her and if she, below, slowly shaped herself to fit that form which hazard had made his, and if, after that, they achieved love, then she was the mirror.

His gratitude was such that she could not bear it sometimes. When they had made a picture of him, a reflection, he lay in her arms sobbing his gratitude, this man who showed only sharp edges to the world. She had told him that gratitude did not enter into her thinking. Only love did, and you could drop gratitude into love's vessel and never hear it light. He never believed what she said. He believed himself the better one at thinking.

Let him have this vanity, she had told herself, but she found it hard to allow, knowing that she was his equal, lacking only the papers with the Latin words on them to prove it. She consoled herself with the knowledge that some of what passes between man and woman must be pride: otherwise they would not be kinds unto themselves, and would lose the pleasure of difference. But it chafed her that he took only her intuition seriously, calling it poetry.

She could feel him struggling beside her, there was no other way to say it, into the position that meant he wanted her to fold to him. She turned when he was still. She pressed her breasts to his back, and she heard him sigh. She pressed harder, the full firm curve of her breasts to the hard knotted muscles of his wounded back, and he sighed as though he had been injected with a drug. She pressed her loins to his buttocks, pressed her right leg out long to the length of his which could not be bent and slipped her right arm beneath him, through the arch in the cage of his ribs, gripping the front of his chest. She heard him sigh again as the last part of the picture was painted, and he lay revealed before the mirror. She breathed slowly, pressing to him, matching the rhythm of her breathing to his, and letting him see. Love, come to the mirror.

She kissed the back of his neck.

"Tell me?" she said.

"No," he sighed. He had almost found himself in the mirror.

"If you want to?" she said, pressing.

"I don't remember tonight," he said, his voice echoing to her from its fall into the dark hole of his sleep which was that vessel she had told him about, into which all the gratitude in the world could be poured and matter not at all. She said, "I love you."

"I know," he said. His voice held the solid ring of belief.

Someday, she thought, I will make him believe. He will come up here cold sober and I will bring him the mirror and he will see and believe.

She awoke to the single, familiar note of a barn owl. It was dawning and she had to hurry. When she came undone from him, he said in his sleep, "No." Sharply in the voice which believed in nothing but torts and writs and the secrets of the craft he practiced.

She leaned back to him and kissed and he said, more softly, "No."

She half ran the last hundred yards along the west edge of the corn, and the outskirts of Henry Bandler's five-acre auto salvage. She had made dogs bark along the way, a white figure escaping into the daylight in a ridiculous, frilled nightgown. She had stopped once behind an oak while a busload of migrant fruit pickers passed, heading south on state road 429. Safe in her own kitchen, she made coffee, but did not feel much like drinking it. She wanted the sleep she had just given away. She climbed into her own bed. It felt delicious to lie unencumbered. She drifted into guilty pleasure, awakened, drifted again. She heard the antique rumble of the lawyer's old Cadillac passing slowly on the road and she looked at the clock by the bed. It was eight. She drifted. She awoke once with a start, hearing the boy call out to her, "Mudder?" the morning summons she couldn't have heard.

She could ask the lawyer to do something. He would law for her if she asked, but if he started a fight with the State, who could say where it would end? And she would once again be the subject of local discussion. She had been chewed in the mouth of the town for years after Mayfield left. Let gossip have other food.

She and the lawyer did not discuss Roland. She was a Warrington and he was a Sawyer, and that was part of why. She could sleep in his bed but could not ask for help without drawing old lines, bloodlines and boundary lines, ink and blood that flowed from the day her great-grandfather, Corporal Warrington, had driven a caisson home from the battle of Olustee, and the lawyer's great-grandfather, Colonel Sawyer, had lain bleeding in the bed of the caisson with a minié ball in his eye. They had placed the colonel's plumed hat on the seat beside the corporal for the troops to see.

She did not know when it was that she had drifted out past the markers and so when she heard the hand in the mailbox, the screen door's rattle, she was frightened awake. She looked at the clock; it was after ten. She walked out and opened the door, shaking the waters of sleep from her eyes. Tom Bayard's blue shirt and leather mailbag were just now disappearing around the corner of the house.

The letter was headed Tae Nin, another strange word, a different place from the last one:

Dear Mother,

(Mommer, she could hear him saying, in his slow, deep voice. That voice the Reverend Tillman had tried so many times to get into the choir.)

I received your last package in good health with letter enclosed. Thank you for the westerns. I have read all the others you sent, and ever other one I could get my hands on five times over so they were specially good to get. That one called guns at devil rock looks to be the best, but will see.

(Here she paused: you'd think they'd get enough of shooting and guns over there, but Bull liked her to send the westerns. He wrote that he traded them around with the other boys so there must be a bunch of them over there that liked to read the cowboy books.)

The Vienna Sausages and sardines are very welcome here too. It's strange you can't get a hold of stuff like that here, especially not out in the boonies. A whole Army eating out of cans and you can't get potted meat.

(Jungle lunch. That's what Mayfield had called it. "Merelene, fix us up some jungle lunch. We gone bird hunting." And she would put some cans of sardines and sausages, which Mayfield called Vy-eeners, in a paper poke and off they would go, the three of them, to borrow the lawyer's dogs if he could lend them, to kick fencerows if he couldn't, Mayfield striding out first with his long legs busting September cornstalks, then Bull, head down, shoulders hunched, toting the two shotguns, and then Roland bringing up the rear, just big enough to carry the jungle lunch. She smiled at the troupe of gypsies in her memory.)

It is not too bad where I'm at now, not when you compare it to where I was. I didn't write you from there because I didn't have nothing good to say. I won't say nothing about this now either. More when I'm home.

She closed her eyes and saw him home, across those miles, safe at home. Bull had spent the year after high school graduation busting his knuckles under the grease rack at Lum Smalley's Esso. Having no aptitude nor any love for machines, he had come home evenings saying he was unhappy, that there must be more to the world than the next oil pan gasket, that he wanted to travel. At nine-

teen, he had enlisted when Vietnam was still a rumble in
the back of Lyndon Johnson's throat.

The war had overtaken him as a senior NCO five years
later when he was just beginning to enjoy the privileges of
rank. He had gone from Hawaii to Saigon and had written
her he had gone to hell. It had been his first and last dis-
couraging word, at least to her. As she read his letters, she
feared his death, but next to it, she feared his doing something that would change him the way the Second War had
changed Mayfield and the lawyer. Mayfield would never
say what it was, but she remembered him taking her out to
the mouth of the river, standing on the bank and heaving
his decorations into the water. She had asked him to at
least tell her what they meant before he threw them away,
and he had said that was why he was throwing them away.
He didn't know what they meant.

I know you are worried about Roland. (They ain't
going to take him, so don't worry.) If they mess with
you two, I'll come back and take some names. I just
wished I could see him, and you. I am fine so don't
worry about me. Dry feet and good teeth. My love to
you and the little one.

Love your son,
Bull (Ethridge)

"They ain't going to take him, so don't worry." Her
firstborn's sweet voice whispering in parentheses across
those miles, those hours of time. She put the letter with
his others in the drawer that held his high school diploma,
birth certificate and the letters from colleges offering football scholarships.

She opened the morning paper to look for mention of
the place this letter had come from. The paper was full of
the war, which was proceeding as it usually did—numeri-
cally. The yellow dead exceeded the white by a power of

two, and the war dragged on. She could find no mention of Tae Nin.

When she had first realized that this war was a war of numbers, of attrition as the papers and the politicians said, she knew they were hiding something. Working in the law had given her experience of deception. A column of figures always hid something. The truth was in the pictures they let through, and in the absences. Kenny Griner was gone, and so was Billy Rappanecker, and so was . . . but she had forgotten the names, remembered only the faces, that they had played football with Bull, and then were faces in *The County News Leader*, boys in uniform with smiles and bright brass, that their mothers had walked with sloped shoulders for a while and seen Swinford through red eyes, and then got over it, the part the town could see, that some families could not farm or fish for lack of hands, and so had moved away. But you couldn't forget entirely. The town of Swinford had its own clarion, Louise Bates.

Louise Bates lived on a one-lane dirt track that junctioned the river road, not far from the limestone quarry pits that had been Swinford's industry for a while. Her son, Harold, who had squatted beside Bull in the football picture, had gone to the war for the adventure of it, or so he had told it around town. When Harold came home in a plain gunmetal coffin, Louise went to Bainesborough in her pickup truck and came back pulling behind her one of those trailer signs, with rows of bulbs that light the shapes of words. She parked it on the road as far from her house as five orange extension cords could reach, and every week she composed a new light bulb sermon for the town to read. Merelene still remembered the first one. NO MORE WAR IN VEET NAM. NO MORE DEAD BOYS. THIS IS WROTE IN A MOTHER'S GRIEF.

Four

It was cool in the lawyer's office, but outside, the sun battered the hoods of automobiles, and made the tar crawl in the cracked sidewalks. It drove the old men from the benches in front of the courthouse to the shaded granite pedestal where stood the brass boy soldier in tattered Confederate drill. The old men braved birdlime to avoid the sun, and even the soldier lifted his right hand to his brow in the way of one staring into brilliant light. Merelene knew the words chiseled in stone beneath his feet: *Look Away*.

She heard the clock behind the lawyer's closed door chime twelve times, and heard impatience in the lawyer's voice. He was in there with a pulpwood contractor named Harrelson Tasche, whose former wife, locally known as Shackjob, was suing for nonsupport. From their medley of rumbles and pauses, Merelene had learned that the pulpwood "bidnis" was in decline, and so was Tasche's generosity. The lawyer, in measured but stern tones, was holding that contractual commitment did not fluctuate with personal fortune.

Merelene was closing up shop for lunch, covering her

typewriter with its plastic hood, when Tasche made his last declamation: "Got damn that round-heeled home wrecker. Excuse me, Miss Merelene." All of this through the closed door.

Merelene marked the irony that her own scandal had placed her in this office where she could not avoid hearing the confidences of the town. It oppressed her. There was no privacy in Swinford. She looked down at her own shoes which had walked well past the possibility of another heeling at Mercer's leather shop, picked up her purse, and stepped out into heat like water. Today, she was invited out to lunch.

She had managed to work the morning away by putting Roland out of her mind. Those times he called, "Mudder?" and was admitted, and she felt the sudden movement of tears in her eyes, she pressed both hands to her face and told herself, save it, save it, as though sorrow were a thing in short supply. She had not met the lawyer's eye, except with a brief shy touch.

Now as she stood by her car, holding her purse to her middle and plumbing in it for her keys, she felt giddy, flattened by the sun. She leaned on the car, seeing on its muddy sides the miles she had driven with Roland, and then the lawyer coming toward her in blue seersucker with sweat shining on his forehead. Watching him hurry, she tried to make the last two days add up to something she could understand.

Close to her, he slowed and tugged his jacket where it had climbed his bent hip. She looked at the pavement while he arranged himself. He said, "Where are you going so quick? I was going to ask you to lunch." She tried to read his face. Had he planned to take her to the General Baines Hotel in Live Oak and offer shrimp salad to her anguish?

She said, "Thank you, but I've got an appointment."

He closed up a little. "Of course," he said, "an appoint-ment."

They watched his client, Harrelson Tasche, erupting from the office toward his pickup truck across the street.

"That's right," she said, not ready to admit him to her plan. Because it was no plan. Because it was half of some-thing that would probably come to nothing. She wanted to reach out and touch his hand where it tugged the lapel of his coat, quiet him, control *something*. Of course she couldn't touch him here on the street. She smiled at him. "I'll be late."

He came on and opened the car door for her with a rusty groan of hinges. As she stepped past him to seat herself, she let her fingers brush his on the sill. He was framed in her window, calmer now, his eyes assessing her. "Can I help you, Merelene?" He looked around at the town, the secretaries and clerks drifting toward a greasy lunch at Fable's Cafe: Harrelson Tasche burning his tires out of town. His eyes told her there was a way to fight this.

She put her key into the ignition and smiled, already too much in his debt.

She drove toward the water, watching the tipping mast-heads of the three big motor sailers moored at Draper's Fishcamp by the confluence of river and Gulf. They were three sticks of gleaming aluminum, turning quicksilver circles above the roofs of the stilt houses along the water. The boats were pretty, but the town resented them. The town said they were owned by rich men from Baines-borough who drove out weekends with reed-thin, chain-smoking women in indecent bikinis, and with children they had gotten out of different women, by the look of them. They sailed off to play on the placid waters the town of Swinford worked for a living. The only people who spoke well of these professors, lawyers, doctors from the county seat, were the merchants who took their trade.

At the boat landing, she turned and drove the half mile to the river road, and then angled inland, following the gentle northeastward curve of the river she loved. The Suwannee was an esteemed personage, a grandmother, an old vessel of memory. She was restless when time passed and no errand brought her to its banks. Seeing the yawn of its mouth, the curve of its throat, her eyes rested upon kin and history. One of their nights, she had told the lawyer about it. Of course, he had said. Of course. The poet always loves water.

She was going to meet the doctor in charge of the "unit for special care" in a new hospital near the old Noble's Ferry Bridge. She had a letter in her purse from this Dr. Reid full of brag about the "new facility," and a lot of talk about special people, special education, and therapy for the special. It was bewildering. She had heard Roland called slow before, and an imbecile a time or two, and she had accepted these words when they weren't used in malice. She knew what was special about him, and special things about others like him, but to see him written down this way, as a category, baffled her. She hoped it was just a way of talking, a doctor's instrument of some strange kind. She wanted to like Noble's Manor.

Using the lawyer's stationery, she had written to them, choosing Dr. Reid's name from a brochure. She had made the words double-edged, so that she might be taken for a lawyer herself (. . . we are interested in investigating the possibility of . . .). When they saw her, in her best dress, and wearing the silk scarf Bull had sent from Saigon, knotted at the side of her neck in the way of the models in *Vogue*, they would not be able to tell differently; nor would they when she spoke, for she owned a host of voices.

There was the legal voice of the letter, used against creditors, and aimed at the world of official rectitude that sat beside her in church, and watched her walk the streets with the lawyer, wondering. It was a make-no-mistake voice, scrubbed of its country accent. Another was the voice that sang in her head even when the others were in her mouth, a confusion of tones and sourceless thoughts, and words which struck sparks from each other. It was the voice of the country autodidact, of the woman who had a mind and could find no way, save by talking to herself, to make anything. It was the voice of that power the lawyer called poetry.

The first sign of the new place was a small shopping plaza, an uncertain condensation of stucco and Spanish tile, early warning that further on someone was paying a wage.

The shopping plaza violated a particularly beautiful stretch of riverbank where an old man named Harry Salver, a swine farmer and cane presser, had lived. Salver had been a legendary fisherman and amateur naturalist, and a man to whom miracles happened as a matter of course. He had caught the longest alligator gar, photographed the last ivory-billed woodpecker and seen the ghost of Edith Packer. He possessed, or had before he died and it all went to antique shops in Bainesborough, the brass binnacle, wheel and running lamps of the Confederate gunboat *Madison*, whose officers had scuttled her in Little River Springs rather than see her rejoin the Union. One night Merelene and her brother had limped into this place in a catboat after their five-horse kicker had struck a rock. He had said he could show them, if he cared to, where was sunk the steam locomotive which had been on Noble's Ferry Bridge the night it had given way. He was a foulmouthed old man who didn't moderate himself for children, which made him popular with children, and, on this particular night thirty-five years ago, the bottle had lubricated his rusty hermit's tongue.

As he rummaged by lantern light in an old, slanted outbuilding for a new propeller, he talked long and loud, blowing a fermented breath that Merelene had prayed would not strike the lantern wick and explode them all into the river. He cursed the museum shit-asses and antique-selling nancy boys who were after him to show them where to dig or dive. God damn them to hell; he would die with the old world in his head. The things and the bones that owned them would stay underground where they belonged. As she passed the shopping plaza, she saw the little clearing where his house had stood, still spotted with holes dug by plunderers who thought he had buried what he knew.

To Merelene's eye, Noble's Manor resembled a cluster of condominiums whose builders had worked hard to make it look old. The stucco had been slathered on in a fashion to remind the eye of St. Augustine, and the red tile roofs were meant to gleam in the sun with a haughty Spanish fire. At least she was impressed by the solidity of the place. It seemed to have resolved itself just as quickly as the shopping plaza but out of firmer stuff.

Dr. Reid made a church and steeple of her fingers and leaned back in her swivel chair. She wore a blue raw silk blazer in this office air-conditioned cold. Merelene was freezing at the places where she had sweated in the car. Dr. Reid said, "The patient Roland is your son?"

Dr. Reid was a surprise, a woman, a Yankee, young and pretty, but with a severity that seemed more a matter of nature than profession. Her squint was an instrument as sharp as anything gleaming in the cabinet behind her desk. And, Merelene reminded herself as she sat across from Dr. Reid, this was not the kind of doctor who treated flesh; with these sharp eyes, she entered the mind, the heart.

"He's mine," she said. Dr. Reid was waiting. Merelene did not know how much to tell. Sometimes medical people only pretended to want your opinion. The silence wid-

ened and so she began to fill it up, with words and phrases
she had memorized over the years, things she had found in
encyclopedias and medical journals, facts which were, because they were irrevocable, Roland's indictment. "We, *I*
hoped at first the damage might be in just one place. I've
heard about operations, procedures to freeze tissue and
restore normal function, but that isn't the case, apparently. The scar tissue is everywhere and so what is needed,
it seems to me . . ." Here she paused, knowing she was
on disputed ground. Was she presuming to diagnose? Perhaps she should just let it falter, leave it to this complex of
skills across the desk.

"Go on," said Dr. Reid. Her eyes had narrowed, two
dark points under the black bar of her glasses.

"Well, it seems to me he is trainable. He needs custodial
care, at least, and whatever vocational training he can sus-
tain. Also, I'd like to see his medication adjusted so that he
is as alert and responsive as he can possibly be without
danger of seizure."

"Where do you have him now?"

Could she say that she didn't have him? "At the Sunshine Center in Crescent."

"Are they doing any of the things you describe down
there?"

"No." She did not know what they were doing. Perhaps
they were doing what she wanted. Could she say she only
wanted him out of that place of blind tongues and shambling feet, wanted decent food for him and people near
who knew him? If he couldn't be home, at least he might
be closer.

Dr. Reid leaned a little closer and smiled, but the smile
was a speculation. She tapped her fingertips together
twice. "What is your . . . relationship to the boy?"

"My what?"

"How do you get along? How *are you* together?"

For a moment, Merelene wondered what trap this was,

but Dr. Reid's eyes held curiosity, not guile. She let herself think about Roland. He was twenty-four years old and a child in his mind. He looked younger than he was and carried himself in solemn bliss. They were to each other . . . companions. She looked at Dr. Reid and wondered again what was the right answer. All she could say was: "I love him."

"I see." Dr. Reid let the church and steeple tumble and leaned forward. "Would you like to see the facility?"

The rest was easy. They walked the grounds and Dr. Reid mentioned the trees and grass, the artificial pond, the beautiful riverfront decked out like a backyard on Miami Beach, and it all spoke for itself.

Until they came upon a man in a summer suit, sitting in the shade of an oak holding a book and staring as though he had just read a particularly arresting passage and had paused to reflect upon its application to this day, this place. As they passed, Merelene turned to watch him, and when he noticed her eyes, he dropped the book and shrugged so violently he seemed to break the strings that held him erect. Merelene flushed, and turned quickly to stare ahead of her.

Dr. Reid put a hand on her shoulder. "That's Professor Trandy, from the university in Bainesborough. He holds a chair, or did until recently."

It was all she said, as though a chair explained this, and they walked on. The sound of Professor Trandy's deep sigh followed them into the bright afternoon.

Inside the cottages, each like the house of a wealthy ranchero, they mingled with the patients, and spoke to the pert young attendants. They ate lunch at the head of one of the tables. Merelene saw nothing that was unhappy. It was a slow dream of life, a little uncertain, but with its glints of insight and absurdity. A dream money could buy. A certain antiseptic odor was the only disagreeable thing.

In the office again, she said good-bye to Dr. Reid, whose

instrumental demeanor had not ceased to gleam, who handed her the same brochure from which she had taken the name "Dr. Reid," and said, "Let me know what you decide. I'm sure we can accommodate Roland here. We are not, as you can see, a strictly custodial facility. We would do some diagnostic testing to determine what might be done for him in the way of training and treatment."

They shook hands, Merelene's nervous palm in the doctor's, cool and dry. She walked out among the pines and oaks, along the cypress boardwalk to the parking lot and looked back at the Spanish fantasy, incomplete through the trees. Then she was surprised to be standing beside her old Plymouth, dented and dusty, and she knew she had just seen the world as it was when the miracle was good.

Five

Now she waited out the month they had said must pass before she could visit Roland, and the days and weeks went by and the world did not end. She kept her routines as best she could without him, and tried not to begrudge herself the small joys of his absence. She could sleep later in the mornings, and watch her own television programs, could come and go without worry. She killed time in movies in Chiefland and Lake City, and drove to Bainesborough wandering department stores. At the grocery store she forgot and filled her cart with the things Roland liked, and then slowly traveled the aisles in reverse, discarding all but what her new life required. She took up her reading habit again furiously now that she could go to the branch libraries and browse, but waiting was mostly what she did.

She waited for the season to change, hoping that May might give a blessed two or three weeks of temperate wind before the town became the sun's anvil. She went to the river when she could, knowing the way to the old spots, hers and Mayfield's, where they had swum, or fished or put skiffs in at midnight to drift along the rocky banks tangled in an army blanket, turning in the moonlight like the one hand of a mad clock while the radio tinned out country love. Some of the old places slept now beneath the floors of fancy riverfront houses; others were the haunts of high school kids who drove trucks to the river's edge rutting everything, banishing the secrecy. A few were left, known only to the fading generation of grandparents.

She would stand on the riverbank remembering all the postures of fishing—how you hand-held a line, how you jigged with a cane pole from the bow of a catboat, which was the tug of a channel cat just before you set the hook. She watched the surface of the river hoping for signs of a week's cooler weather, the north wind that made cat's feet on the water, a soaring red-shouldered hawk, a fleck of foam from upstream. Any of these, if it was just so and not otherwise, was a sign. Sometimes, looking out at the bright, tannic water, she would think she saw Mayfield and that wild friend of his, Jack Rappanecker, returning from one of their flatbottomed trips down from the Okeefenokee, where, they would tell her, the river was a hundred channels and you could get lost (winking at each other) and never come out. There. There it was, there just at the bend where the big fallen oak threw its branches into the blue vale between high rocky banks. Two figures, a mound of gear, the sharp quick movements of a man casting into the eddy under that leaning oak. Soon they would be landing, full of a morning's whiskey, and some of that from the night before, and full of stories—who'd shot the biggest cooter, told the worst lie, taken the fewest baths—and resenting the end of it even as they could not stand another minute, and smelling all too much like they had been working at their pleasure. Soon she would take one man into her arms and tell him, when his own pleasure at telling had waned, what she had done while she had waited, and how much she and the two boys had missed him.

The man in the boat at the bend stooped and started his kicker and off the boat went upriver not down. It was 1973. Mayfield was sixteen years gone, but still she felt the strange pull toward him, the eddy in her loins.

And there was more to wait for. She waited for the war to end before it took Bull or changed him. She waited for the world to turn, the stars and moon to align in that last right way which would bring the peace that surpassed. She waited for all like herself who believed, and wanted and waited, to say so, and she waited to say so herself. When would their time come?

Swinford, by most indications, stood solidly behind the war. If the DAR and the VFW, and the flags and bumper stickers and songs that rolled from the honky-tonks at night were most indications, Swinford cherished the President's purpose in the conflict overseas. But what did the mothers of the boys Bull had played with, fished and hunted with, and planned with, the women who gritted their teeth and stared into a hollow middle distance when oh say can you see was played at baseball games, what did *they* signify? Were they nothing? Was one of them, her absent gaze and grinding teeth, less than a bumper sticker that said love it or leave it? Merelene waited to find out.

The town gradually came to know that Roland was gone, and made its feelings known, either in expressions of regret (a few of them genuine) or in sighs and nods of satisfaction. She knew that most of her neighbors were glad to see him gone. He was something they did not understand, and so, could not tolerate. Even as the village idiot, that time-honored and assimilable thing, he had threatened them.

Encountering Mary Heatherton brought the day of Roland's error back to Merelene, and to have it back was the last thing she wanted so soon after he had been taken. It was one of the things she waited for, to run into Mary Heatherton.

Merelene was leaving the Big Star with a load of groceries. Out of useless habit she had bought all the things Roland liked. She had just reached the car, was opening the trunk when Mary Heatherton parked in the space next to her. When they saw each other, and couldn't pretend otherwise, Merelene cursed her luck through the teeth of a smile.

As Mary stiffly put on her glasses and adjusted a shopping list to her eye, Merelene smiled hard. "Hello, Mary," she said, stepping forward while Mary levered herself, tall and ample, out of her car.

"Why, how are you, Merelene? It's been such a long time." Mary smiled the big blond smile that had never needed dental work.

Looking up at tall Mary, Merelene said, "I'm just fine, and how are the girls?"

"The girls are doing right well, thank you." It was the last amenity, the necessary one because of Roland.

Merelene made to pass, but Mary stood in her way, blond and solid and certain. When she saw Mary's hand coming toward her shoulder she almost flinched. "It's for the best, Merelene, you know it is. And it had to happen. You don't need to blame yourself. It's just one of those things He sends and we have to do with it. We all know you'll make the best of things. You always have, haven't you?"

Mary waited now. An answer should come. Merelene stepped back so that the hand was lifted from her shoulder. Her mind swarmed but words wouldn't drop to her tongue. Finally, she was just tired. "I have always made the best of things, Mary. I have." She looked up at the hot blue heavens. "And with His healing, helping powers, I guess I always will." Maybe she had let her voice roll a little like Mary's favorite radio preacher, but Mary hadn't noticed. Mary nodded big blond approval.

She watched Mary cut a smart wake into the supermar-

ket, her leather bag thumping her hip and the shopping
list waving white in her hand.

The town knew that Mary had undergone an expensive
and tedious course of hormone therapy so that she could
have children. The issue had been identical triplet girls.
She called them the three lights, the lights of her life.
They had come to her at age thirty-six, and she called
them the late fruit of the season, doted on them in a man-
ner almost fanatical. And they *were* three beautiful identical blond girls who would become three lovely women,
tall and straight and ample, just like Mary.

What had happened was perfectly predictable, and not
at all ugly if you knew Roland. It had been gossiped beyond all proportion, which was predictable, too, if you
knew Swinford. This was the part Merelene could not
forgive; it lay on her heart like a stone. The town had not
believed her when she told Roland's real intention. She
had thought the town knew him. You live in a little place,
forfeiting privacy, and when trouble comes no one knows
you. She had been wrong, and had paid the price of the
stone for her error.

One day, Roland had walked off. She had left him
watching *Emergency!* (He liked the quiz shows and the dra-
mas in which people talked on radios. He wouldn't watch
anything else.) She had told him, as she always did when
she had to leave him by himself, to stay put. "Yes, Mudder."

Who knew why he sometimes did not stay put? Who
knew? Was there a doctor in the world who could tell? A
social worker? A gossip-mouth busybody? When he
walked off, followed by the dog, he homed on the nearest
house with a freestanding bathtub, shucking his duds, as
the town said, at the front door. He didn't care who was
home, or if anyone was. People didn't lock their doors in
Swinford.

The Heathertons lived in a large frame house, not far

from the town's block of commerce. It had been a long
walk for Roland that day. Merelene often reflected that
she would give a lot to know what made him select the
Heathertons' after passing so many other houses, empty
or occupied, houses he had visited before, all with bath-
tubs.

As it happened, Mary Heatherton was bathing her three
little daughters in organic soap bubbles like those she had
seen on TV. Everything she did with the children, Merelene believed, despite (or perhaps because of) all those
hormones, was perfectly natural. She received her guid-
ance in these matters from the TV. Certain—this was how
Mary later told it—that she could hear anything that
might arise amiss, Mary was on the phone down the hall
from the bathroom. Listening to her lights, their little
squeals of delight, she chatted with a friend about salad
dressing.

Roland had been in the tub for quite some time, playing
patty-cake, his narrow middle ringed by a white daisy
chain of bubbles, before Mary finished her conversation.
She fainted dead away, striking her head on a towel rack,
when she discovered him there among the golden three.
He had the girls out, and toweled off and dressed by the
time Mary crawled to the phone and spoke in tongues to
the police.

Apparently, after waking up, she had been unable to
talk to him, had seen him stretching their little limbs as
though they were rubber, or so she said. The truth was
that he had not hurt them, had only sported with three
mental contemporaries, toweled and dressed them, proud
that he knew a little more about the subtleties of toiletry
than they did, and ignored their hysterical mother. He
had not hurt anyone until Troy Haber arrived on the
scene. Roland did not like policemen, despite the fact that
they frequently talked on the radio.

When Troy came running at a squat, his pistol in both

hands, Roland took it away from him, and broke Troy's trigger finger. Troy ran howling to the cruiser to radio for help and looked up, sucking his bleeding finger, to see Roland, fully dressed, followed by a worried dog, walking off in the direction of home. Troy didn't want to charge Roland. He was embarrassed at being disarmed by a slow learner. It was Mary Heatherton's story, a magnificently magnified fiction in the ear of the town, which sealed Roland's fate.

It took every power of persuasion Merelene possessed to convince Bill Ebert, the rest of the town's police department, a man she had graduated from high school with, not to lock Roland in his office overnight. She had promised she would not let him out of her sight, and had been as good as her promise, even taking him with her to work and sitting him in the lawyer's file room, little more than a closet, during the days that preceded the hearing.

A few days after the Big Bath, as the lawyer called it, she had received a visit from the county mental health man, who told her Roland would have to go. She had listened, while he rattled the sheaves of complaints in his hand. An unctuous little man who said, "You know how it goes when we investigate, Mrs. Durham." He made as though to hand her his fistful of paper. "Give folks a chance to talk and things just seem to come out of the woodwork." She had listened, believing with time it would disappear. They would not send him away for his one mistake.

Now she waited, and did it about as well as she did most things. They had told her one month, then a weekend visit.

Six

She passed the place where she had spun from the hot asphalt into the ditch a month before. She slowed, stared at it. Her sign. Her black tracks in the soft, wet earth still slick and dangerous.

This hot flat road, she realized, would become theirs, hers and Roland's, a place for her at one end, for him at the other. She saw herself cutting this rut across years into her old age and Roland's too—his medication, they had told her, would age him until he caught her. Far ahead, where parallel lines met and the road ended in an illusion of water, she could see the future: the two of them in roadside stops and on lonesome stretches of Gulfcoast, places where there was take-out food. Herself, an old woman making fewer trips and then, finally, none, and Roland, aged by the burning drugs, old among grown men in diapers, spending his years waiting. She saw Mayfield there at the watery intersection, who had helped her make this boy. She saw him old in places where broken men were found late at night laying their faces into their hands.

All this because the State said so. Because in epileptic

seizures he thrashed and chewed his lips and swallowed his bloody tongue. And because of his one mistake. She tried not to think of him as she drove, but she could not help it. She hoped he would be the same. She could bear a change in the way he looked, if such were necessary, but she wanted him to behave as before. She wanted him glad to see her, but not too glad; that would only make her leaving worse. She must make it plain to him this was a visit, that he could not come home with her.

But the more she thought of him, the more she wanted, until it made her tired, like this journey, this broken-backed road, the sawing insects at its shoulders. Too much, too long. Then, she thought, why not? Why not take him home?

In the counselor's office, she waited, watchful, guarding her resources. When the young man came in punching his glasses flat to his face with an inky index finger and huffing his breath as though he had been running, she sat up and put on the face she used in the lawyer's office. She crossed her legs, right shin out—the left had a dog-bite scar—made her mouth into a pucker as efficient as the one the young man pouted with as he read Roland's folder.

"It took me a while to pull your son's file, Mrs. Durham. They just sent it from Receiving today."

"I see," she said. She had made her request, if that was what it must be, and now let him make up his mind.

He mumbled, moving his lips as he read. (Roland didn't even do that.) "I see here he runs away." She would let this pass. Roland did not run away. He walked, no, he strolled of an afternoon into a friendly distance, knowing the dog would mark his progress, knowing she would come when his new friends found her. His new friends always called. *Mrs. Durham, we hate to bother you at work, but he done done it again. In the bathtub. Yessum, just walked in and*

*took a bath. Kind of sweet if you ax me, but Felton don't like it.
Says he might have fits in there. So I thought I better call.*

"Occasional seizures. Phenobarbital. Mellaril. Heavy
dosage. Mrs. Durham?" The young man looked up at her
out of that educated assurance some college had taught
him, a supercilious condescension and the suspicion that
what was on the other side of the desk was dirty. "Mrs.
Durham, it's only been one month. I don't see how we can
allow it. The boy has to have time to be acculturated . . ."
He offered her a pained face. She sat straight, kept her lips
firm, and thought: *Kiss my ass.* She smiled: "Mr. Deloach,
or is it *Doctor* Deloach . . . ?" She waited while he fin-
gered his tie.

"I have a bachelor's degree in psychology, Mrs. Durham. Please just call me John."

"I see. But your rules state that after one month a ward
may be taken home for a weekend. I have requested that I
be given time off from my job. I am taking my vacation
early so that Roland and I may have this time together."
(It wasn't hard to lie to this snot.) "I have come three
hundred miles, Mr. Deloach." She sat firm, straight, her
body a prim exclamation. She knew what he would do
before he did it. He would look at her as long as he could
stand it, then, for want of anything else, he would pretend
to read some more.

When his eyes slid away from hers to the file, his lips
did not move and she knew she had won. She waited a
space. He sighed, reached for a pad and began to write. He
pushed a permission slip across the desk to her. They both
stood.

"It's against my better judgment. I advise you to recon-
sider even though you are within your rights."

"No," was all she said, leaving him standing behind the
desk.

She drove to the infirmary, where she was given Roland's medication and her instructions. She nodded as the

woman in starched white explained the instructions on the bottles.

They were taking their time with her because they were preparing him. The moment she had walked out of the counselor's office, she knew, he had made the telephone call that gave them fifteen minutes to get Roland ready.

When she pulled up in front of the cottage, peering down the long walk before the car had properly stopped, she thought she saw his face at the window, his mouth forming a word behind the glass. Then he was drawn, or moved himself away. She sat in the car as the hot, brutal chemicals began to gather in her eyes. Why, Lord? But she had to be nice, not communicate alarm for his sake. She smiled: the word at the window was, *Mudder. Mudder. Mudder.* She pulled the rearview mirror down and opened her purse, searching for her compact.

"Roland?" The attendant smiled. One big happy family here. "Oh, Roland's in the dayroom, I think. Let's go see." As though she had not just seen his face at the window.

At the far end of the room, in a window seat where filmy white curtains fanned him, they had composed Roland. He held a magazine open in his lap, but he looked straight at her and made no sign of recognition. Even from this distance, she could see the little piece of toilet paper on his face. Her worst moments came, always, when she saw him at a distance, silent, calm, and knew that to a stranger's eye he might look completely normal. Now, he might have been a student musing on some library bench, leaned a little forward, about to rise decisively and go about his business. She turned to the attendant beside her.

"Where are his things?"

"You can take him in to get them." The man pointed toward the dormitory.

She drew several long breaths. What was wrong with her anyway? She was thinking: I still have time to get out. She said aloud, "No," and walked to the handsome young

man whose mind was a strange shell-holed country where
a war had been lost and a life forfeited in four days of
sickness. She sat down beside him in the window seat. She
let her hand rest on his knee. "Roland." He stared into
serious philosophy.

"Roland?"

He turned and flashed her his master of ceremonies
smile. The attendant smiled too. Something had worked.
Roland took her hand and led her to his cot, the chest of
drawers where his things were kept.

Later, when he stood beside her, holding his bag while
she signed the forms, all the young men appeared. They
came out slowly, pushing across some boundary. She saw
the man across the desk bite his jaw. Some of the boys
wore football helmets, others rocked and sighed as they
came, some had the blissful Oriental look she had come to
know. They crowded around her. How much new could
there be here? She was the visitor.

They all wanted to touch her. She stood at the desk
encircled, while the embarrassed attendant stared at her.
Then, as though into water, she walked to them. She felt
something unnameable in the glow of them, all patting,
hugging, until the man said, "Mrs. Durham?"

"Yes," she said. She hurried then, and some of their
hands came off roughly.

She did not look back from the steering wheel, the road,
the blue sky. She could still hear them saying, "The
mommy. The mommy is here."

She pulled out of traffic at a rest stop only a few miles
from the Center. She got him out and embraced him,
squeezing quickly and then thrusting him roughly away,
looking him up and down; a bruise on his forehead, the
razor-burnt cheek, dirt under his fingernails. She softened,
kissed his nose, his eyes, then ran her hands along the
sides of him.

The trip back went quickly. When she glanced over at Roland from time to time, he looked at her and smiled his confidence. She placed her hand on him, taking the feel of him unchanged. His flesh neither shrugged nor accepted hers. The greeting was over.

"Roland, baby," she said.

He turned to her, his head lolling a little, drowsy with the music of the tires. "Mother loves you," she said. She could not stop the tears from coming.

She stared at the highway ahead, then saw in the corner of her eye, something slick and bright. He held out to her the picture. There stood the two of them above his thumb, the front porch behind them. The dog. The house halved.

Bull had held the camera on one of his leaves from Hawaii. His big hands dwarfing her old box Brownie. She had called him into the picture. No, he had told her. Just you and Roland, he had said, smiling. You two are soul mates.

Seven

Roland sat out in the living room watching *The Price Is Right* and smoking a Camel cigarette, a recreational activity he had learned at the Sunshine Center. Standing in the kitchen, Merelene could hear the near-crazy happiness of the master of ceremonies saying, "Now, Betty, all you have to do is guess how much this little item costs." And Roland talking right back like he always did, like he hadn't even gone away. Except for the cigarettes and swearing some, and shaving himself so hard his face broke out in blisters, he was the same boy she had seen carrying a satchel up that walk a month ago.

"Eighty dollars!" Roland said to the television. Then, as though it were an afterthought, she heard him mumble, "By God."

She had confiscated his cigarettes but he had kept looking for where she hid them, and fiddling as though he didn't know what to do without a butt in his fingers. They had compromised at five a day. She was about to go out and tell him it was time for bed, when she remembered Saturday was the lawyer's night. She was an hour late.

She was heading for the phone when she heard the unmistakable rumble of his sixteen-cylinder Cadillac in her oystershell drive. She touched the wet strands at her temples and tried to see herself in the mirror of the maple highboy as she detoured for the front door. His knock was firm, and she opened to his shy smile.

He looked back over his shoulder at the lighted windows along the street and winked broadly at her: "Hello, Merelene. I was in the neighborhood and thought I'd drop in for a chat." His voice was loud and musical. He winked again.

She swung open the door. "I see your eyebrows, now come in before you get us the audience we deserve."

When he saw Roland in the silver of the TV, he looked a question at her.

Merelene said, "I brought him home for the weekend."

"I see that." He stepped into the living room and stood beside Roland, and she liked him standing there.

"How is he? He doesn't look much the worse for his trip down south."

"Why don't you ask him how he is?"

The lawyer said, "How are you then, son?"

Roland did not turn from the television. "I read you weak and garbled. Say again."

The lawyer chuckled at Roland's radio talk. He used his own microphone tone. "I say again, how are you, sir?"

The master of ceremonies was getting the hugging of his life from a short, fat woman while the audience cheered. Roland said, "Betty, you're a *winner*!"

The lawyer stepped back and they both watched Roland. "I was expecting you earlier," he said.

"Be patient," she said, "I'll be along as soon as I get him down and quiet. You know I'm not supposed to leave him alone."

The lawyer went to the door. "I'm the soul of patience and its body too." She looked at his body, and he smiled.

* * *

She found his back door open and let herself in. She did not hear him, but knew he was in the house. She liked to be alone here, to wander and marvel at what he possessed, to suppose what each object meant, a history going back to the day Great-grandfather Warrington had driven the caisson home from Olustee with the plumed hat on the seat.

She had not wandered far among the horsehair sofas and Tiffany lamps and strange war relics when she heard his shuffling gait on the landing above and then on the stairs. Listening, she reflected that life with him would have a strange rhythm. She knew from Roland how to pace herself to another's hardship. At work, she gave the lawyer's body head starts while his mind waited for hers to catch up. Lately, she had lain awake nights trying to imagine the combination of their two disabilities in her house, Roland's and the lawyer's. The two of them had not discussed Roland.

When the carpet softened his footfall at the bottom of the stairs, she let Roland into her mind, the picture of him asleep where she had left him. One of the conditions of his visit was that he would not be out of her sight. It was partly to spite counselors and laws and the State that she had walked here tonight.

"Merelene?"

She did not speak.

"Don't go."

She stood still, knowing he had sensed her, wondering at this web of intuition, his and hers.

He could see her now. He slowed his pace, and she saw his relief. She smiled, with a sudden flirtatious happiness. She said, "What do you want with me?"

He laughed again, and broke the straight line he was making toward her to head for the walnut highboy where his other love was kept. He took the decanter and poured himself a generous portion of the whiskey whose merits he was always declaiming. She watched his pale dome of forehead, the house of those awesome brains, tilt back and take on a red coloring as he drank, then saw his eyes come alight as he poured himself another. His brow was as red as his hair when he turned to her, the smile of their flirtatiousness on his lips. She tried not to show him the anger she felt. She held herself, chilly, feeling the effort fail.

He sat down in a big wing chair by the fireplace. Now he did not look at her. "Kick up the fire for me, Merelene, before you go."

"Yes," she said. She took the brass poker and turned an oak log up to the air, spurring its red alligator hide until it burst into flame. She banked a few pieces of lighterd around it and added two more small sticks of oak. He needed the fire, even in summer his bones were cold. She let herself hum a little of "Aura Lee" while she worked and he watched.

He often watched her move, do chores, things at the office, with some mixture of envy—of her careless grace—and love. Sometimes she looked up and he was stupefied at the sight of her and this made her blush. Now she did not look at him, only prepared her skirts around her legs and made ready to leave. She said, "Don't fall asleep down here. You'll wake up with a hitch in your get-along worse than you already got."

He laughed and his hand struck out and caught her arm. He pulled her close to him with the strength that always surprised her. She stood by his chair while he held her arm almost painfully, and they stared into the fire. "Fire gets me, Merelene, trances me. I see things in it the caveman saw. Gods that made him do horrors and blood. When I stare into a fire, I see a need for myself in this world. All the exalted meanness that brings people through the doors of my office paying for my worthless education. I'm the priest to the fire. Do you understand me?"

She smiled. His hand still held her arm. "Yes."

"What am I saying?"

"You're telling me that you want to do horrors and blood but can't let yourself."

He laughed. "That's part of it."

"A goodly portion," she said, "and if you keep drinking that whiskey, someday you're gone do some of that exalted meanness, just to see what it's like."

Awkwardly, he raised her wrist to his lips and pressed a kiss to it. "You keep me from it," he said in a churchy tone.

"Yes," she said, tired of this. She needed rest. Tomorrow was Sunday and Roland had to go back.

"The meanness," he said, "not the whiskey."

She pulled her arm away.

"Don't go," he said for the second time.

"What do you want from me?"

"I don't know, just to have you here standing in the portrait with me. Go over by the window and look at us. You and me and the fire."

"All we need's a dog."

"I don't keep animals in the house. It's a thing city people do because they don't know what animals are for."

"You'd keep one in the house if you had to. You'd do a lot of things if you had to."

He said, "If I had to and if I could. Is that what you mean to say?"

"I said exactly what I meant to say."

She stood beside him, wanting to give him back her hand to kiss, or to kiss his, unable to do either. She left herself and went to the window and watched them, two stiff, correct figures in an old daguerreotype picture, tinted amber by the fire, the colors in the flame playing through the filmy fabric of her nightgown and robe, revealing the shapely legs that walked for both of them in his office and were his pleasure in the nights of their strange conjunctions. All she had to do was say a word now, any time, and they would become the portrait, man and wife, and immediately, she knew, the image would begin to change. If she said yes to him, when the question was in every glass he drank to provoke her and every word he spoke; if she said yes, then the picture would compose itself just so, and immediately it would change and she feared what it would become. After all, it was she not he who had been in such a picture before. She bent down to kiss him and heard him sigh.

She went to the window in fact now and drew the other wing chair to the fire. She placed the chair as close to him as it would go and sat down. She took his hand from the arm of the chair, feeling the fluttering pulse in it, the small film of sweat on it from the fire or his excitement. She placed it carefully in her lap. She stared into the fire, look-ing for the trance he said was in it, and feeling his hand separate the folds of her robe, trace the curve of her belly, find the lattice of scars that two children had drawn there. She felt the hand grow more insistent and she covered it with her own, moving it downward and adjusting the po-sition of her thighs on the chair. With her own fingers she told the hand to slow, to go gentle. Both of them started when she drew a sharp breath and he gave one. She kept her hand above his and said, "Talk to me," knowing that it might not please him, but knowing, too, that the trancing fire was in her belly, had crept up her legs into every limb, and had found her throat where things demanded to be spoken.

In a choked voice, he said, "Goddamn, woman," and she knew that his own power of speech had been defeated. They had gone to separate places.

She began to let the words come, slick with the motion of his hand, midwifed by his fingers, and it was not long before she realized that she was speaking what the lawyer called her poetry. She heard only portions, knew that she would remember almost none. From time to time, she heard him say, "go on, go on," and did not know whether he spoke to his own hand, or to her voice. She felt his arm sometimes, where it crossed her thigh and plunged, a hard insistent presence, the thing that conducted her dance, her song. "Down by the Suwannee River," she said, "my love and I did meet, and he twisted my hair in his fingers and made me lie at his feet."

They came to something like a conclusion together. His was exhaustion, hers was the plunging of her limbs to the fire until the flame in the hearth was the flame that powered her tranced singing, her rolling thighs. She looked down as though from a great height and saw him grasp the muscles of his own forearm and withdraw the hand from its nest in her. She felt the fire pour from her limbs back toward the hearth and felt the poem tumble down. She seized his hand before it was gone from the warm aura of her lap and pressed it to her lips, tasting its salt hardness. Feeling the last of the fire in her long, long legs, stretched toward the hearth, she pressed the hand to his lips and then, its fingers into her mouth. Drowsy now, she closed her eyes, saw blood, horror in the fire, and told herself she was sorry that another night had passed without his asking, without her knowing the answer.

Eight

As she walked the damp, moonlit pasture, the dusty roadside, then along the fencerows at the back of Henry Bandler's junkyard, she could not compose a charm to keep the dogs from barking. She had used up the night's magic. A dry, sweet breeze was holding the methane gas from the mangrove flats offshore. If the night stayed cool, the lawyer's fire would be a pleasure to him. As she walked, Roland came into her mind, and the pace of her heart quickened a little. She would soon open the door and go to his room, and see him panfaced and mumbling in the moonlight that rolled in at the window. He might say in his sleep, "Congratulations, Mrs. Grimes, you've won a year's supply of Cheer," or some such, and she would smile, and whisper, "Thank you, Mr. Barker."

Roland did not wander at night. Did not, never had; whatever mechanism it was that sent him off in search of a new bathtub, shut itself off at night.

She lifted the backdoor latch, and knew all was right by the sound of the house, a humming refrigerator, the sighs of old boards beneath her feet, and the quiet, warm breath that touched her cheek as she swung the door inward. She

was crossing to Roland's room when she remembered the
wet muzzle of Hall, the dog. Why wasn't it pressed to her
hand now, guiding her in the dark? A chill replaced the
last of the fire glow in her limbs. Then she saw Roland's
head above the headrest of the overstuffed chair. With a
rushing of chemicals to her heart, she snapped on the
light. He was sitting with his back to her. Why didn't he
have the TV on, why the light off? She heard him call,
"Mudder?" not from the chair but from his bed, and a
man, not Roland, but with the same choke of black hair,
lifted himself from the chair. As a smile split his face, her
one thought was: I have not finished my letter.

He said, "Hello, Merelene. Long time, and no see," and
gave a dry laugh. She pressed her hands to her bosom and
spoke the name of Jesus, and swayed there, hoping the
awful bath of chemicals away, knowing what she must
look like in this flowing gown, an illustration from *A
Child's Book of Bible Stories*. It was some time before she
knew she would not fall, and all the while, Mayfield only
stood watching her with that bemused, healthy smile on
his face and Hall the dog pressing against his leg in trea-
sonous rapture.

When she had collected herself up in the awful blank-
ness that followed, she could not speak, could only notice
in second sight that his smile, his hair, were the only
things healthy about him. His face was drawn, not the
lean, tight face she had known. There was a sallow cast to
his blue eyes, a bleached look that was pitiless: like Roland's, a gaze that could be aimed at the sun and not flinch.
His clothing was of solid kind, a pair of boat shoes, khaki
trousers, a webbed belt, a dark windbreaker open down
the front, a white shirt, and strangest of all, he held a
knitted watch cap in his hand, the kind shrimpers wore.
His clothes were dirty. She could see the beard growing
on his cheeks in the same whorling pattern that con-
founded the razor she had put to Roland's face a thousand

times. But this Mayfield had left before any beard had appeared on Roland's face. She wanted to tell him about it.

She said, "Did you go look at him?"

His face quit smiling, and he turned away from Roland's bedroom.

Roland called, "Mudder?" from his sleep. She said, "Yes, baby."

Roland said, "Night."

"Yes, night love," she said.

"No, I didn't," he said, and it was as though nothing had passed, no time had disappeared over the lip of a flat world, since she had last seen his hard resistance to Roland. She was certain of one thing. There was nothing hard left in him as hard as what had grown in her in his absence.

"You been out?" He tilted his head back again, and laughed, bouncing the shock of black hair in the light. He pointed at her gown, wet around the fringes, the fanciful smile returning to his lips.

She thought: I don't account for my coming and going to anybody in this world, least of all, last of all, you. She said nothing, only lifted her gown a little, looking at its wet hem. Then she stared at him, taking him in all in all.

His smile, the flirty look in his eyes, the casual cast of his limbs did not hold long as she watched him. He shuffled a little, seemed to shrug without actually doing it. He reached down behind the chair and picked up a cheap canvas duffel bag, its zipper broken, dirty things sticking out of it in black and white and red clumps. He held the duffel up before his chest. "I need someplace to sleep tonight." His eyes asked her.

She shook her head once and he nodded, unsurprised. He dangled the bag at his knee. "I want to talk to you."

She thought, what could we possibly find to talk about? Then she remembered how it had come to her, that one question: Did you go look at him? She had thought the

place that conceived such questions was gone. Was a scar
that time had worn from the surface of her heart.

"What do we have to talk about?" She did not sit, did
not move, made no gesture of welcome.

He said, "I don't know. Everything. Everything we
never talked about when I was here. Things I never said
and you never said. All the things we never finished."
When he saw her face changing, he said, "Don't think this
is easy for me." He weighed the duffel bag again as though
it held all his weary travels.

She was weary. Even his return was old now. Without
thinking very much, she said, "The road was always easy
for you. It was staying home you couldn't do. It was looking at him"—she pointed hard at Roland's room of sleep—
"you couldn't do." She had let her voice rise, and now she
pulled it back down. She did not want to hear herself
again, after years, in that high tone of complaint. She had
lived without complaint. There wasn't much else to be
proud of. She and Roland, until his banishment, had been
easy mates.

He said, "I want to talk about him. Maybe that's what I
come back for."

In a low tone, she said, "I remember talking to you,
Mayfield. It was listening is what it was."

She could see he was not listening to her. He had inclined his head, not so much in sorrow or shame as in
what he used to call meditation. "I'm meditating, Merelene," he used to say, and she'd leave him alone for hours
at a stretch. *And Mayfield meditated upon it, and then he said.*
Only he never quite said, at least not when she was within
earshot of him. He kept them all in, his meditations. They
were one of his moods.

She remembered his other moods. The sourceless, light-
ning anger and a useful, shrugging easiness. Each had en-
gendered its own trouble, for him, for her. She had loved
the easiness, taking it for that thing she loved in the river,

in the pines, a kinship with the persons of trees and waters. What she had discovered after all, was a collection of
traits loosely slung together out of the history of the town,
and from the songs they both liked. He was the shrug of a
Hank Williams tune, the brave, shaded stare from the face
of the Confederate monument, a Bible story or two, the
exploits of a few favorite uncles, dead or in prison, or old
enough to show scars to little boys without being properly
ashamed. It was the stuff of every local character she had
known in this town, give or take a shred, until she had met
the lawyer.

She said to herself: charity. Show charity to this man,
and show him the other virtues you can still afford. And
live by the rules his absence has taught you. She said to
him, "I'll talk to you some other time, when I'm not so
tired. Call me here, in the evening, after six. I'll be home
from work. If you still want to." If you aren't gone, she
thought.

Holding the duffel to his chest, he walked to the door.
She could see his eyes, despite his best intentions, fasten-
ing themselves to the wet hem of her nightgown. She
could see his easiness giving way to anger. What gall, she
thought, watching him struggle with himself, with the
gown, what damned gall. To think, after all that had happened, and all that had not, he still had the right to his
jealousy. She said, "Please leave."

He smiled again, the smile of his easiness, but older,
more frail, and pressed a hand to his forehead for a beat or
two. When he took the hand away, he looked at it, as
though it held more than his temperature. Then he held it
out to her. To shake? She looked at it, and repeated,
"Please?"

He stepped toward the door. "You're as lovely as the
day, no it was a night, I met you. Remember that night,
Merelene, when you stopped for me?"

She shook her head, no, and he smiled. She had meant,

no, I will not think about that now, will not let you bring it up between us now. She knew what the smile meant.

"I know you remember it. Neither one of us can forget it." He turned at the door and dropped the duffel and in two steps was close; she was in the circle of his odor and the warmth of his skin and these were memories whose teeth she had tried to pull. Now they bit at her and she reached out to fend him off. He held her shoulders tightly and talked low and slow and cold in the way that had started fires when she was his. His face was a blur before her eyes: he was pine trees and backseats and midnights and man hair and he made her legs weak and her hackles rise. He said, "Tell me you remember," and pressed his lips to hers.

She could not give herself to this kiss. She shoved at him. He let go of her and stood with the look of challenged pride and crazy victory on his face. And suddenly she was angry, her fury as strong as his spell. She dug both hands into the front of his shirt. "I'll show you what I remember." She dragged him toward Roland's bedroom. He saw what she was doing, and twisted her hands and tore them from his shirt.

"By God," she whispered harsh and breathless in the quiet house with the dog dancing in anguish around their legs, "I'll show you what I remember."

Then she heard the complaint of bedsprings and Roland's feet slap-slapping the linoleum. And then Mayfield was out of her grasp and there was nothing but the windy night in the door frame, and despite herself she ran to the window with Hall whining at her feet.

He must have used the same stealth that had taken him away in the first place, had kept him alive and moving all along, for when she had turned off the lights to see out, the starry field was empty. A hundred questions clattered into her mind. Where would he go now? Was it true what she

had read about him in the Jacksonville *Times-Union*? Why
had he come back, why?

Roland stood beside her at the window, pooling her in
the warmth from his bed. With the hot print of Mayfield's
kiss on her lips, she turned and looked at him. But he kept
his face to the window and when Hall finally broke the
silence with a bark, Roland petted his head and said, "His
master's voice."

Nine

Monday morning, she was at her typewriter waiting for the chemical whitener to dry, when the lawyer called, "Merelene, come in here, will you, please?" When she stood beside his desk, she saw that his hand shook, holding a letter. His forehead was pale and moist, and she could not check the alarm that began to sound in her nerves.

"Look at this," he said.

The letter was written in a hand she had not seen for years. It asked the lawyer for legal services in the matter of custody proceedings. It was signed, big and bold at the bottom—Mayfield Durham.

"What is this?" the lawyer asked. "Is this what I think it is? That man wants your boy? Now, after all this time?"

She said, "Apparently," trying to hold a legal secretary's voice.

She told him about Mayfield's visit, out of the starry blue, the same night she had been with him, one world tipping its contents into another. She didn't mention Mayfield's eyes on the hem of her gown, the flirty way he had taken with her, his trying to kiss her, his disappearing so suddenly. She told him Mayfield had given her no indi-

cation that he had come back for Roland. He sat rigid as
she told it, tapping a pencil on the blotter, the color rising
in his face until it crept across his parchment forehead
into his hairline.

"Where is the boy now? You took him back to the state
home, did you?"

She watched him, watched him squint, wondering now
if she had made some terrible mistake. "No," she said. "I
didn't take him back. He was supposed to go back Sunday
afternoon, but I didn't take him. I called him in sick."

"You what?"

"I called that snot psychologist, Mr. Deloach. I told him
Roland had contracted a cold. I said it would be better for
him to stay here for a few days."

"And he *accepted* that?"

"Well, I brought up the subject of contagious diseases. I
said it was probably a cold, but there had been a lot of the
swine flu around here and . . ."

"Damn it, Merelene, you ought to been a lawyer. You
temporize with the best of them."

She didn't know what *temporize* meant, but she could see
admiration and worry combined in his face.

"I asked you where he is now, right now. Did you leave
him home? Is he likely to wander today?"

"He's at home like always." She said it a little coldly,
from a tight mouth. "What does it matter where he is?"

"Have you ever heard of kidnapping, Merelene?"

She had heard of it. "I am *not* a kidnapper. All I did
was . . ."

"I'm not talking about you."

"Who are you talking about then?" She was lost, maybe
in more ways than one.

"This exhibit here"—he tapped the letter with a finger-
nail as rough as tortoiseshell—"tells us that Mayfield
wants the boy. People like Mayfield sometimes take what
they want."

Then she remembered the children whose faces were pinned to the bulletin board at the post office, and magazine articles about divorced couples, children found in South America and Australia with one parent or the other, years older than the pictures that the police had been given. "I'll hide him," she said.

"You'll take him back to the Center," the lawyer said flatly.

"I'll hide him . . . somewhere."

He sighed and shook his head in exasperation. "We'll talk about hiding things later. We've got this to deal with now." He hit the letter again with the flat of his hand.

She reached for the letter but he held it away. "How can he take Roland? *Can* he? Tell me, you know the law."

"I don't know, Merelene. I know he can't by the means of my services."

They stared at each other. She said, "You're going to have to help me now. You know that?"

"Yes," he said. She could not read his eyes, what was behind them in that cave of mind. He said, "You know I've always wanted to." He smiled, and a little mischief came into his tone. "Even from the time you were the child bride of Mr. Mayfield Durham, local rakehell and scoundrel. You know it, don't you?"

She knew things about him. She remembered the rich boy whose expectations had always set him apart. He had been wild in the isolation of brains and money, coming home summers from prep school in crested blue blazers and white buck shoes with fast cars and faster girls and his eyes aiming far off. Never at Swinford. Certainly not at her own self. Later, after the war had torn his body and labeled him a hero, the town loved him and wondered why he didn't leave for Bainesborough or further, where people would appreciate his elevated talk, and he could make a living doing the law he liked. She knew *something* had kept him here.

She said, "Wanted to help me?"

"Wanted you," he said. His face coloring again.

She laughed or shuddered. She said, "Don't tease me, just help me get through like you said you would." And she wanted to go back to her typewriter before his eyes could work on her more. He cleared his throat, and his eyes changed. "There are things that . . . give him a case, if it's a case he wants." He watched her.

"Things?"

"You know what I mean."

"You mean he'll say I'm unfit."

"I mean he can say it, can try it. It's the usual stratagem. You have to be ready for that."

"And what about the things *I* can say. Was it *me* that went off and left a family, one of them addled and the other two without one skill between them to get their daily bread." Heat rolled over her as she remembered herself last night taking Mayfield into her hands to drag him to Roland's bedside and make him see. Intending, maybe, to beat him with a handful of Bull's letters and say, "You got a son with bullets flying at him right now."

He looked at her. She knew he was thinking law, confining them to things provable, testifiable, so she said, "Do you know who he is?"

"I know who he is."

"I'm talking about his wonderful new self. Mr. Money-bags."

"I know who he is," he said. "Believe me."

At noon he came out to her cubicle and took the plastic hood and covered her typewriter with her hands still on the keys. "Come on," he said. She took her purse from under the desk and followed him out to his old Cadillac.

He drove straight to her house, and, without the usual courtesy of letting her out of the car, got a head start up the walk to the front door. She was beside him before he had made the stoop. "What do you think you are doing?"

"Unlock the door."

"Answer me or we'll stand here making a spectacle of ourselves in front of Sligh Street."

"I'm acting as your attorney, Mrs. Durham. The one you asked to help you. I'm telling you it's your best interest to unlock the door."

She hesitated for a moment, but her hand was already in her purse.

Roland was watching reruns of *Rescue 8*. He didn't turn his face from the fishy glow of the TV when they opened the door. She said, "How are you, baby?"

"Fine, Mudder."

"What you watching?"

"Male Caucasian, aged thirty-two." He still hadn't turned toward her.

"See," she said to the lawyer, who seemed a little less determined standing beside her now, "I told you everything was all right."

"Does he have a suitcase?" The lawyer was hobbling toward her bedroom. It was territory she protected.

"Of course he does," she said. "Wait here and I'll get it."

She could see the yellow glow of the sign a half mile before they reached it, and at two hundred yards she could read the words. THEY SHALL BEAT THEIR SOWARDS INTO PLOUGHSHARES AND THEIR SPEARS INTO PRUNING HOOKS. She turned and looked at Roland in the backseat beside his suitcase. He looked worried. The first time she had packed him for a trip, one month ago, he had gone willingly; this time it had taken a little persuading. "It's just Mrs. Bates," she had told him. "You know Mrs. Bates. That keeps the children."

"Miss Frances of Ding Dong School?"

Lord, where had that come from? Could he remember

that far back? But remember wasn't what his mind did. It was a switchboard connecting all calls at once. "Yes, honey," she said, because, in a way, he was right. "Like Miss Frances and Ding Dong School."

When the engine stopped, Merelene could hear the shouts of the children from behind the house which was Swinford's unofficial, unlicensed day-care center. Louise Bates came out to meet them on the neat, swept sand under the live oaks. She stood by the lawyer's door, waiting for him to steady his feet on the ground. She was a tall, thin pretty woman with a narrow face and slender hands. She stood holding herself, arms across her chest, long wrists stretching from the cuffs of a pilled old cardigan. It was cool under the live oaks that shaded her dooryard, and the blinking orange lights from her trailer sign flickered on her face. She shook the lawyer's hand. "Hi you, Mr. Sawyer." She peered across the car hood at Merelene, "and Mizriz Durham." Then she looked into the gloom of the backseat where Roland sat. "Is that the television boy the lawyer told me about? How are you, honey?"

Roland didn't speak.

Louise Bates went to the window and stuck a long arm into the backseat gloom. "Give me your hand, sweet, and we'll go inside and see what's on TV."

Roland slid over toward her and opened the door. When he was standing on the swept sand in front of her, he said, "Captain's log, stardate 3457 point 4."

Louise Bates looked at the Timex on her pale wrist. "That's not until later, honey, but you can sure watch it when it comes on."

When Roland was settled in the glow of the television, Louise Bates gave them her tour. It was a clean little frame house whose only purpose was children. There was nothing of value that could be broken; the floors were spill-proof linoleum, the wallpaper was washable, the cups and plates shatterproof plastic. The odors were talcum and pine oil and just a hint of innocent urine. The backyard was more shaded swept sand, but covered in a crisp, amber layer of pine needles. On a swing set and slide and monkey bars, seven county children, aged from five to twelve, occupied themselves in what seemed like harmony.

Louise Bates reserved one room as an office. It was no bigger than a large closet and held a metal desk, two chairs, a filing cabinet and an adding machine. She led them to it, and seated herself at the window overlooking the backyard. The lawyer insisted that Merelene take the one other chair. On the desk, reposing at an angle, was a framed photograph of Harold, Louise's son, in his U.S. Army PFC uniform. Under it was the legend *Suffer the little children* . . . in a scrolly script. It was very much like Merelene's own picture of Bull, and yet the two could not have been more different. Harold was a shrine now. Her picture was the living blood and life of a young man who wrote to her, who promised her he would stay safe, who received her packages of goods and books and sent back his thanks, who was coming home.

Louise looked at the picture, then out the window at the children. "Tell me again, Mr. Sawyer, what I'm doing with this boy."

"Why, you are keeping him," the lawyer said, with a raised eyebrow, and pointing to the neat yard beyond the window, "just like the ones in the back there."

"But thosens in the back are picked up at night and this one won't be?"

"Oh," said the lawyer, expansively, "that's just for a day or two, until we get a little problem of ours solved."

"Which it's what? This problem?"

"Well . . ." The lawyer's face colored. Merelene leaned forward across the table, shutting him out. "You remember my husband, don't you, Louise?"

She watched Louise Bates' eyes. Hadn't she known

Mayfield? Hadn't everybody known him some way or other?

Louise watched the backyard. With quick energy, she threw up the sash: "Now you *stop* that, Tommy C., or I'll have to come out there." Tommy C., who was about to ski backward down the slide, sat down.

"I known him some," said Louise. "By reputation mostly. I remember that business with the waterworks out to the city limits." She looked at Merelene in a puzzled way. It had all been so long ago. Even the words *my husband* were strange.

She waved her hand between them to sweep away the old memories: "Anyway, he's back here, and he's asking about Roland."

Louise's face changed. She stared at the children in the yard, most of whom, Merelene supposed, were from what the social workers liked to call "one-parent families," and then at the picture of the moon-faced boy on the desk. It was a color photo and Harold's skin was turning orange in the light from the backyard. "So you just want to hide him a little bit." She looked at the lawyer when she said, *hide him*. "Here with me?"

"And Mrs. Durham will pay whatever you ask for room and board . . ." It was the lawyer coming in again. But Louise was looking into Merelene's eyes now, and Merelene could feel the deep search. She looked straight back letting the examination happen.

Finally, Louise said, "I think we can make an arrangement for a few days. I can't tell you how long. Pends on how he"—she gestured toward the flicker of the television —"works out here. You know, how he gets along with the other kids." She hadn't taken her eyes from Merelene's. She must have heard about the Big Bath at Mary Heatherton's house, everybody had. "And you know, some of these parents have heard of him . . . I reckon."

Merelene firmed her eyes and said, "Then *some* of them have heard he gets along fine with other children."

She went to the living room and stood beside Roland in the glow of the TV. "Momma's going now, baby. You be a good boy and do what Mrs. Bates tells you."

He looked up at her. It was the same look she had seen in his face the day he had got out of her car three hundred miles south and ambled up the sidewalk with the attendant's hand on his shoulder. He raised his chin a little and touched his beard. She said, "Mrs. Bates has Rice Krispies."

"Rice Krispies," he said. "In the morning?"

"That's right."

He turned his face back to *The Price Is Right*.

When she was riding again with the lawyer, she couldn't help it, the same empty feeling, the same panic fear. She turned her head toward the window and ground her teeth, swearing she wouldn't, but a tear rolled. He left her alone until they had stopped in front of his grand old house.

"Would you like to come in here with me for a minute, Merelene?"

He was thinking, probably, that she couldn't go back to work, nor to her own empty house. She said, "All right," keeping her face to the window.

When they stood in his parlor, her cheeks were dry and there wasn't much to say. But she had to know one thing. "Why did she do it for you?"

"Louise?"

"Yes, Louise."

He went to the decanter on the Queen Anne table. With his back to her, he said, "She owes me one, I guess. I did some work for her one time. However, I suspect she did it for you, Merelene, after you let those eyes of yours go to work on her."

"What kind of work?"

"Probate work, when her husband, Pete, died. I did it
pro bono. It wasn't much." He turned and pressed a crys-
tal glass of amber whiskey to his lips. "But Louise is like a
lot of these people around here. She thinks my mumbo
jumbo is magic." He flourished the whiskey. "Holds herself forever in my debt." The smile he gave her across the
top of the glass said that he and his secretary were a con-
spiracy, and the others were "these people." Merelene
could remember when a will had completely baffled her.
As Mayfield's letter did now. She said, "I want to go lie
down," and headed for the stairs without his consent. She
barely heard him whisper, "Of course," as her foot
touched the carpeted stair.

But lying in his high old bed, high in the silent house,
she could not sleep for thinking about surprises. This bed
was full of them, his and hers together, all their nights.
Here in the early afternoon shade with a wind riffling the
curtains and the jays churring in the yard, she found herself remembering their first time, how it had happened
after years of their working together without hint of its
coming.

As her long love affair with his mind had grown, she
had accustomed herself to the knowledge, persistent and
bedeviling, that to him she was only fingers at a typewriter, legs to go to the post office. The day it had happened, it had seemed to follow from his first notice of her
mind, his first in their years together, and her first remark
about his body.

She had been typing letters to his tax clients, and she
had changed some of them, correcting him when his ele-
gance got the better of logic. It was a late, quiet afternoon
in the office, and she had changed his words as much to
alleviate boredom as to make sense. Still, when she took

him the letters and walked back to her desk, she was a little afraid.

He said, "Merelene, this is very good work here. I could let you *write* these letters, not just type them. You'd do as well as I do."

She had said, Yes, she supposed it was true, and allowed herself a moment's levity. "If you'd get up and walk out here more often,"—shouting this through the door—"you'd *see* how much I do without your stamp of approval." The heat had started immediately in her face as she realized how hard she had said the word *walk*. The silence grew and the distance between their two rooms increased by miles before she heard him getting up from his chair.

She did not know what face would show itself at the door, anger, hurt; she did not expect the smile that came gyrating around the corner. He said, "I didn't think you liked it so much—to see me walk, but . . ." He raised his hands as high above his head as they would go and rattled his heels like a flamenco dancer. It was minutes before they could stop laughing.

And still that might have been all had he not come out to the street a half hour later to find her with a dead battery and only three dollars in her purse. He called the Esso station, and said he would take her home. But he didn't turn at her street; he continued out the cowtrack to his own high old house and unloaded her with great ceremony saying it was time for them to get to know each other better. Her only thought was that it was pleasant to be abducted, and that now, perhaps, they would have a good talk, perhaps the first of many.

He was not pleased when she turned down the whiskey he drank with such pleasure, but they sat in the parlor and he sipped and stared at her, while she stared at the dusty old room. He owned a real Tiffany lamp with brass tassels dangling from the painted china shade. There were Persian rugs, gorgeous in their patterns, moth-eaten but still lustrous and thick. There were portraits and emblems of his family. Straight-backed stern ladies in high Victorian collars and long skirts and laced boots, and men, mostly in military uniform, going back to his great-grandfather, General Colquitt's aide-de-camp in the 1st Florida, and hero of the battle of Olustee. The colonel wore an eye patch and Merelene could see where the leather of its strap had stained the flesh of his temple a parchment color. He stared at her from the one eye that had seen everything, his right hand crossing to rest with his left on the hilt of his sword. He was not half so stern as the women.

The most recent of the pictures was of the lawyer's father—a youth in his twenties—a neat little man with an accountant's spectacles and an accountant's evaluating gaze. He wore a seersucker suit, a bow tie and a boater raked low in a way that made him a little ridiculous.

The lawyer had finished his first whiskey by the time she had finished her survey of the room, and still they had not spoken. She did not want to be uncomfortable with him. That was over, she had decided, because he seemed to be trying to tell her so. He rose to pour himself another and she watched him cross the Persian rug, thinking, what are we going to do?

She said, "It's a lovely room," aware that her voice was quiet and far away like the voice of someone standing at the window peering in. He poured the whiskey carelessly, spilling some of it on the lace cloth that covered a Queen Anne table. "A lovely room," he said, "which has not seen a lovely woman in many a year." It was not like him to deliver one of his lines with a sigh, and his back to her. He usually offered them up like the jewels he thought they were. She began, for the first time, to think about getting home. It wasn't a long walk, and was by no means an unpleasant one this time of day, so she wasn't worried

about his getting too soaked to drive. She said, "Well . . ."
He was still standing with his back to her, but now he
drank very quickly and she heard him strangle a little. She
stood too. "I . . ."

"Merelene?"

"Yes."

He turned, flushed at the throat and under the eyes.
There was the clearest plea in his eyes and it was at war
with his pride. He began to walk toward her and his struggling was unbearable to her now, because now she knew
what he was going to do when he had crossed the long
room. She waited until he was near, then turned her back
to him. She was not certain why she did it. She stood
watching the live oak in the yard, a bluejay worrying a
yellow cat lounging in the crotch of the tree. She felt his
hand at her waist, the angular press of him against the
curve of her back, and the light touch of his lips at the
nape of her neck. Still, she did not turn, and he murmured
to her things she did not hear for the clamor in her ears.
Perhaps they were not words anyway. His touch was
tender, the caress of his lips light upon her neck.

She let him turn her then and kiss her on the lips, long
and deep, and with this kiss she knew it was what she
wanted. The whiskey on his lips burnt her, and it was as
though she had been signed by him, the seal of a new life.
After this first long, satisfying kiss, her first man's kiss
since Mayfield, he turned and walked toward the stairs
and she followed, slowly, watching him walk with new
eyes, the eyes of a lover. It was a long way up but it
seemed like nothing.

His bedroom was a monk's cell. She knew without his
saying so that downstairs was a museum to him now, and
that this place was where he lived in a bitter and austere
spirit, alone with his disappointment. Her heart rushed
out to this room and its severity. She had the urge to cover
it all, and him, with herself, with the decoration of love.

He took her to the bed, a big high bed, which he had to struggle to mount, and began fumbling with the fastenings of her clothing, his eyes never leaving her face. It was as though her eyes held the instructions he needed to undress her. She helped him a little, here and there, blushing as she came loose from her fetters and stood before him naked with her expectancy coursing in her. Then, she felt the sudden need to cover herself again, to bolt from this room, not because it was wrong, but because she knew it was not going to end here, it was going to be from now on. This moment passed. She made it pass by closing her eyes and refusing the impulse to press her hands to her breasts and cover them from his feeding stare.

She made herself reach out to his vest and begin the buttons, which seemed to her to break from their beds as loud as pistol shots. She laughed at herself, at last, at this last of her timidity and then with hands almost rough, she took him out of his clothes. When he was naked, she saw his wounds, long incisions where the flesh was as neatly cleft as by surgical instrument, and others, crude and brutal, as though he had been beaten with some blunt thing. And there were two bullet holes in his right thigh. She stared at their small, starry entrances and large cauliflower exits. He watched her looking, as he sat on the edge of the bed, his right leg stiff as it forever was. He said, "They shot me down," and he put his right hand on the two punctures, "here and here," and he raised his hand to wave in a general way at the rest of him, "and I couldn't use the parachute; my leg was holding me in and the ship went into a treetop." He touched the other places thoughtfully. "The rest of this is glass and metal. They found me on the ground. Somehow, I climbed down from the tree. The parachute was full of holes anyway." His smile was wry and bitter. He had abbreviated the story so terribly, perhaps to save her the real horror. And what did she know about flying an airplane in a war, about going down in flames. He had been a well-built young man of average height with a handsome face and a fine mind when he had gone away to fly, and he had come back bent and five inches shorter. He had been standing on his toes to kiss her neck downstairs. She tried to keep herself from crying, but couldn't and knew that she would spoil it all for him, for them. He said, "Now don't do that, not now. If there was any way without showing you this wreckage, we'd manage it, but there isn't. Please don't cry."

She took up his shirt from the floor and wiped her eyes, and said, okay, okay, I won't, and she leaned close to him and he kissed her cheeks where the tears had been. She said, thank you, and he said, "I'm going to have something to thank you for, ain't I?" She bundled him in her arms as best she could and nodded, yes.

Ten

She had been born of farm people and raised to know what farmers knew. She had bucked tobacco bales, loaded and unloaded barns, and watched a few burn to the ground with a family's whole life hanging in racks inside. She had topped and suckered tobacco plants, and cropped the leaves in the August heat when the touch of the tobacco resins to the skin could make blisters rise.

She had ridden the yellow school bus to Alligood County Consolidated Junior-Senior High School with the children of crabbers and shrimpers. Looking up the aisle she had noticed their hands, dark brown and sticky like her own, or chapped raw from the shells and smelling perpetually of fish. None of them had thought much of it.

The road to Bainesborough, to the university, to department stores, supermarkets, and the county seat, was the way to another world. It was only fifty miles, but its truest measure was time, not distance.

Merelene had been a tomboy. She wore jeans when she didn't have to, and her brother's flannel shirts when he let her. As a young girl in the 1940s, she went without brassieres because she was small-breasted and in her brother's flowing shirts no one could tell what she was wearing. She was never certain why she dressed as she did, walked as she did (without all the unnecessary wiggles) or liked what she liked, fishing, hunting, driving long distances by herself at night with a ballad on the car radio and the moon in the treetops. She was certain that she was going to be a woman, though there were a few who whispered that she was not, and she never lacked the attentions of men, for men could sense better than the whisperers what she was and would be.

She had met Mayfield one night in the summer of '46 when she was seventeen years old. She was on one of her midnight drives. She had stayed too late, purring along on the powdery crest of a county secondary road watching for deer at crossings only she knew about. She had lifted her eyes from the edges of the road and aimed them at the moonlit canyon between the trees and was picking up speed to get home quick when she saw it, a brief flicker of white at the road's edge. She had passed a good ways beyond it before an afterimage, more or less complete, composed itself in her head of a young man in a white short-sleeved shirt, carrying a duffel bag.

She was never sure why she stopped. Girls by themselves did not pick up hitchhikers, even in those days when soldiers were on the roads and the country was grateful. But she had been certain, as she shifted into reverse, her arm resting on the cool metal of the windowsill and her hair flying out, that she would help, do whatever this chore demanded. Later she had reckoned it was nothing less than the hand of fate (sometimes she said to herself, cruel fate) that stopped the car that night.

He stood still at the window in the dark and they could hear the engine ticking, and the june bugs were flying through the high beams like tracer bullets. She did not have to add much to the image she had composed a moment earlier. He was slender, she could see now, a very dark young man with hard, sinewy arms in a white short-sleeved shirt open at the throat, and khaki trousers, probably his from some branch of the service, which reassured her a little. He did nothing but stand, and for a moment she feared he might be feebleminded; there was something about the stillness of his limbs, the simplicity of his stare. It was as though he did not believe what he was seeing.

Finally, he stepped toward the car and looked into the backseat. She looked back there too—nothing of course. What did he expect? That she was playing some trick? His face, his eyes, had the look of one who took no chances. He took another step toward her and leaned in to the window and she could feel the heat of him, sudden and vital there with her in the car. She swallowed and said, "Get in."

He placed his bag on the floor and sat lightly on the seat beside her. The shifting of springs and straps beneath them was somehow intimate. They drove some distance in silence before she remembered to ask where he wanted to go.

"Just along this way a ways." He said it firmly, in a tone that contradicted the uncertainty of the words themselves.

She said, "Do you know where you are?" She tried not to keep stealing glances at him from her driving.

"I'm about five miles outside of Chiefland, just before the cutoff to a little place called Swinford."

She said, "You are that, but where are you going? Into town?"

He said, "You can drop me in town. That'll be fine."

She said, okay, but she kept thinking, the way he'd said it, he didn't seem to care where she took him. One place was as good as another. And yet he seemed definite in other ways—the straight way he sat and stared at the on-rushing night, rested his hand along the crest of the old bench seat so that it almost touched her shoulder, and lit a cigarette without asking her was it all right.

She dropped him under the eyes of the Confederate

monument on the courthouse square. He stepped out of the car, stretched, leaving his bag on the floor inside (otherwise she might have driven away immediately and things might have been different) and looked up at the monument a long time. It was lighted by a small flood mounted on the courthouse wall and he shaded his eyes to see it, which made him look a lot like the figure on the pedestal.

He flicked his cigarette in the general direction of the inscription on the granite pedestal, blew a plume of white smoke into the night, and turned to her. "The fool that put that up ought to have to take its place for a year or two." Which was in those days nothing but blasphemy. Merelene savored this heresy, even as she said, "Boy, you better not use that attitude around here. It's some who'd put you under the ground if they heard it."

"Come one, come all," he said in an even tone. She picked up the bag to hand to him, noticing that it was light. It couldn't have held much more than a change of clothes. He bent into the car, taking the bag from her and leaning closer than he had to. "You operating this taxi service tomorrow night?"

She said, "Not hardly." She did not know how to take him. Did he think she drove around in the middle of the night looking for the likes of him? She decided it was just more foolishness from the opposite sex. She had enough experience with boys to know they said whatever floated on the cerebral surface when they got next to girls like her.

He withdrew a bit and said, "Is it a rooming house around here, or a hotel?"

She said, "Not that's open this time of night."

He chewed his lip a bit over that piece of information and then said, "Just as well," and backed out of the window. She put the car in gear, thinking about taking him home and putting him in Eddie's vacant bedroom, Eddie,

her brother, who was still in Yokohama with the occupa-
tion, but only thinking about it. She was in enough trouble for getting home at twelve-thirty.

As she drove away, letting herself look at him one more
time, one time too many, she supposed, he smiled a little
wickedly, and called out, "Be seeing you." And he was as
good as his word.

She had seen him all over the place after that. It was the
summer after her graduation from high school and she
had seemed to be everywhere herself, driving the car fast
and hard and enjoying the freedom and danger of being
loose from school and into her future.

She never knew where he had slept that first night, but
later he took up residence with Mrs. Henderson, who ran
a small rooming house. He took a job as a Cat operator in a
small pulpwood operation. The town suddenly began to
talk about him. She caught snatches of conversation about
"the new boy who worked for Hardy Parker, out to
Steinhatchee." They said he had connections hereabouts,
but never seemed to visit them, never said exactly who or
where they were. They said he could hold his liquor with
the best of them and often did with the worst. They said
he had gotten into a tussle with Hardy Parker's younger
brother, Rodie, and had made pretty short work of him.
They said he had come to church once and unloosed a
beautiful tenor voice, but only once. He was a crack shot,
they said, and knew how to repair things and could handle
horses and dogs. They said he had been in the service but
didn't talk about it, because they supposed, he had seen
dark things. You didn't cross him, they said. No sir. No
ma'am.

Yes, she had seen him all over the place that summer,
and she had said a cordial hello and gone about her business, until, one afternoon, when she was getting some gas
at the Esso station, and he was standing around in the

shade of the grease rack with the local motor buffs while they all pointed at something underneath a '37 Chevy.

He had broken away from the group and sauntered over to her window, carrying a dope. He stood outside the window, just as he had done the night she had given him a ride. He tilted the dope back and drank it off and dropped the empty in a carton slanted against the gas pump. Then he reached down and opened the door and got in. She said, "Well, get right on in. Don't stand on ceremony." He said, "No, I don't stand on it. I fly over it. Where you gone take me this time?"

She said, "Son, I ain't taking you serious, let alone take you in my Daddy's car."

He said, a little less recklessly now, "Let's drive on out to the river and cool off. It's hotter'n a two-dollar pistol on this concrete. How bout it?" He smiled a smile that said at least he was asking, not telling. So when she had plucked her change from Lum Smalley's greasy fingers, she tucked it into her jeans and just drove. It felt good to get off that hot concrete and have the wind streaming through the car.

When they got to the river road, she decided to head out to Sale Spring and he didn't seem to mind where they went. Every so often she would glance over at him while he did his best to act like he didn't know she was looking, or maybe he didn't know. She didn't know which was worse. It was practically impossible to talk over the wind and the engine and she supposed that was just as well. What would they have to say anyway? They hadn't gone far along the river road when they passed Larup's, which had just opened, nothing but a tar paper clapboard shack with a jukebox and a pool table, and a hand-lettered sign hanging in a live oak over the hardroad that said WHISKEY. For the types that hung out at Larup's it was sufficient.

She had never been inside Larup's, nor had any inclination to be, so she concentrated on driving and thinking and was surprised when he said, "Here," as though she should know what he meant by such an exclamation. He slid over closer and inclined his head to her ear and said, "Stop here. Something I need to get."

She pulled in with a spray of sand and the burr of tires that brought a few of Tom Larup's patrons to the open door. She sat in the car with her ears burning while they leered at her and the jukebox boomed. He got out and parted them like waters. He wasn't inside but a few minutes, and emerged with his straw hat knocked back on his head and a paper bag in his hand with its top twisted like a cornsilk cigarette. She could just hear the rumors racketing their way up one side of Circuit Street to the Mt. Horeb Baptist Church, and down the other side to the First Presbyterian. She had connections enough in both denominations to generate a small-to-medium scandal. Her only hope was that the faces at the door might be from the other side of the river, Isle Hammock boys.

When he got into the car, he put the bottle on the seat beside him, and looked over at her for a judgment. She was too busy leaving Larup's to give one right away, but when the wind was whistling in their ears again, she said, "I ought to know better than to do what I'm told."

"You're fine," he said, as though that was the end of it. Didn't he know what a seventeen-year-old girl's reputation was worth in a town like this? Yet she found that she could take comfort from his certain tone. You're fine. Maybe he knew the people inside, and what they would say, or not say. Maybe he knew the times (though he could not know the place) better than she did. He had been away to war. She sensed with everyone else that the town was waiting for the lesson its returning sons would teach.

She knew his name was Mayfield Durham. She'd heard it from some talkers, but never from his lips. She said, "What's your name? If we are going to be riding in this car together with a bottle of whiskey on the seat between us, I believe I have a right to know." She smiled to show that she was half joking, but he stared straight ahead and said, "I'm Mayfield and you're Merelene. You're the prettiest girl in this town and you got a pretty name, Merelene." Now he looked over and she blushed, damning herself for not controlling it. "Why, thank you, sir," she said.

He picked up the paper poke and put it on the floor between his boots. "The bottle don't have to come between us." He was watching her. The power of his gaze was such that she could not look at him, and so drove on, concentrating, and feeling herself inspected by the inch as though she were in a doctor's office. It was not altogether unpleasant, this doctoring of his. And another thing: she found she wanted to know what was in the brown paper bag with the twisted top. She had never tasted whiskey.

She took them to Sale Spring. Going in on the rutted track that would allow only one car to pass at a time, they encountered a pickup truck full of Truscotts, parents and children, six girls and three boys crouched in the truckbed and swaying like ducks in a shooting gallery. She had to back into a little side way to let the Truscotts pass and she had to wave and speak to as many of the stair-step kids as she could remember, Herbert, Delvin, Marie, Eddie, and smile at the mealy faces of Howard and Sue in the cab of the truck. And know that she was to be talked about now for sure. The Truscotts were powerful talkers.

When they got down to the spring and parked on the bluff above the spot where the cool blue water boiled up from the sandy earth into a limestone bowl before flowing to the river, she saw that it was the one day in a thousand when no one had come. The Truscotts had had it to themselves and now so did she and this Mayfield Durham. They sat in the car for a time and she made silly remarks about the history of the place, and its ownership and its uses, all obvious, or nearly so and she was ashamed of herself for pattering on like a tour guide and making it obvious to him that she was afraid to be alone here with a man of twenty-one, a veteran, a person of superior experience and new to the community. She regretted the whole thing. But he reached over and took her hand and tugged it and said, "Come on," and she was sliding with him across the seat and out the door and they were running down the sand bluff like two children and suddenly, he seemed no different from a hundred boys, simple creatures, and she was safe again.

It was a beautiful day, deep in summer, the cloudless vault of sky arching the chimney of live oak branches above the blue sinkhole. A rope hung from an oak branch with a loop in the end for the brave few who could swing out and drop. Now it turned slow circles, writing its shadow on the roiling surface of the spring.

She knew how many thousand gallons per minute of pure limestone spring water made the surface of this pool stir and turn, but she did not tell him. She felt clear and cool and blue herself and she had finished being his guide. She let go his hand and walked to the edge of the pool and slipping off her shoe and sock, put in some toes. He was behind her, reflected in the water. She felt him reach for her waist and take her as though to throw her in, a boy's usual doings, to make her scream and plead, and she was disappointed, and then she felt him slowly turn her with powerful hands she could not have escaped had she wanted to, and she was facing him, the two of them standing on the limestone shelf which still held the half-dried footprints of little Truscotts. He confronted her for a long moment with eyes that stated clear intentions. He was going to kiss her. There was nothing she could do. She wanted to do nothing. She found with surprise and guilt and a great surge of something else she could not name, that she wanted this kiss, and more, had wanted it since the night she had seen a flicker of white shirt on a roadside not far from here. It was a good kiss. It fit.

* * *

That first time by the spring, when he had kissed her
with the kiss that fit, she had known more would follow
and quickly and she was ready for her life to begin. The
long time of growing up and of waiting among children
who waited too, of graduation and coming to this summer,
poised as she drove the midnight roads under the white
moon; the time of her search was over.

Habits followed quickly from that first kiss. They saw
each other every night, until her mother stopped her, saying that it was all right to have a beau, but not to give him
the knowledge that you wanted no others. It wasn't wise.
She must go out with other boys.

Hating it, she accepted dates with the slow-witted sons
of pulpwooders and shrimpers, and had her first bitter
arguments with Mayfield about them, offering up her
mother as her excuse. And she snuck out late with him
after being dropped off as early as was decent by the other
boys.

She would leave by her upstairs bedroom window, barefoot, her toes finding purchase on the mossy cedar shingles, and go swinging into the branches of the live oak that
shaded the back gallery. It was not easy, especially since
Mayfield insisted she wear dresses. He would have none of
the tomboy she had been. He wanted a woman who
looked like one, walked like one, and later, he said, loved
like one. He would teach her.

In the mornings, she practiced walking in her bedroom
mirror, toeing along the straight oak flooring like the New
York models she had seen in the Movietone News. It made
her slim hips turn with each step and gave her a few of the
wiggles she had hoped to go without. It wasn't long before
she could do it without fear of falling in the high-heeled
pumps he had brought her from Bainesborough.

So she would tuck up her skirts into her underdrawers
and sling the new shoes by their straps over her shoulder

and climb into the high, windy night hurrying to meet him on Wilmott Avenue under the streetlight. Terrified of being seen, she would stand casually there like a woman of the night. He would pick her up in the new Packard he had bought with his Caterpillar money and drive with her as close as warm air on the seat beside him until they were in the next county, going from one cut-and-shoot dive to another where he always seemed to have laughing, dancing, dangerous friends.

Or sometimes they would not cross the county line. He would drive straight to Sale Spring, into the heart of the circle where the water rushing upward cooled the air, and they could almost hear the dying echoes of the day's swimmers. Occasionally, they met a car or two at the spring; it was a place lovers went. There was a decorum about these meetings. The cars were parked as far apart as possible. Mayfield always dimmed his lights, never attempted to discover who was who. She liked this consent of outlaws, and imagined girls like herself in these other cars, who would not be bound by the edicts of mothers who did not understand love. For she was coming to understand love, its power, its strong demands.

They knew each other for the first time one night at Sale Spring. She was dressed to kill in a Mexican lace blouse, off the shoulders like Jane Russell, and a dirndl skirt of bright cotton and hoped to go to the roadhouses to kick up her heels and show herself off for him. But he drove to the spring instead, and she did not complain. It was as though their directions were written out on the night in front of his rocketing Packard.

At the spring they were alone. Even so, by habit they left the car and walked into the woods, heading first in a false direction to cover their way from anyone who might be watching. When they were well into the tall pines, they turned and circled the spring, and took a downhill grade to the south following the underground run of the spring until they came to the mouth of a little cave hidden in a bower of cedars. They had discovered it together one day when a sudden rush of cold air on their faces had made them curious and Mayfield had stepped forward to part the cedar branches and reveal this fantasy place. They had looked at each other and without speaking, agreed it was theirs.

As she walked beside him on this night, her arm coupled in his, and the blanket he had taken from the car in his other hand, she knew something would happen. Nights here had been growing more and more pleasurable, and more dangerous. She hated to fight him, because love was not combat, but there were times when she had resisted with more than gentle force, and these times she loved him all the more for the fierceness of his need. She was life to him.

When they were inside their grotto and he had spread the blanket for her in his funny, courtly way, he stepped to her and kissed her deeply. Then he began to unfasten the buttons of her blouse, and she stepped back and said, "Whoa, son." She could not see his eyes, where lay the message she needed. He stepped close again, placed a warm hand on her neck and whispered, "It's tonight, Merelene."

At first she thought she could pretend ignorance of what he meant, but this stupidity passed and she fished in the whirl of her thoughts for what to do, to say, and caught nothing. Finally, the whirling slowed and she covered his hand with hers on her breast and said, "Tonight, then." She began removing her clothing, and watched as he began to do the same. She had seen him before in bathing shorts, but this, the white trunk of him, emerging legs, somehow was different. She was standing in her brassiere and underpants, cold and wishing for the comfort of the blanket, when the panic began to rise in her. If only he would put his hand on her again, gentle her now, say it again, "Tonight," but he only continued his undressing. She did not want to think about his confidence. She said, "There's something I got to do," and stepped away, and out of their place, leaving him to think what he would, that she needed privacy for a woman's reason.

She ran quickly back to the spring, her heart clattering against her ribs, straight, not by their circling route, and stood at its lip by starlight regarding her dim image in the water. She had not been ready back there, and how could she get ready here? The cool breath of the water spread gooseflesh across her thighs, and she ran her hands along them, fiercely chafing the flesh to warm it. Then she let her fingers touch the place that Mayfield wanted, would have soon if she could get the panic down. She pressed herself there, asking this secret flesh how to be ready.

She did not know why she went to the river, left the cool clear pool below the white limestone shelf and walked to the leafy bank. She lay her underthings on a cypress knee, parted drifts of warm mist and walked into the river upstream of the spring run, and somehow, knew this was right. The river was quickly deep in this place and she struck out in a strong breaststroke, upstream, keeping the white flicker of her brassiere and underpants in sight. She beat against the current, not making way, until she was out of breath. She rested for a moment, but fearing to be carried down to the cold mouth of the spring, she turned and swam to the bank.

She was cold again when the night air touched her and shivering like a dog, so she waded upstream searching with her feet for a piece of sandy bottom where she could sit shoulder-deep in the warm water and rest herself. She tried to clarify her thoughts as the warm currents pulled at her buttocks and thighs, lifted her breasts with a gentle tug. She tried to think of what was surely coming, and to do so, again she let her fingers find the place that Mayfield wanted. She parted herself and felt the waters enter. She stood and walked back up the bank, gouging up hands full of leafy marl, faintly sulfurous and black as night. Fiercely, she rubbed these two gouts of the river's body across her smarting breasts, her belly, and down into the cavity between her legs. She felt the leaves curl and break against her secret skin, the rake of gravel and twig, and knew that she had found it. She rubbed harder, until she had scored her flesh, thinking all the while, trying to understand why she needed this.

She had gone back into the river to clean herself, and was walking back to Mayfield when it came to her. The river was a woman. As she passed the spring, returning, she knelt and saw her face in it.

Mayfield was a little angry when she reached him. She was dripping wet and his first words were from his need and harsh, but she did not hear them. She was still full of the wonder of what she had learned. The rest was simple. He took her into his arms and using his shirt dried her. When he touched the welts she had made with his fingertips, tracing the name of her new condition, she said, "Never mind, just come on." Then he was over her and it was what she had learned it would be, and what she had learned, she learned to use.

It wasn't long after this night with Mayfield that the lawyer returned from the army hospitals. His homecoming made quite a convulsion in the little place. He was announced by newspaper articles numbering his exploits and clamoring for the proper welcome, calling him the true-blue son who had sacrificed. As a seventeen-year-old who was newly in love with a stranger, also a soldier, Merelene did not pay much attention. She had known the lawyer only as the young man whose family owned damned near everything. The young man had come and gone mostly—to Choate and then to Yale. She had seen him driving around the county summers and holidays in a fast and flashy car with Italian writing on it, and like as not, a pretty girl in the curve of his arm. Naturally, the town resented him. Some of the boys, sons of shrimpers and pulpwooders, who would have changed places with him in a minute, called him Lord Faunt Lee Roy, which got shortened to just Lee Roy—*there goes Lee Roy in that car of his.*

When she had thought about him at all before the war, it was to envy him a little like everyone else, and occasionally to wonder was he as stuck-up as some people said he was. She had passed him once or twice on some dusty midnight back road when she was fifteen and out learning to drive, the sound of his racing engine harsh in the canyons of pine trees. And she had caught his eye a time or two and seen nothing in it for her, for any of them in this place. It was an eye trained on something in the distance. She supposed, a brilliant future. He had enlisted in the Air Corps after Yale, an item in *The County News Leader*. She had followed her brother's progress (nothing in the paper about *him*) across the Pacific, read his strange letters with little square holes cut in them where the censors had been, and forgot about Lord Lee Roy.

He had come by private plane to the airport in Bainesborough hardly more than a pasture in those days, and had ridden in an ambulance the fifty miles to Swinford, bypassing the town and its greeting, and pulling up under the tall oaks that shaded the family home to be unloaded like so much beef, a consignment for his ailing father and their Negro houseman. It was almost a month before anyone saw him. He did not leave the house until he could leave it walking, if walking was what you could call it.

She had seen him at a distance once or twice, moving around experimentally in the shade of those tall trees, learning the stiff, halting gait that had carried him ever since. And once, when she was well into her courtship

with Mayfield, the three of them had met on the main
street of Swinford.

It was late one evening as the movie was getting out. It
was *Mildred Pierce*, she recalled, and she had just seen it for
the third time (having made Mayfield sit through it twice).
The lawyer was coming along the street stabbing the concrete with his two canes, sweating and concentrating, his
father walking slowly beside him in a white Palm Beach
suit. She and Mayfield were among the last out of the
movie house, and so there were only a few to see the
strange spectacle. She supposed they planned their walks
to avoid stares and kind gestures. But they were a little
early this night.

The lawyer did not look up until he was close, and Merelene silently cursed herself for not giving way while she
could have. And she was disappointed in Mayfield, who
stood rooted beside her frankly staring. She supposed his
interest stemmed, at least in part, from the local lore about
Lord Lee Roy. He had heard all the talk, read the papers
about the fighter pilot who had made twenty-eight kills in
just three months while Patton raced to the Rhine. Perhaps he had a soldier's interest, maybe even a little of the
comradely feeling. Mayfield had entered the lore too.

The lawyer looked up at them and blanched, then, as
best he could, greeted them. She would always remember
how pitiable had been his attempt to tip his hat to her. His
father, standing beside him in agony, had finally reached
out to stop the hand that dropped a cane as it tried to
reach his hat brim. She whispered, as though they were
alone in church, "How are you, Enos," ignoring her manners and his father. He looked at her from under a knit
and glistening brow. "I'm fine," he said, and laughed, she
thought, a strangely hearty laugh. "I'm just fine, and
you?"

By now, she was lit by her own deep blush, and thinking he was making fun of her, thinking stupidly, only of

herself, tried to make the rest as brief as possible. "Everyone is glad you're back."

"I'm sure," he said, and it came out curt maybe because he didn't really know any of them, nor did any know him. It was all manners and politeness and just too much trouble. He wanted to be on his way, such as it was.

But he said a strange thing. "You are looking pretty as a princess, Miss Merelene. You certainly are." He smiled big, watching her and Mayfield too, and she blushed deep, and through the shock of his knowing her name, could think of nothing more to say. She only nodded as Mayfield tugged her away. When they had walked on down the street toward the ice-cream parlor and a little treat before the big one, she realized that Mayfield had not spoken. She thought it odd, but did not mention it. She supposed to him it was all too useless for comment. As far as she knew, he had no capacity for embarrassment.

And later when she and the lawyer had become what they had become, she realized there had been something in his eyes for her that night, though she had not had the experience to see it. It was a blessing, she had decided, that she had not seen it, for she'd had enough on her hands then, and for years to come.

Eleven

One night not long after the lawyer's homecoming, Mayfield came to her bedroom. In her warm sleep she was
flying the watery element from no departure and with no
place to land. She felt a hand on her face and woke gently
to this touch. Even before she was properly awake, she
knew it was he who touched her. She moved her head on
the pillow, and saw his shape in the dark, that he had
placed a chair by her bed, that the window, the same one
she sometimes flew to him from, was open, that her filmy
curtains rolled in the night wind. Taking the words from
her recent dream, she said, "You flew in my window."

His hand, moving now on her forehead, said yes, yes,
yes.

She lay for a time under the searching pressures of his
fingers, letting him trace her like a blindman.

"You have a beautiful face, Merelene." He whispered
this, and when he did, she was conscious of the house, of
her parents piled beneath them in sleep, all the sweet vapors of their dreams rising to the dark heavens, and she
and Mayfield, together in the highest room, awake in il-

licit meeting. She whispered. "Thank you for the compli-
ment."

His voice went on low and soft and sure now. "Your
cheekbones are high like the Algonquins"—he placed a
thumb-and-finger tripod on her eyes and nose, measuring
—"and your nose is slim and slightly tilted up and your
lips are full but not overripe and your chin is the work of
principalities and powers."

She had never heard him talk this way. Tranced on her
pillow with his fingers wandering her face, she believed
she had returned to her dream. "I feel the skin you washed
before you went to bed tonight. It glows alive. It don't
need powder and oil and paint. The first time I saw you
was at night, and I knew your skin. I know it now."

"You see with your hands?" she said.

"I do," he said. "My hands are eyes."

"Why do you drive a bulldozer with them. That's a
rough way to treat your eyes."

"I want them blind for the time being."

He stood abruptly, and his hand leaving her face was
the loss of all the pleasure of the world.

He was at the window.

"Where are you going?"

"I don't know," he said. "Out to get blind, I guess."

"Don't get blind without me?" She hated the plaintive
note in her voice.

"I want you just where you are," he said, "lying in your
warm bed, with your perfect face in the cool air from the
window, and sleeping the night to death."

"What a strange thing to say, Mayfield."

"Not so strange, Merelene. Not when you know where
it comes from. I will see you."

His last words awakened her completely. He had said he
would see her. She lay still, listening, and heard him in the
rustle of live oak branches and then his feet soft on the

grass and light on the pavement, and then the grind and cough and rumble of his Packard going into the night.

An hour later, at first light, she heard his car pass again, flying, the radio loud and the laughing louder. She recognized the high squeal of Roark Drawdy's voice. Angry and abandoned, she reminded herself that he made no bones about his friends in three counties and the things they sometimes did after he let her off. She reminded herself she had no claim on him, nor he any on her, not yet anyway, and tried to go back to sleep. When she was sure that sleep had abandoned her, too, she lay in the dark watching the panes of the east window take on the shine of visibility. She heard the awakening whistle of cardinals in the live oak, and then from far away, the smallest whine, like a mosquito in her ear, growing louder, becoming the siren of a State patrol car out on the Chiefland road. She pictured two men in the car wearing Sam Browne belts and campaign hats low over the grim determination on their faces. The phone rang downstairs and she heard her daddy groaning his way out of bed.

He worked part-time for the county utilities. People called him Tom Warrington, the water man, or sometimes just Tom Water. These calls came sometimes, a broken pipe, a storm drain plugged in heavy rain. He even did a little moonlighting in blocked septic tanks. As she lay watching the dawn light solidify on the windowpanes, she knew it was water that had brought the two grim-faced men in Sam Browne belts, one of them wrenching the steering wheel now through the sharp S-curve on the old Kincaid Road. And her daddy would be going to meet them.

She heard the Water Man answer the eleventh ring, and her mother, drowsy but rising: "What is it, Tom?"

When her father said—"They *what*?"—Merelene put another piece into the picture. Mayfield's Packard. The loud radio and Roark Drawdy's high, pig-stuck voice, and downstairs, her father's outrage, and the siren which was just now lowering to a slow grind as the State car slowed at the town's one traffic signal.

Merelene was out of bed and into a skirt and blouse and shoes and standing by her father at the phone. "I'll be there as soon as I get dressed," he said, and slammed the receiver into its cradle.

Later, when he was hurrying into the car, she slid in beside him. "I'm going with you."

She could see him start to be her daddy, but her eyes stopped him. He clamped his lip and slipped back into just Herbert Tom Warrington, determined public servant. "I don't want you underfoot."

"Don't worry about that," she said. "I'll be in the background."

The tallest thing in town was a giant silver tulip bulb on four girder legs with SWINFORD, FLA painted on it in flat black letters three times the height of a man. You could read it five miles out on the Chiefland road. Now Roark Drawdy dotted the I in SWINFORD as he clung to the rungs of a tiny ladder halfway up the bulb.

Her daddy's eyes had been on the water tower ever since its silver eminence had risen above the tops of the live oaks at the edge of town. When they pulled up next to the road patrol car, in a peanut field a mile outside of town, her daddy got out, his eyes still on the dangling dot which was Roark, and walked toward a group of people standing just outside the chain link fence that ringed the base of the tower. A woman Merelene didn't know was saying, "I stepped out here to let Jimmy give water, and thrown my eye up and there he was." She spoke earnestly to the State patrolman, who took a pad from under his Sam Browne and began to write. "Here, Jimmy," the woman said, "come to mommer!" Jimmy, a beagle, raced down the peanut rows wet to the eyeballs in dew. He

panted at the woman's feet while she explained that she
hadn't meant to interfere if the man was *posed* to be up
there, but . . .

Merelene knew Roark Drawdy from high school. He
had been the class criminal, a sly boy who was always
taking things out of his pockets to show the other boys,
things that made them blush and get quiet and incline
their heads toward him. His people were smugglers, had
been since the Reconstruction. The town accepted their
way of making a living—or it resisted outsiders so well
you couldn't tell the difference. She had never liked Roark,
not the way he walked, a toed-out, slap-footed swagger,
not his wet little close-set eyes, nor his high-pitched voice
like the call of a peahen.

Her daddy huddled with the other road patrolman, and
that was when she noticed Mayfield's car. Its dew-shiny
hood was snubbed under a loblolly pine by the fencerow
on the other side of the tower. Then she saw Mayfield. He
had already climbed the fence and was headed for the ladder.

Before anyone could stop her, she ran to the fence. With
her fingers dug into the chain links, she shouted, "Mayfield! Wait!" He was thirty feet above her. He stopped
climbing and turned and smiled, hooking an elbow in the
rungs. "Hush, Merelene. You'll get me in more trouble
than I'm already in."

She didn't know what to say now. Finally, she said,
"What are you doing?"

"Just what it looks like. Going after Roark."

"What's *he* doing?"

"Roark?" He turned and shaded his eyes from the sun
that had just broken over the tops of the pines. "Roark
says he *thinks* he can fly. He ain't *sure*, but he's gone give
her a try."

"What do *you* think?" She shaded her eyes now, too, and
for some reason felt herself smiling.

"Me? I don't think he can. I think it's the law of gravity or the road patrol. That's why I'm going up."

"Can I come?"

"Not this trip. Sorry."

And he turned and she watched his legs and arms take him up the ladder, his body foreshortening until it was a blot no larger than Roark there dotting the SWINFORD "I."

She ran back out to where her father and the crowd had finally seen Mayfield. One of the road men shouted through his gauntleted driving gloves, "You better not climb any further, bud!"

Merelene shoved her head under her daddy's arm and whispered, "He's going up to get Roark before he flies."

"Flies?"

Before Merelene could explain, they saw Roark's arms flap and heard him call out, a high and reedy sound, "I'm bout to go airborne. Watch me." Merelene remembered high school. It was always watch me and the pockets full of nasty little mysteries. And now Mayfield went with him at night, ranging over three counties and doing God knew what. She couldn't see what Roark had that Mayfield wanted. Now, she was about to watch Roark fly or bury himself at her feet. She closed her eyes and prayed him safely back to earth.

She stayed curled in the curve of her father's arm, listening to his breathing, her eyes locked to Mayfield's arms as they swam up the ladder toward Roark. Why did Mayfield have to go up there? Why not one of these officers of the law? She shrugged off her daddy and spoke to the State men: "What are you going to do? Aren't you going to do something?"

The nearest one didn't even take his eyes off the tower. The other said, "Missy, I don't like high places."

The nearest one shaded his eyes with the gauntleted glove and said, "Fool goes up there, fool can come back down. Then we'll deal with him."

"Lot of use you are," she said. Then she felt her daddy's hand on her shoulder: "Hush, Mer. It's not their job to climb up and collect that trash." He didn't say anything about Mayfield, but she knew what he was thinking. Let the man who rides around at night with him go up and get him down, two of a kind. She stepped away from him then and stood by herself on her own piece of ground.

Mayfield had reached the little catwalk that surrounded the silver bulb of the tower, and she could see him stick his head through it just beneath the big D. Halfway through, before pushing himself up and stepping out onto the narrow walk, he turned and surveyed the countryside. She could see his tiny head sweep an arc that gathered the whole of Swinford, and then sweep back again higher, across the horizon. She thought: I have to remember to ask him how far you can see up there.

When he was on the little walk, he moved casually toward Roark, and stopped beneath Roark's perch, and again looked out across the fields and forests. Then he found Merelene and waved to her, and she waved back so hard her shoulder hurt. Then he turned and she knew by the way he stood, hip canted, one hand plumbing his pocket, that he was talking to Roark. Roark was above the equator of the silver bulb and sitting on the ladder, waving his arms and keening. Sometimes a word floated down on the wind, ". . . fly, . . . you believe, . . . I can . . . stop me or . . ." Some of it just sounded like howling. She could not hear Mayfield. Neither could Roark, by the look of him. Mayfield started to climb the ladder.

She put both hands to her ears, and they slowly came around and covered her mouth to contain the scream she felt coming. At Roark's feet, he stopped and she could see him reach out and touch Roark's shoe, very lightly it seemed. And she saw Roark's face snap down and look at him. Roark's arms, straight out from his body, stopped flapping when Mayfield touched him. Then she heard

Mayfield, heard him speaking in her thoughts as clearly as though she were beside him on that ladder which could hold only one.

"You bout finished going solo, Roark, ole buddy?"

And more nonsense from Roark, more about him flying and don't try to stop him.

And Mayfield again, calm. "Roark, you just want to get above the rest of us. You always did. Only thing, you scaring the hell out of the road patrol."

And Roark looking down now, "I can fly."

"I know that, bud, but you can't show it to the rest of them. Now why don't you come on down here with me and we'll go have us a drink of whiskey."

And Roark: "Flying makes you good. Can't have no more truck with whiskey."

And Mayfield laughing, "Maybe you *can* fly if you gone that far off plumb."

"I can."

"All right then, big'un, amo go back down to the ground and watch you take off."

And Roark, looking at the ground again, his voice breaking. "Mayfield."

"Yeah, big'un?"

"I can't get down."

"Sure you can, darlin. All you got to do is turn around and climb. You climbed up here, didn't you."

"Up is different from down."

"Not all that much. Not all that much."

"You help me?"

"Sure I will. What you want me to do?"

"I don't know."

"Well, turn around and put one foot where my hand is and I'll do what you need me to do. We'll get her done."

All of this she heard as though she were there beside him on the ladder.

She watched, holding her mouth with both hands, as

Roark slowly turned and started down. The silence, after all his calling and keening, was strange. Merelene knew, without seeing it, that the crowd had grown. She could feel the gravity of bodies rooted to the earth around her. She could hear a few mumbles, a few voices she recognized.

She was about to release her mouth and breathe when Roark lost his grip or let go. She saw him turn in the air, squirming, and grab for Mayfield and miss and heard his peahen cry of terror as his arms flapped and then Mayfield's left hand struck out like a snake and took Roark's belt and in her mind she heard him say, "Christ let me hold," and saw Roark swing below Mayfield whose right hand was welded to the ladder, and then Roark lay curled on the catwalk and the people around her screamed the words sacred to their hearts.

Then, as little conversations, fervent and breathless, broke out around her, and she heard her father say, "My Lord and Savior," Mayfield knelt above Roark and unbuckled his belt. He tied Roark's hands and then secured the belt to the floor of the catwalk, and then took off his shirt and twirled it and then tied Roark's feet. They could see Roark struggle briefly in his hands, and Mayfield leaning over him speaking and Roark going limp again. After he had knelt over Roark for a space, he rose and turned and filled his lungs with air, she saw him look out to the horizon again, again the long arc of seeing, and then, with the morning sun shining on the hard plates of his bare chest, he cupped his mouth and called down, "Send up a rope."

Then he walked slowly to the hatchway in the catwalk and lowered himself to the ladder and came down to them.

When he was down, and the crowd pressed around him and touched him as though each could seize a piece of him, he was quiet. Merelene held him close, announcing to the town whose he was. The road-patrol man who had talked about fools came over with handcuffs and Mayfield only looked at him and held out his wrists.

That was when her father stepped in. "Wait a minute. Municipal Water don't want this man arrested."

"How do you know that? You ain't Municipal Water."

"In this town I am, and what I just seen was him solving a problem for me and for you too."

At this, the John Law hesitated. Mayfield stood simple and straight and calm with his hands held out and she had the feeling he had been in those cuffs before, somewhere, sometime. She said, "Why don't you take a rope up there like he said. Did you forget about the man up in the air?"

"Fool you mean," the Law said, and tucked his hand-cuffs back under the Sam Browne belt.

"You got a rope, I'll take it up," Mayfield said. He was still holding his hands together in front of him. That was when she noticed the blood oozing from under the finger-nails of his left hand and the long blue welt growing at his left shoulder.

The Law looked hard at him. "You done enough for one early morning, bud. My advice is go home and have your breakfast off a plate and not out of a bottle. Let us take care of the rest of this."

But they stayed. She took a blanket from her father's car and draped Mayfield, who could not move his left arm now. They watched her father go up and lower Roark from the tower, trussed up like a yearling bull at castra-tion time. He came down silent and still, and when his feet hit the ground, they gave under him and he lay curled up like he had been on the catwalk while the two road men discussed his arrest.

Again her father interfered. "He's had his lesson. Look at him. He ain't going to be climbing nor flying for some time."

"You speaking for Municipal Water again."

"No, for common sense this time. Can you hear it?"

"All right then," said the gun bull, only too happy to get shut of little Swinford and Roark Drawdy and his sunrise solo flight.

She said, "Mayfield, let me take you home," watching her daddy for his approval. He looked neither yes nor no, only necessity. It was Mayfield who solved things. "I got to take Roark home. I started out with him and I got to finish with him."

"I'm coming," she said, watching her father turn away to his car.

She and some of the crowd helped Roark to Mayfield's car. He was trembling and walking now, but not talking yet.

When she was driving them out to Roark's remote pasture, she said, "How is it?"

Mayfield tightened his fist and winced. "Like to jerked my arm out of the socket."

You want me to take you to the doctor after we let him off?"

Roark groaned from the backseat.

"No, it'll be all right. It just takes time."

"It's against my better judgment."

"So is most of the things I do."

She laughed, feeling her chest fill for the first time with the breath of relief. "I judge this morning pretty good. You shouldn't have let him go up, but you sure God brought him down. Of course, you could have brought down a better cargo."

He laughed at this and glanced at Roark, supine on the backseat and mumbling now, "I known I could do it, I just known . . ."

"He was all that was stirring at five in the morning. 'Sides, I thought he could do it."

"Do what?"

"Fly."

She knew Mayfield had flown, straight into the heart of the town.

Twelve

They made their vows in the Mt. Horeb Baptist Church a month to the day after Mayfield had brought Roark down from the tower. She had named Mayfield that day as hers, knowing he had flown into the lore of the town, and that she was there with him, the girl he had waved to from the air, who had run to the ladder and begged to go up with him, the one who covered him with a blanket and drove his car off to finish the errand of mercy.

There had even been a small item about it in *The County News Leader:* "Swinford Suicide Rescued from Tower." The story was garbled. It told that Roark was despondent and Mayfield was a police officer. It said nothing at all about flying.

Roark didn't like being called a suicide. He swore he had made three clean passes over the crowd and around the tower and a perfect four-point landing back on the ladder before Mayfield started all the ruckus that got him trussed and lowered like a common lunatic. He told any and all who would listen that he had never known a blue day in his life and suicide had never entered into his thinking. He had gone up for fun and fun was what he'd had.

Mayfield's left arm, which had fastened him to the ladder while the other held Roark in the world, never was the same. He couldn't manhandle the bulldozer a full day in the pulpwood operation without pain, so he went in with some of his wild friends on a mullet boat. They worked like demons from the moon of December to the moon of January, making almost a year's wages in that space when the mullet roe turns red and the fish bolt crazy to deep water where the pressure of atmospheres strokes the new generation from their bodies. After the red roe run, he did some crabbing and guided some for the sporting gents from Bainesborough, but he wasn't happy fishing.

She encouraged him to look for what he liked, to find what he wanted. She told him she was in no hurry for him to make his fortune. They did not need a fortune to live.

The first year of their marriage was a night out that never ended. They could dance, and run with his friends to the roadhouses in three counties and then come home at sunrise to their own legal bed. She lay these early mornings while he slept with his torn arm thrown across her breasts, thinking herself the luckiest woman in the world.

The town loved Mayfield, at least for a while, and forgave his nocturnal habits until they reflected discredit on his family. For now there was a family. They had not talked about it, but like the fish the moon made crazy, they had made themselves again twice, in two babies, the second and third years of their life together. And they had made the house too small, filling it with cries and smells, and chores and ending forever the long night out they had both loved. What Merelene discovered that took its place, as easily as the moon changes shape in the sky, was happiness in her two pieces of Merelene and Mayfield. She loved their faces and feet and how they woke each morning ready to be filled with more of the world. And she loved their differences. At the ages of two and three, they were carefree and serious, light and sober. Two very different little boys. She knew less and less of what Mayfield discovered. He was still waiting to hear his calling. It was not to bulldozers or fish, or farming. And there wasn't much else in little Swinford, except Roark and the work he did, supplying pleasures.

Five years passed and she had two shirttail boys and Mayfield picked up a living where he could. She had embraced what he was in his fast car and his fast life, the mystery of him climbing the tower, and the fact of him in her bed at night, hard and wet as trees and the river. It was a long time before she worried about that other Mayfield, the one he had been before she had seen him standing in the dark on the side of a road. She had told herself those things would come with time, but they had not. He kept the past locked. When she tried for a key, he joked or brooded or deflected her in some other way, and so she did not persist, only knew that someday he would need to tell her.

Mayfield loved his children. He was a good father when he was not looking inside himself at the secret he kept there. Sometimes in a brooding mood, he would go away and come back with grease all over him, and tell her he had fixed something for somebody, a transmission, a carburetor. Exhaustion soothed him, but he was strangely tormented by the dirt on his hands. She knew from the few photographs and military papers he had saved, that he had been a mechanic in the Army Air Corps, but he didn't like to talk about it, and showed no inclination to return to such work. In his good spirits, he took the boys hunting or fishing, and often the four of them spent weekends in the woods in an old army surplus tent. It was in the seventh year of this life that Roland was sick. A mosquito bite. Brain fever. One of Florida's five recorded cases of encephalitis that year. Six days he lay in the isolation ward, near death, then slowly rising and seeming all right, then the seizures and the tests, the trips to Bainesborough where the doctors said his brain was a constellation of wounds. His age would never change. She went through it all stunned and Mayfield stood with her quiet and brooding and strong.

When Roland was home with her again, and seeming only tired after his illness, only a quiet, confused little boy, perhaps less interested in mischief, she believed the doctors had been wrong. But she confused belief and hope. Six months showed her how profound was the disorganization of his mind. He didn't grow, and the things he learned were fragments from the radio, and the things he said were these fragments and bits and pieces of his brief past. He seemed to float in time. His mind was like the radio which could tune in anything and connect nothing.

As she watched the distance grow between him and his older brother, and the estrangement that came with it, her love for Roland grew fierce. If he was to be marooned on some island alone, at least she could provision him. At least she could translate him to the world when the world cared to know. Sometimes in the afternoons when the house was quiet and Bull, who was Ethridge then, was out playing with his friends, she would lie with Roland pressed to her heart and listen, imagining she made sense of him, speaking strange inventions of her own. She was never sure what had happened between them in those months after she knew he would be different. She had thrown herself around him as a barricade, a house. He lived in her, cellar in the mansion of her love. And that was what Mayfield could not understand.

At first Mayfield was with her, day and night. He would not leave the house when Roland was awake. He stood by the child's bed watching the face that was flushed with the heat of summer sleep and waited for the return of the life they had had. He spoke to Roland for hours, begging for the words and sentences they had shared before. Tell me this or that story, he would beg the boy, who would wake and look at him in wonder and speak radio talk about laundry detergent.

Mayfield seemed to believe that he could bring the boy's mind back by exercise, and for days he tried and it broke her heart to stand by and watch him lean over the bed and coax up the sound from Roland and then bite his jaw in anguish when it was only babble. Sometimes, she came into the room and found Mayfield crooning to Roland in the tenderest way, and rubbing his own arm at the spot where Roark's weight had torn it, as though he could heal himself and Roland, too, both at once with his hands and the exertions of his beautiful voice.

Sometimes during this period, she would come in to him and touch him and he would start as though she had arrived from another world, an unwelcome emissary from the place where no amount of singing and calling out could recall a child's brains. Sometimes, just in the second when he realized it was her, she would see anger in his eyes, resentment she could not understand. The anger would fade and he would reach down and trace Roland's cheek and touch his blank eyes and say, "Ain't he the most handsome boy? Ain't he, Merelene?"

But he couldn't stand by Roland's bed forever, talking and singing to the fragments and broken bits of what they had been. Finally he left the bed and the duties that went with it to her, and traveled into himself. She was exhausted much of the time. She gave as much time as she could to Ethridge and tried to set aside a part of herself for the hours when Roland was sleeping, and Ethridge was playing, so that she and Mayfield could be together as they had been before. It seemed years ago now, the time when they had been on their long night out and she had awakened to him in the morning knowing the day held nothing but more of the same. But Mayfield could not be easy with her, even when she called him to bed, to remake the old world for a space.

He complained that she had grown cold to him, that Roland's illness had made them strangers. She knew she had been less attentive to him; her love, which had been divided by three, was now split again and given to this new self of Roland's, a self she had to study, had to hold close and understand. She asked Mayfield for patience, and he gave her silence and his absences. And then one day, he disappeared.

She believed he would come back. Absence was his way of telling her he had his pain too. She was ready to say yes to him, to say she would hold him to her as she had held Roland these months since the fever. But the days became weeks and she was alone in the house with two boys and no money, and the story of her abandonment going up one side of Swinford and down the other.

Later, she did not remember well that first month after Mayfield's going. It seemed that she had wandered the house in a nightgown, and mirrors were everywhere and her face in every one was the red wreckage of some other woman, old, resourceless, finished. She had cared for the children, but barely. She remembered little Ethridge asking for meals, saying it was time, and seeing what she had become, quietly setting out pans and food for her, taking her by the hand to the counter: "Can you start, Mommer?" The beginning of his lifelong silence and self-sufficiency was in that month.

With help from her parents, she waited that first year on a lean living and hope. After that, she knew she had to take the mirrors from the walls and organize a new life, and that was when she bought the secondhand typewriter and taught herself to use it, and bought the books that taught shorthand and office management, choosing work she could do at home, at night while the boys slept.

Sometimes, when she was tired from her studies, and

Roland had gone from the radio to the mysteries of his stone-blank sleep and Ethridge was asleep, too, his puzzled face on a pillow in the same small bedroom with Roland, sometimes, when the whole town was quiet except for the barking of a dog or the rush of wind in the palm fronds or the jittery call of a whippoorwill, she would let herself think about Mayfield. She did not ask herself why he had gone. That was a question she saved. Instead, she tried to remember a time when he might have told her, in his own way, that he was going. Some moment, an action of his or theirs together, when he had signaled and she might have intervened between him and his demon. One of her sleepless nights she found it in her memory. It was the evening that Roland had spoken a complete sentence for the first time.

She had been sleeping that night, a month before Mayfield's sudden departure. She had awakened to find him gone from the bed and the clock telling her it was early morning. She had walked through the dark house, knowing where she would find him, unsurprised to see him, tall and narrow, leaning over Roland's crib holding a lamp. She stood in the doorway and watched him.

He pulled a small table to the edge of Roland's bed and put the lamp on it and plugged it in making a round pool of light that crosscut his chest and bathed Roland's sleeping face. Then she watched him examine his own hands, rubbing them together in the light that cut across his chest and left his face in darkness. "I got grease on these again," he said, using the voice he had used for months to try to bring Roland back. "It gets under the fingernails and rubs in the knuckles and you cut yourself and heal over and it stays under the skin. Years later you can still see somebody's transmission in the palm of your hand." He reached down and pushed a lock of hair back from Roland's forehead. "You don't mind, do you? My greasy old fingers?"

Then she thought she should announce herself at the door and walk into this scene and stop it or join it, at least let him know he was watched. She felt tears in her eyes and could not understand why. He was talking about nothing, a grown man, her husband in the middle of the night explaining his hands to his son who wasn't even awake. But she didn't move. She could not enter the circle of that light, nor could she make herself go away and leave them alone. It was as though she had come upon them praying.

"These hands have seen a lot, Roland son. I want you to know that." He touched the boy again, this time with both hands, taking his face and shaping it a little, and through the bars of the crib, she could see the boy move under the covers waking up. "I'm a young man yet, but they have seen and done. I want you to know what you can know. "There"—Mayfield flexed his arms, moved his hands— "you can know that, can't you. I want you to know I've did what I can for you and for your Mommer. I want you to know that." And she heard Mayfield's deep, musical voice break and become a sorry, aching croak. "I wisht I could *feel* it into your head, just . . . *put* it there. I wisht . . ." He lifted his hands from Roland and looked at them again. Scrubbed them in the light.

"I used to put faces back together, make heads where there wasn't anything but . . . God help me, never mind what there was. You don't want to know, and He don't help. I did miracles. They all said it. What a vocation I had! They all said it. But I couldn't stay with it. You can't, a man can't keep on with a thing like that. It breaks him down. It's too much responsibility in it for one man to keep doing and doing. I had to get away from it. I want you to know that. That's why I put my hands in somebody's carburetor or differential gears. It's about all I deserve."

Then, distinctly, she heard Roland's old self speak.

"Daddy's up the tower." And she shivered, thinking: maybe it *is* a miracle. She pictured him lying there quiet through his father's crazy speech, his eyes staring up at Mayfield knowing only what they knew. And then him rising out of his malady.

Mayfield's body was rigid, his hands hovered inches above Roland's face as he listened. His voice croaked, "Yes, Daddy's up the tower? What's he doing up there? Tell me son?" She did not know how long Mayfield waited for more. She stood at the door, a silent spy, waiting too, hoping too, and then Roland said, "Lux gets clothes whiter."

Mayfield sighed, a deep sigh. Then he leaned down and his head came into the light, and she could see his face stricken and running with tears and he kissed Roland's eyes, one then the other, and she hurried back to the bed where she lay awake and waited.

When Mayfield came back and laid his weight beside her, she lay rigid, arguing with herself. She tried to reach out, only inches across the warm counterpane into his agony. She tried to think of what to say. She could draw him to her bosom and hold him and he might tell. But she didn't. She was afraid. Of what he might say, of more of the mad words, of his burden, whatever it was. She only lay pretending to sleep, in misery, and felt him lying the same way.

In the morning he rose early and went to the mullet boat. She could hear him finding his clothes in the half darkness and brewing coffee and leaving before he had time to drink it. And he rose just the same way one morning a month later preparing the same way and departed for good and she never knew whether he kissed his sons good-bye.

The bed was hers and she lay in it years, awakening from sorry dreams to find her hand stretched across that little space and the name of Mayfield on her lips.

Thirteen

When she pulled into Lum Smalley's Esso station on Tuesday afternoon for gas and to discuss getting the front end lined up (or whatever it was), she noticed the usual crowd of layabouts lounging in ladder-back chairs in the shade of the grease rack. Only now there was something different. When she pulled up, they all stopped smoking and masticating tobacco and looked at her until Lum's familiar forearm was on her windowsill. "What can I do for you today, Miss Merelene?"

She told him to fill it up with his cheapest and tried her best to describe what had happened to her car in a muddy ditch not far from the Sunshine State Training Center.

"That's easy enough," Lum said. "Just drop it off tomorrow morning and I'll have one of the boys drive you on to work." And then, because it was her, and he knew it was necessary, he said, "It won't be but about thirty dollars, pending on whether you bent your tie-rods." He watched her for a nod of agreement, the only contract needed at Smalley's Esso. "I won't need any of the boys to drive me to work." She did not know why she was feeling so strange and passing it on to Lum. It was just the way they had all looked at her. Lum's greasy odor disappeared from the window and she could hear him banging the nozzle into her gas tank. She'd had half a mind to ask him: Lum, what is different?

When she handed him a twenty and then took her change from his gasoline-smelling fingers, she saw that one of the grease rack sages was on his way to her car. It was Roark Drawdy. She always thought of him (and of many like him she hadn't seen much since then) as fixed in the identities they'd let happen to them in Alligood County Consolidated Junior-Senior High School. He was still sly, shoat-eyed and full of nasty little mysteries. He took his time about crossing the concrete to her car, and she considered slipping the clutch and leaving him at the mouth of the shady cave where he was chairman of the board.

Instead, she sat, anger mounting, and waited for him to press the blade of his hip against the car door. He looked up and down the street before leaning in at her window, too close, smelling of last night's whiskey, a smell she had not forgotten in these sixteen years of single life, and of something else, the combined uselessness of that brotherhood of gas pump ne'er-do-wells.

"Hi you, Miss Merelene?" He put a sarcastic stress on the *Miss*.

She said, "I'm fine, Roark."

"How's Bull and all them?"

She said, "Bull's fine." She did not mention Roland. The town knew about Roland.

"That war is *some* bad," Roark said. He heaved a troubled sigh and rocked his head as though to say: What can we do? Nothing.

She said, "Yes, it's bad." She thought: Let's write to Congressman Corey about it, the two of us. She stared straight ahead, waiting.

He was still nodding. "Ole Bull's a hard one. He'll come through fine, you'll see."

She didn't speak, only wished he hadn't mentioned Bull's chances.

Roark straightened up with a groan of leather and a muffled belch. He looked up and down the street again, taking his time, and then leaned in, inspecting her. After a few seconds of his cold eyebeams, she sent him an impatience even he couldn't ignore. He said, "Guess who I seen down at Larup's?"

She might have known.

Mayfield had appeared to her like a ghost. Why had she thought he was the property of her own midnights? The old mistake. He had never belonged to her. His home had always been the mind of the town.

"Who, Roark?" She was grinding her teeth.

"Why, Mayfield Durham, that's who. He's back." He waited for her reaction. When she didn't give one, he looked up and down the street and leaned into her window to hand her something. "He axed me to give you this." He winked. "I was gone come on by your house and give it to you but now you're here . . ." His hand fumbled at hers while she tried not to take it.

She looked up at him, hating his height, her own confinement in the car. It was a piece of paper, folded into a hard little square.

She remembered Roark up in the air one early morning almost thirty years ago with his peahen trills raining down and half the town laughing at him. She dropped the piece of paper on the seat next to her and said, "Roark, I don't think he ever left. I think he's been around here all this time."

Roark looked down at her, pulling his chin in and beetling his brows. "*Around* here?" He stepped back and she could breathe.

"You kept him here. You and the crowd down at

Larup's. I bet a night doesn't pass but you yammer the life back into him. Tell me about the time you and him went up for your first solo flight, Roark. I bet you tell that one all the time." She smiled at him.

His face was a condensation of every mean thing in him. Slowly, she let out the clutch so that he slid away behind her.

In her mirror, he was standing on the hot concrete with his snake lips thrust forward, his Moorman's Feed cap pushed back on his head, and an empty oil can coming to his lips. She saw him spit.

At home in her kitchen, she read the note. It was from the same neat hand that had written the letter she had seen in the lawyer's office.

> Meet me at Sale Spring. You know
> our place. Eight o'clock tonight.

She had some thoughts as she stood holding his hand-writing. Sale Spring was their place. Eight o'clock was just before dark this time of year.

Her feet took her into the house without benefit of conscious thought. She sat in the kitchen over a cup of coffee, her nerves coiled, unable to focus her mind on anything but the place, their place, the small grotto of limestone and cedar at the mouth of a cave where the cool breath of underground deeps and springs whispered across your naked body on a warm summer afternoon as you lay with a man learning things so fast you couldn't hold them, until they were scattered around you on the mossy earth like so many bright jewels.

There was no car by the spring. She parked where they had always parked. She had only been back once or twice since their times—those few months when they had made this place a habit. Later, when they were married and owned a bed, Mayfield had been pleased to sleep between sheets, but she recalled a little disappointment. She had asked him a time or two could they go back to the spring, just for memory's sake.

And feed the skeeters? he had said. Not me.

She left her car and walked, as surely as if she had been here yesterday, to their place. She found herself hoping that he would not be there, so that she and her memories could have it. When she approached the little declivity flanked by two crouching cedars, she was sure, even in the failing light, that no one had touched it since them. It was still full of its secret.

She parted the cedar branches and the cold cavey breath of the underground river whistled in her face. She remembered it, cool on summer nights—he had called it nature's air-conditioning—but full of the smell of blind fish and wild mushrooms and things that had drowned in the river miles from here. Love in this place had always been fearful. She moved into the little room and saw something lying on the mossy earth. A squarish something, a briefcase. She picked it up. It was heavy, of good dark leather. The initials, MD, were affixed to it in brass that reminded her of the collar studs soldiers wore.

Her fingers were on the clasps when the cedar branches behind her parted. He was dressed as he had been that first night. The beard grew in gray whorls on his lean face and he stood with his arms folded across his chest, calm in the gray light that slanted through the branches.

"Swinford ain't changed," he said, his voice full of admiration.

She felt like a thief with the briefcase in her hands. She turned and put it down in the place where it had been lying.

"Have you been walking up and down in it?" She asked.

He winced. "Don't quote the Bible to me, Merelene. You never did that before." He took a step closer to her and stirred the ground with the toe of his boat shoe. "I've done some walking, been around a bit and seen a few things. But I been keeping myself a secret too. Traveling in . . . cogneeter is what they call it, I believe." He laughed at himself, a small chuckle of self-congratulation. "Sometimes I do that."

She said, "I know you do. I remember."

The light was failing, but she could see that it hurt him to receive her meaning, to remember his first experiments in secret flight. She removed the letter he had written from the pocket of her skirt. She held it out toward him, a white flag in the gray light.

He leaned forward to it, then rocked back. "Where'd you get that?"

"From the office. You didn't think you could write a letter like this to him and me not see it, did you?"

He thought about this, stirring the earth with his shoe and massaging the old pain at his left shoulder. "Naw, not really. I guess it was to both of you. Of course it was."

She was surprised at his quiet voice and at her own. Perhaps it was this tree room and its breath of dead things and cave mysteries that spelled this quiet. Whatever it was, she liked it. She looked at her hands now, and at his chest where she had twisted her fingers into the fabric of his shirt thinking to drag him to Roland's bedside. She remembered him at Roland's bedside once long ago and how he had tried to sing and talk and touch the right mind back into his son. She felt her eyes going small and hot at this recollection and knew she must expel it. She shook the letter in her hand.

"Mayfield, what is the meaning of this damned letter? Did you think you had to talk to me this way?"

He grabbed the front of his shirt and spoke with some heat. "The last time I tried to talk to you, you like to tore the shirt off my back."

"Never mind that, I want to know." She shook the letter. "What does this mean?"

"It means what it says." His voice was low and firm and she could see his eyes shift to the briefcase. He stepped past her and picked it up and cradled it to his chest and a strange cast came into his face. "It means I want my turn with Roland."

"Your turn?"

She was angry now and knew he could see it. He stepped back and held the briefcase firmly. "What kind of fool do you take me for?" she said in cold fury, "the same one I was when you left me with two shirttail boys?" She stepped toward him making the little bower small and hot, too close for all the memories it held.

Quickly, he opened the briefcase. "Merelene, look at these."

She did not know what to do. He was holding papers out to her. It was almost too dark to read. Her anger did not want paper. But there was something in the way he held the sheaf of disorganized leaves toward her that made her reach.

"What is it?" she asked, her voice low again. What could this briefcase hold that he thought invited him back to this place.

She accepted a handful of documents and used her legal eyes on them. They were medical reports. Roland's name was all over them. They were his case. Some were dated the years of his early illness and some were recent. When he spoke, his voice was almost prayerful. "Maybe there are things that can be done now. Procedures."

For seconds, she felt her heart race, and hope run with it, but only seconds. Even in this half dark, she recognized the doctors' names, some of them, the clinics, the procedures. It was research she'd done years ago. She knew what was possible for Roland. And here stood Mayfield with hope high in his face. She was two women. One gave him his hope, forever: the other wanted to scatter these useless white leaves at his feet, throw them in his face. She clutched them until her hand was a claw and they dripped blood. He watched her stuff them back into the fancy case.

He stepped toward her. "You see," he said. He took her shoulders in his hands. She let him touch her, still tender for his hope, and still two women. "You see what I want?"

So this was his booty from the years, what his money had bought. God, she thought, as his hands caressed her arms, and found her face and hair, God, what a hopeful, helpless fool.

"You're still beautiful, Merelene. Just like when I left. When I said Swinford hadn't changed that was most of it. You haven't changed. You're still the prettiest woman in this town, in the whole place. I know you are." His hands were all over her now, and one of the two women was ready to sink down to this mossy earth and lie with him in the loop of time. The other woman's voice was cool: "You want me, don't you?"

His heart was against hers. "Yes, of course I do."

And she said, "You want what comes with me too. You want Roland now."

"Yes," he said, but she heard the smallest hesitation.

"Because . . . because you think they can fix him, the doctors?"

He caressed her. She felt him nod his head in her hair. The darkness was complete now, and swarming around them full of cold cave air and the slow, writing movements of the cedar branches and the wheel of stars in the chimney above them.

She pushed him away, and pushed out of her mind the woman who lay with him on the mossy earth at her feet. She placed both hands on his chest and pushed hard, surprised to find him bony as a bird cage under her palms. She made him let go with little effort. She did not know what to feel: sorrow for the loss of his power or joy for the rise of her own. "You didn't learn anything away from here."

He stood in front of her shaking, expectant, wanting her. She said, "You just want what you always wanted here."

He looked at her, at the mossy ground. Perhaps he could see himself and that other Merelene in their habitual poses. He smiled. "What's wrong with that?"

"Well, you're not going to get it."

"Who is?" he asked. He stepped toward her, hands on his hips now and jaw shot forward.

"I don't see that it's any of your business."

"You're still my wife, Merelene."

"Only by the thinnest legal thread you can imagine." And she thought, God knows what you can imagine.

She had hurt his man's pride and she knew what was coming now. His voice had the manscorned derision in it that only made her tired. Made her deride him more. He said, "The last time I saw you, you were in your night-gown. How come you didn't wear it to this visit if it's your nighttime traveling outfit? You did come intending to meet *me*?"

She said, "I came for one reason. To tell you whatever was between us that could call me by an unsigned note is over. Dead. I don't come when you call. Not again. We're none of yours anymore, Roland and Bull and me. You haven't changed a bit. You came to my house in the middle of the night and didn't even look at Roland's grown-up face." She stood with her own hands on her hips, her pulses hammering, staring him down.

He turned away, back to the mouth of the cave as though to take his breath from it. "Oh, I've changed, Merelene. A man doesn't go away sixteen years from his home and not change. A man don't live that long and not change."

"I'm waiting," she said.

He turned back, his hands inert by his sides.

"I'm waiting for you to tell me about the changes. If that's what you got me here for."

He smiled.

She said, "Now that we know it isn't going to be for anything else."

"About the changes?" He seemed to concentrate now, very hard, as though he would be explaining it to himself. And what he said was not what she expected. She expected a conversion from drink, a long descent to the bottom, and then the pledge in some city salvation center and the first steps of his rise. She expected, though it was not a thing to be hoped for any more, religion. He stepped toward her now and said, "Merelene, I'm a wealthy man. Rich is what they call it. You see me here in these old clothes because I want you to. I wanted to come back to this place as I left it. Merelene, there's a story in a magazine about me; it calls me an eccentric because I sometimes wear my old clothes. And here's another change, Merelene. I didn't come back here and bust into your life. I been meeting you late at night to save your character. You're a respectable widow. You know how people talk in a little place like this."

In her rolling thoughts kept rising the image of him as she had first seen him on that midnight country road, a young man, tall and slender and hard, in a white shirt and canvas trousers, yet with the seed of this night in him somewhere. Here he was now, standing across from her on the mossy crest of the limestone, dressed exactly the same, and for a reason. To come back and appear to her as he had appeared that first time. As though no time had passed.

"The magazine is called *Fortune*, they call me the diamond in the rough, the pyramid man. I sell franchises. They say it ain't nothing but dreams. I sell dreams. Someday soon, maybe tomorrow, a woman, she'll be one of your neighbors, she'll walk up to your door carrying her sample case and show you lipstick and blushing powder, lashes for your eyes. To make up your face, to make you over . . ."

Merelene could not help it; she touched her face as he talked.

"Beautiful. She'll offer you the opportunity to do what she does." He stopped, angry. "They say it's wrong."

"Why do you keep telling me what they say?" she asked. "Who are they? It's what you say I want to hear."

"I tell you what they say because they write about Mayfield Durham, in a magazine called *Fortune*. They do it because I've made one. I'm fortunate. It amazes me, still."

He stopped now and looked at the stars in the chimney above them, marveling at himself or at fortune. And she thought of Bull where the hot metal was flying and of Roland and misfortune and what money could buy for him. Maybe Mayfield had changed. He had stopped turning under the stars, and now held his hands out to her like a salesman, like a preacher, a lover. He still owned his powers. He was grappling for her, using hooks and ropes from the heart, and she knew it, and feared it, and damned herself for the old warm feeling.

"I came back for knowledge, Merelene. Knowledge of you. A man can run away from a lot, but not from his one true love, not forever. There's something inside you I want to find before it's too late. A man is lucky if he comes back and she is still where he left her, still as he left her. Knowledge of you is what I want."

She spoke quietly, her face a torch in the darkness. "I was never your one true love. Nobody was but yourself."

"That hurts me, Merelene; it does." His face hung narrow and pale and pained before her in the darkness.

She was about to speak, to tell him this was their last meeting, at night or otherwise, but he raised his hand, pained and priestlike, in the space between them. He bent and picked up the briefcase and cradled it to his chest like a treasure box, and stepped past her and disappeared into the trees. She was left standing in the fetid breath of the cave, her thoughts rolling with pictures of him, of their young bodies sweating at her feet. She reached out to the close air and waved her arms in it but there was no proof of him.

Fourteen

The next morning, when she uncovered her typewriter, she found a sheet of paper in it. It was addressed to her from the lawyer. She stared at it for a long time before reading it. He had never done such a thing before. She recalled leaving work the afternoon before, worrying about her morning encounter with Roark Drawdy, and seeing the lawyer still at his desk. "Go on," he had told her, "I've got a few things left to do here." This morning, his office was empty. She was alone with this letter full of typing errors. She imagined him painfully pecking it out, maybe at the very moment she was in the cedar grove with Mayfield.

Dear Merelene:

I am a cripple, a gimp, a freak. I have lived in this comic skin almost thirty years since piloting a P-47 Thunderbolt into the top of an Austrian linden tree. And now I am going to ask you to live in the comedy with me. Are you surprised? For all my knowledge of you, I cannot think what will be in your mind as you read this message. I leave it for you to find in your typewriter because I don't have the courage to speak these things to you out of my mouth.

But what is courage? I cannot even remember anymore what it was to fly against German fighters; I have only my dreams. In them, again and again, my one piece of luck is canceled. The ship catches fire and makes a torch of a linden tree on an alpine skyline and I am released from this world. As you know, the ship did not burn, and here am I, luckless until now.

I live in my father's house, his father's house before him, alone and making do for myself without even the manservant my father had. I live this way because the struggle uses time, and time is the last thing I have wanted lying on my hands. There in the treetop, I understood eternity. I did not want it on earth. I have sometimes dreamed of the resurrection of Woman in that house, and in my dream, the very walls shrink from Her touch. She is alien, unwanted in that Man's redoubt, that place which reeks of an illness so old its causes are forgotten. It is from the search for the germ of this illness, and from the certainty that you are the hope of cure, that I come to you now with my suit. The illness is not these twisted legs, this disarrayed flesh; it is a soul bumped out of true, imprisoned in a skin which is its emblem.

My family were soldiers and statesmen. They believed they were people of character and consequence. My great-grandfather, the hero of Olustee, took a minié ball in the eye but came home from his tree a whole man. We were the Sawyers of Swinford. We made a fortune cutting down pine trees in the place where the pigs crossed the river. I heard my grandfather speak of *noblesse oblige* and the *droit du seigneur*. My father never did. The diminishment of character which has been our trouble can be read in the eyes of the portraits that hang in the rooms of that old house. I am the bloodline gone bad.

Oh, I have not done badly for myself. I have managed to hold what little of the family land came to me from my father, and have done so without farming on the backs of black men. I have practiced law these twenty years since the war and my convalescence. I am known hereabouts, I suspect, as a better legal mind than this town can use, and as a wit who has no one to talk to. I have not done badly—for a cripple.

I have lived in this town, in this house, and done my work, and nursed the pride that has kept me here, whose other face is fear. It has been bitterly easy to be fast in a slow place. Bitterness threatens to swallow me up.

There are things you do not know about me, things no one knows. I was not brilliant at Yale, much less than good at Cornell. I was no hero in the war. The Germans I killed were boys. They had little fuel, less experience. They expected to die. It was 1945 and history was against them. I am sure they knew it. I was a good pilot, but only by pitting will against terror. I flew with my gorge in my mouth, and my grandfather was never far from me, ghosting through the piney woods on a pie-bald stallion, his gray coattails tattered by Yankee bullets. The great-grandson of a county colonel, I fired tracer bullets at the great-grandsons of Bismarck's dueling dandies, knowing that my grandfather's one eye had seen more than my two could ever see, had understood the Yankee ball that blasted its vision away. When a boy in a Focke-Wulf got behind me in an Austrian sky, I did not know what it meant. I still do not know. But I know that I see courage every day. You bring it with you, Merelene. I see it in your every act.

Now that your old husband is back among us, for God knows what reason, I feel the press of time and will finally do what I have misfired for years. He forces me to it. If he has any sense, he has come back wanting you. I want you too. Give me an answer in the haste I never gave you.

When he walked in the door, she was reading his signature, the same one she had seen on a thousand legal documents, but now different. She watched his face flame with pride and embarrassment, as he made his way to his office. She was stuck holding the paper, watching him go past. She heard him sit and clear his throat and begin to ruffle papers.

She went to him and bent to kiss his forehead. He still didn't look at her, only moved his head toward her kiss. She sat in the chair by his desk where his clients sat. Staring straight ahead, he said, "Give me an answer, Merelene. I can't follow you around like a moonstruck boy forever."

"I thank you very much for the beautiful things you wrote to me."

"And my answer?"

"I can't answer. Not yet. There are too many things . . ." She groped for the right word.

"Things?" he prompted. He still had not looked at her. His flaming face was full of pride and love.

"Unfinished things. You know it's true."

He turned his red, hawk's face to her. His eyes were stories. "I know that I've shared enough with Mayfield Durham. I know I've lain down in a bed with you and he was there. I know I'm tired of it."

She wished she could tell him that he had shared nothing with Mayfield: they were different women, Mayfield's wife and this one who loved him.

"I'm tired too" was all she said.

"So you won't answer me today?"

"I can't." Her words were no, but her tone was the same

one she used to say she loved him late at night in his high old bed in his monk's room miles from here.

Suddenly, with all his energy, he pushed himself away from the desk. He was heading for the door. "Come on, I got something I want you to see."

She said, "What?" holding back as he steadied himself in the doorway. "*What* do you want me to see?"

When he turned from the door, he was smiling. "Do you want to see it or don't you?"

"I don't know." What was he trying to do to her?

"When was the last time you saw your boy?"

"I been sneaking to Louise's at night," she said, "and calling that psychologist every day to tell him about the progress of Roland's cold."

"Well, come on then. We'll pick him up from Louise and go for a drive in the country. You're not too tired for a ride, are you?"

Fifteen

They were rocketing up the river road in the lawyer's antique Cadillac. The way he operated the special hand controls gave her the feeling on this bright morning that anything was possible. Roland sat in the backseat looking particularly interested in the scenery. Louise Bates had seen to it that he shaved, and somehow had kept him from sawing his belt into his middle too tightly. When they had picked him up, Louise had said, "It'll do him good to get out for a while. He's gone get a tan from that TV."

When they were all in the car, Merelene had asked the lawyer where they were going. He had started the thundering old engine, made it roar with a subtle motion of his fingers on the controls and winked broadly at her. "All in good time."

And she thought, yes, good times, as they struck a line as straight as a ray of light up the east bank of the Suwannee River.

The lawyer began to hum, in his croaky baritone, an air she had heard somewhere, perhaps it was "Annie Laurie." She settled back and let the wind ruffle her hair, and the front of her blouse and felt the best she had since this whole thing began, months back with the Big Bath at Mary Heatherton's house.

The lay of the land was uphill; they were rising out of the Suwannee basin. The water oak and cypress hammocks gave way to pastures and fields of tobacco whose sticky white flowering suckers would soon have to be cut.

When they turned, onto a still narrower road, hardly a cart track, winding off uphill under the branches of tall oaks whose roots knobbed the earth under them, her curiosity was too much for her. "Where are you taking us?" she shouted above the noise of the jouncing automobile. He said, "You got your secrets." He glanced in the rearview at Roland's face. "I got mine."

She muttered, "riddles," and surrendered to the mystery.

Soon, they entered a clearing and she could see, far off at one end of an old pasture, a large barn or shed, with clumps of machinery heaved up around it, grass and scrub growing through its ribs. It wasn't farm machinery. An old pickup was parked by the shed, and she could see a man moving around in the shade of a tin roof. He was wearing blue bib overalls, and a green baseball cap, and a white rag hung from his back pocket. A small dog followed him in and out of the darkness beneath the tin. They were nearing all the time, and what she finally saw inside the barn, great God, was an airplane. It had four wings, not two, and a red paint job and two holes for people to sit in and as they neared, she could see the man in bib overalls working on it. He climbed up a little pedestal made of old fencing and shoved himself armpit-deep into the engine. Just as they rocked to a halt in a cloud of dust and chaff, sunlight glinted on the red body of the thing and she saw that its skin was of thin metal, dented and whorled and scarred in a hundred places. How could such a thing ever preserve life in midair?

The man in overalls pulled his arm carefully out of the

engine, and turned, regarding them with a squint from atop the platform. The fice dog sidled behind him, in the shade of the airplane, and barked twice. "Hush, Pissant," said the little man.

Merelene wondered as she sat in the car in the settling cloud of dust, whether she had heard right. Hush, Pissant? She looked at the lawyer for some sort of confirmation, but he only stared out the window at the airplane. There was something like mother love in his eyes.

Finally, after another bark from the dog, and more of the lawyer's moony-faced gazing, the little man got down, somewhat uncertainly it seemed to Merelene, and walked toward them.

"What say, Delvin?" the lawyer called out, throwing open the car door. Before she could stop him, Roland was out and standing beside the lawyer. Merelene kept the car between herself and any dog with a name like that.

The lawyer and Delvin shook hands in the embarrassed way that was common among men she knew and she lost sight of the dog. The lawyer called, "Merelene, come and meet Delvin Sweet."

She heard Roland say, "Jet Jackson, the Flying Commando," while he pumped Delvin Sweet's hand.

The little man held Roland's hand, and regarded him for a moment, then stood on his tiptoes and glanced across the car at her: "It's all right, ma'am. She don't bite."

Merelene slapped at her skirts and walked around the front of the car thinking, that's one I heard before.

She shook hands with Delvin Sweet, but not before he made a pretty big thing out of transferring grease from his hand to the rag in his pocket and back again. When he pulled the rag out, a pint bottle of Walker's Ten High hit the ground. The dog sniffed it and sneezed, and Delvin Sweet took his time about picking it up. He brushed the label of the bottle, smearing it black, then held it off away from his face as though to read what it said. Then he shook it, watched it bubble up a bit, and turned to the lawyer, "You want a bite of this?"

Maybe the lawyer didn't really want to, not in this morning heat, but he was a polite man. He took the bottle, and let several large bubbles slip up its neck. His eyes watered as he handed it back to Delvin, who took what he called a bite, which was a long obscene suck that ended in a wheeze and a little buck dance that made the dog bark.

"Hush, Pissant!"

As she knew he would, Roland had started to pursue the dog. He had to touch things, especially animals.

The lawyer said, "How's she coming, Delvin?"

"Oh, I made a right smart of progress on her these last few days. You know, since I got that bunch of parts from Sanford. I'm still having some bad times with the valve guides. I had to get plumb unruly with them boys over at Melton's machine shop. I 'spect you'll hear about it."

Roland was sitting flat on his bottom in the dust with the dog in his lap: dog and boy had the same familial look in their eyes.

The lawyer said, "I expect I'll pay for it is what I'll do. But that's all right, Delvin, that's all right. You get what you need, hear? I want this thing to *fly*!"

"She gone fly all right," Delvin Sweet said, squinting off into the blue sky where someday soon, his eyes promised, they would see a bright red gash. "Don't you worry about that now, she *gone* fly."

Delvin excused himself and walked to the shed, the dog followed, but stopped halfway and looked at Roland, who said, "What's your name, dog?" When Delvin Sweet was gone in the dark shade and making some grinding sounds, she leaned over to the lawyer and whispered, "You *want* a sot mechanic working on your airplane? Is that right?"

He kept the same stunned smile he'd had on his face since they had broken cover at the far end of the field. "Whiskey sharpens a man's perception, Merelene. Delvin

is a visionary. He knows more about that airplane than the
man that drew the plans. You give him the tools and the
money and the time and the whiskey and he'll turn it out
better than when it was new. I believe in few things like I
believe in Delvin Sweet."

He stared at the airplane the whole time. "Come over
here and look at this, Merelene." She helped him drag the
little platform around to the side where they could climb
up on it and look in. She had to admit to a little curiosity
about what was in there. They stood side by side and
looked at a very simple leather seat and harness, and a few
glassed instruments, and some of the same special controls
that were in his car.

"Did Mr. Delvin Sweet, the visionary, put these things
in here for you?"

"He did, Merelene, and ain't it a beautiful job of work?"

She said she supposed it was if it made him happy and
kept him safe. She looked up, through the wires and struts
that were strung above her; if it kept him safe *up there*.
They were standing where the blue wheel of the sky
scraped earth, and this was the red Ferris wheel car that
would pluck him up.

He kept his eyes on the two seats, the instruments, and
one of his hands began to stroke the red metal. "I wrote
you a letter last night, and this is a message too. Do you
understand it?"

She reached out and stopped his hand. "Take your eyes
off this machine and look at me."

With great reluctance, he did. "Yes, ma'am."

"Why are you showing me this?"

"I think you know why. Because it's a thing I always
wanted. Because I'm letting myself have things now."

"This is a heap of old parts until I see it work, and if it
doesn't work, which I suspect it won't, you are going to
end up dead. And I want you to know one thing. I am not
like this thing at all. *I* will never kill you."

"No," he said, "but you've had me airborne a time or two."

He looked away now, at the place where the green of pine and oak gave way to blue, a perfectly blue, cloudless spring sky. "You're going to love it."

She looked off there too, feeling on her shoulders the soft rolling edges of the great wheel of blue which touched earth, feeling stuck here in this place of junction, but stuck, at least, with him. She sighed. "Maybe so."

That was when Roland climbed up on the little platform between them and looked into the airplane, and then at the lawyer and said, "Here we go, bud."

When the lawyer pulled up in front of Louise Bates' little house, a yard dog came out to sniff his tires. Roland got out and followed the dog. She reached for the door handle, but felt the lawyer's hand on her arm. They sat in the heat and vibration of the old Cadillac and he stared straight ahead and she knew the airplane was not all he had to show her. Finally he turned, his color high and his voice a little strangled. "Merelene, did you always think Mayfield came to this town by happenstance?"

Instantly, she saw Mayfield alone by a country road late at night, a preposterous hitchhiker. She had never mentioned that night to anyone. And she wouldn't now.

"Yes, I did." She looked at his red face. "What did *you* think?"

"It's what I *know* I'm about to tell you."

She felt her breathing constrict in the old terrible way; as it had when Mayfield had helped her to the cold thrill of a secret, some chapter of the world he lived in. She felt the years she had suffered the sting of his secrets, the years which had become her armor, hardening around her. "Go on," she said.

"Mayfield came here because I told him to."

"You *told* him to?"

"Yes. I believe that's the way he would say it."

"But he isn't saying it. You are."

"That's right," he said. "I am and there's a good bit more." He settled back on the leather seat, and gripped the steering wheel with both hands. He turned to look at her and she saw him quail at the anger in her eyes. His voice was tender, like a physician's with bad news.

"Mayfield was with me in the war."

"With you?" She found Roland now at the edge of her vision, on the property line with the dog sniffing some scent. She watched him walk the invisible trail the dog followed, stopping and moving on as though he understood. She said, more quietly. "What do you mean, with you?"

The lawyer took a deep breath. "He was a mechanic, like Delvin Sweet there you just met. He fixed airplanes. He was a demon with the P-47 Thunderbolt, Merelene. He could put a ship in the sky nobody else could taxi and he could keep it up there. All the pilots wanted him working on their ships. He had the touch. He was golden. You know how these things get started and grow and it gets to be . . . superstition."

Maybe she knew, but she shook her head, her voice low and dull. "I haven't ever been in any war." She hated the way his voice quickened as he told it. He was excited by his memories; he didn't know they were bullets aimed at her. Here was another man fascinated by her old husband.

"You are lucky for that," he said. "Mayfield and I used to talk. I remember the first time we did. I was an officer and he was a technical sergeant and there was some . . . a little bit of the awkwardness that goes with rank, and we started out with the amenities as I remember."

"Amenities?"

"Polite things, or what passed for it between boys in a war. We were southern boys. We had that to start from. I remember one day I was going up for a check ride. It wasn't a mission. I wouldn't have been talking to anybody much if it had been. It was just up and around the field a few times and down again, to test a new elevator. But they armed the ship anyway, and Mayfield came out to help the armorers with the ammunition belts. It was the first time I'd seen him. I heard him talking grits and greens, you know, and I asked him where he was from. "Nowhere," he said, and smiled that black crow grin of his.

"I said, 'Everybody's from someplace.' I was a cross-examiner even then."

"And he said, 'I'm from a service station at a crossroads. But it ain't named. It's exactly nine and one half miles from another place which is just outside of a place that's on a map.' You remember how he talked? You remember his grammar?"

"I remember my own, too, some of the time." She wanted him to hear her anger and be careful, but he was in his memories now and didn't hear. She felt herself growing cold and sullen. There was a life she had not shared with Mayfield and now, years later, she discovered the lawyer hoarding a piece of it.

"Anyway, so he says to me, 'Captain.' I still blush to think that I was twenty-one years old and a captain in the Army Air Corps. He says, 'Captain. A better question is where are you from?'

"I told him Swinford, Florida.

"I remember very clearly that as soon as I mentioned it, the name, his face lit up. He wanted to know everything about it. Every time we met on the flight line he'd ask me questions about little old Swinford, as he called it. He called me the man from a place that's wrote on a map. And then, after I shot down a Focke-Wulf or two, it was, the man who *put* the place on the map. I remember him pulling his head out of the belly of an airplane, and his face all covered with grease and saying, 'Hello there Cap'n Sawyer. What you gone tell me about Swinford by the river today?'

"I told him. It was a way for me to talk to a sergeant. I was too young to wear my bars easy. I wore them hard, and when I got around Mafe—that's what we called him—when I got around him, all the weight was lifted. We talked about a funny little town and it became an invention, and we invented a little more every day until it was Oz on the Suwannee, Xanadu by the Gulf.

"We had quite a thing going and then one day I went up in a ship Mayfield had just blessed with his greasy fingers and I came down in the top of that tree I told you about.

"I didn't see him again until one night when I was out walking and ran into you two coming out of the movie. In little old Swinford of all places. And I'll tell you something, Merelene. I wasn't surprised."

"Why didn't you speak to him? Greet him?"

"I was talking to you."

She waved this away. "You know what I mean."

"I knew he didn't want me to. I thought: he's found his magic place on the map and I'm from the old world, the war. I know the old Mafe, the one with the greasy fingers. This is the new one. All dressed up for a night out with his princess from Oz and his hands are clean. I could see he didn't want me to. I could see it in his eyes. I knew his eyes, Merelene. I *knew* the man."

She said, "He never told me any of this."

"I know he didn't."

"And you didn't either? You kept it from me."

"I was keeping it for him."

"For him?"

"Call it confidentiality. Lawyer and client." His voice was uneasy.

"Call it that if you want to," she said.

"Listen to the rest of it," he said. "Not long after we ran into each other in front of *Mildred Pierce*—you see, I even remember the movie—he came to my back door and asked my daddy if he could see me. It was night, I remember, on the Fourth of July and I was upstairs lying in the usual heap listening to the explosions and watching the flares and I could hear my daddy telling him to go away. 'Enos doesn't want to see you.' And then Mayfield saying something about knowing me from the war. And my daddy saying especially not someone from the war. I lay there in my bed and hollered as loud as I could. 'Get me my canes. Get me my canes.' The whole damned town must have heard me.

"We talked and he asked me not to tell anyone we were comrades-in-arms."

"Why? Why did he care?"

"Because of what happened after I was . . . taken from the scene. It's what he told me. We stood there on the back stoop. He wouldn't come in the house. I offered him a soldier's libation and suggested we toast the glorious Fourth, but he turned it down. He said, 'It's because of what happened after I known you.' He wouldn't say, 'after you were bagged.' He wouldn't tell me more. He did say this. He said they blamed him for the loss of Captain Sawyer. All the flying fools who gave him the name of magic and believed his fingers could keep a plane safe from being shot to hell and wanted him to work on their ships and even tried to bribe him to stick his wrench in their engines. All these fools descended on him like the very wrath of the pit when Captain Sawyer went down."

"Why?" she asked. The lawyer sighed and sank further into the leather seat. Roland was at her window looking in, the dog at his knee. The look on his face was patience and puzzlement. "Why did they do that?" she asked, reaching through the open window and taking Roland's hand.

"Because his was the last hand to touch my ship before I took it up and got it stitched."

"What did you tell him by the back door of your house?" She squeezed Roland's hand, calm in hers.

"I told him to forget all about it. It wasn't his fault. Metals fail. Stresses push parts past their limits. No one can see all the hairline weaknesses. And the rest of it was nothing but superstition, twaddle and nonsense. I told him it was a better pilot than me, a German boy with luck and guts that smoked my tail. I told him the engine was going like gangbusters right up until that Focke-Wulf put a twenty-millimeter cannon round through it." He rested his hands on his scarecrow legs. "And through me too."

"Was it going, the engine?"

He waited a long time before answering her and his hands reached for the steering wheel and the fingers slowly went white. "No."

"What did he say . . . when you lied to him? Did it comfort him?"

"Not so's you'd notice." He loosed his white hands a little. "What he said was, 'Kind of you to say so, Cap'n Sawyer.'

"I told him, 'Mayfield, all that Cap'n stuff is over. It's finished and I'm glad to have it off me.'

"He said, 'No sir, Cap'n Sawyer, that's where you wrong. It never ends. It never does.' "

She sat in this Cadillac time capsule staring across its shiny hood into the past, until she thought she could see a propeller spin where the hood ornament was. Then she saw the times when this chapter might have helped her, might have kept things from getting worse. These two brothers-in-arms had kept their secrets and she had been left to fight unarmed.

"Enos," she said, "I started with a question and you still haven't answered it."

He stared at her.

"You said he came because you told him to. Did you ever tell him to?"

"Not in the way you think. He felt responsible. He felt bad about what happened. Together we had invented this place, this Swinford."

Then it came to her. "When you invented this place, this Swinford you invented by the river. Did you ever mention me? Did you tell him about me living here?"

He waited for a moment, then stared past her through the window at Roland, who returned his gaze in patience. "Of course. Of course I did. Every magic place has its princess and its fool."

"So he came here?"

"He came here," the lawyer said. "He must have figured that if you could invent a town, you could live in it."

Sixteen

It was churchy cool and quiet in Larup's. Behind the bar the bottles glittered and all the exotic pictures and names on them were a pleasant promise—of travel maybe, or the death of anxiety or the temporary illumination of hope. Louise Bates shucked a pack of unfiltered Pall Malls and a Zippo from her red purse. "Want one?" Merelene declined but with longing. She watched Louise pour a long white cigarette from the red pack and professionally flip the lid of the Zippo and she smelled the first smoke and the lighter fluid at the same instant.

They sat for a space looking at each other while Louise exhaled gray smoke up at the ceiling. Louise had a spell, Merelene decided, and she was captured for the time being. She felt no need to hurry things, to ask what next. Louise picked a fleck of tobacco from her lower lip. She was a Mary Astor with dark hair, Merelene decided, not quite a Myrna Loy. She would have played the dangerous older sister, or maybe the good gangster's moll. She rolled the fleck of tobacco on the tabletop and then looked at it carefully. "They got good grouper sandwiches here. That's what I usually have."

Merelene nodded. "Whatever's good."

Louise drew on the Pall Mall and watched her through a veil of gray smoke. "I seen you was worried when I come in the lawyer's office."

Merelene nodded, thinking, It's my condition of life.

A half hour earlier, she had looked up to see Louise standing in front of her little desk, her wide, dark eyes taking in the office and the lawyer's shut door, as though this were the gatepost to Oz. Louise was all red. A dress, a patent leather purse dangling from her elbow, and spiked heels. Three jostling shades of red.

Merelene had smiled and pulled the plastic cover over her typewriter. Louise still stared at the lawyer's door. "Does he give you a dinner break?"

Merelene nodded. "He's pretty good about things like that."

Louise listened seriously, then whispered, "Let's get something to eat, what do you say? I got my car right outside." She jerked a thumb toward the street.

Louise was on some sort of mission, so Merelene followed the thumb into the heat that leaned against the door. Louise's car was a big Pontiac, bright red, with a peeling vinyl roof and red bucket seats that were hot as a stovetop. As Louise made the engine grind then roar, kicking pedals like a high school boy, Merelene looked up the street at the usual assortment of clerks and secretaries drifting toward Fable's Cafe. No one seemed to be watching them.

With the wind rushing in and the radio playing Tammy Wynette, they didn't talk. Merelene sat with her knees up trying not to fry her thighs on the Naugahyde. As they headed out the river road, she watched the cypress trees fly past and the dotted white line slip under the gleaming hood of the big fast car.

Louise drove with one hand, her head thrown back

keening "Stand by Your Man" with the radio. It was a prayerful face that Merelene studied until Louise caught her at it and shied and they both smiled.

"I love that woman." Louise changed hands on the wheel and patted the radio. "She's had *some* life. She ort to slap the pee water out of that worthless husband of hers." Louise watched Merelene for confirmation. Merelene could not have said the worthless husband's name, but she smiled female complicity. It was harmless to drive and cuss. What else was there sometimes.

When Louise pulled into Larup's, Merelene didn't protest. A few cars and pickups cooled in the sandy lot under the live oaks. They sat for a moment watching the smoked windows of the bar. Louise said, "I come here a lot. It's close and they get good fish sometimes." Merelene nodded, remembering the times she had come here with Mayfield, and then the times he had come alone. You could eat or drink your lunch at Larup's.

Inside, it was all the same. All shadows and glittery bottles and churchy cool. The bartender was making slow circles with a white cloth in front of a farmer collapsed on the bar. The farmer was Charlie Dorneau. She could smell him—beer, diesel fuel, malathion and sweat. Merelene blinked as they passed him. In the double vision of memory and real time, Charlie was two people, a skinny, puzzled boy she had known in high school, and this wind-broken drinker on the lip of old age. At least he had made half a day in his peanut field.

They sat at the window table where they could watch the traffic on the river road. Louise turned to the bartender with a toss of her brown hair. "We'll have two grouper sandwiches, Willard, and don't lean on the mayonnaise."

The bartender called to the back room, "Deuce groper easy mayo." He gave the bar another swipe or two. "What you ladies drinking?" Louise ordered a draft beer and Merelene asked for a Coke.

"You was worried," Louise said, "because you thought, 'Who's taking care of the children?' " She watched Merelene's face.

Merelene looked into her eyes and she saw the shadows under those tall live oaks and the swept sand yard and the children moving around in the shade of bright colors and Louise there too, hugging herself in the pilled old cardigan, proprietress of it all.

"Not so awful worried." She smiled. "I was thinking about it."

"I got a girl comes in to spell me sometimes. So I can get away when I need to."

Merelene nodded again, following the slow movement of the cigarette in Louise's hand, thinking: in your red dress.

"I wanted to tell you about Roland. Well, first off, I never did believe any of that stuff they said about him. He *is* peculiar . . ." Her eyes widened at Merelene, maybe threw a challenge, but Merelene gave back her most receiving smile. Louise nodded at the smile and drew on the Pall Mall with a sucking pop that was not unpleasant. "He's peculiar . . . but not in the way some people says he is. Believe me, I been keeping little boys and some big ones too for a long time now and I know the tendencies. Roland, he's just *very* friendly. He's got the kind of friendliness you don't see in grown-up people. Those little ones back at my place they crawl all over him. They sense him. They know who wants them around and who doesn't and what he's got is . . ." Louise waved her cigarette in circles and her eyes had gone to slits. She couldn't find the words.

"I know," said Merelene. "I know what you mean and I never have been able to say it very well. But I read a book about saints once and I found Roland in it again and again." Louise was her friend now. Always would be now.

Louise said, "I guess I don't need to go on, but I did want to tell you what I thought of that poot-butt Mary Heatherton and her hissy fit about your boy taking a bath. I tell you she ain't all sweetness and light. I'm in a position to know. These mothers coming to pick their kids up, they tell me things. Why . . ."

Merelene touched Louise's hand on the tabletop. She didn't want to hear about Mary's other life.

Louise looked startled, then nodded. "Well, anyway, if all that woman's got for trouble is a coeducational bubble bath, she's in better shape than most of us. . . ." Then Louise eyes seemed to swell and blur. She sipped her beer and smoked, watching a pulpwood truck pass with a ripping noise that rattled their window.

Louise stared at the empty road, and Merelene thought: She's really a pretty woman. She's my age and I remember when we were both pretty. Now she's the sign lady, the one who puts the Bible verses and the Jeremiah warnings in yellow lights out under the trees.

Everybody knew the story of Louise's widowing, not six months after Harold had been killed at Khe Sanh. Her husband, Pete, was a crabber, and by most accounts a good one, clever with his traps, and knowledgeable of the water. He had stepped on the rotten planks of an old dock one day and had fallen through and by an odd chance, had caught his foot between the boards. It was high tide and he was suspended beneath with his head and shoulders in the water, trying to lift himself up. The dock was not fifty yards from a little restaurant on Horse Shoe Beach where the jukebox had covered his cries. They had found him at low tide, hanging under the dock, the bone of his right ankle nearly sawn through, his head a foot above water. He had been one of the few fine swimmers among the men hereabouts. A husband and son in six months.

"I always thought you was lucky to work for the lawyer." Louise looked at her out of shocked eyes that contradicted the controlled tone of her voice. "Pete didn't leave no will. He didn't leave much *property* either, but the lawyer helped me when Pete died. He's a nice man."

"Yes," Merelene said, "he is nice," wondering as she always had to, and hating herself for it, what Louise knew about her and the lawyer.

"Sometimes," Louise said, "I go to that place where Pete used to put his boat in the water and just stare at it. It ain't healthy, I know, but I just have to go do it. And I think about what sticking your foot in the wrong place can do to three people. I don't know."

Merelene had thought about it too. Accidents, mishaps, her blood and Mayfield's mixing to make a Roland and then a mosquito bite. And Bull. Where was he putting his foot down at this very moment? Every time she felt a mosquito on her skin she remembered Roland as the helpless perfect thing he had been for a few years before a bug had bitten him.

"Anyway," said Louise, "I wanted to tell you about Roland. He's got a calling to be with little children. He's practically my second in command. Some of the little ones call him Uncle Radio, cause of that way he talks."

Merelene said, "I needed to hear it."

They ate their sandwiches and watched the river road. A few cars pulled in, mostly local men, farmers whose wives were going to the junior college or selling acreage and Amway and didn't cook the noon meal. She knew a few of them. Not one of them could come in the door without stopping to stare for a moment at the two women sitting by the window. The place got smokier and noisier, and less like the dream visits she had read on the liquor labels. And there was more of the diesel and malathion and sweat smell that Charlie Dorneau had brought in with him.

Merelene was about to bring up the subject of Roland's future at Louise's when Roark Drawdy pulled into the parking lot. She watched him get out of a new Dodge pickup, stretch himself in a patch of sunlight, remove his mirror sunglasses and rub the disks of white flesh that lived behind them. She felt her stomach tighten, not because she feared Roark, but because he carried so much of the past with him, chapters of Mayfield she didn't know. How many of Mayfield's midnight raids had started here in Larup's?

When he came through the door he pretended not to notice the window table. He followed the bar, slapping backs and shaking hands. Louise sank down a little in her chair and set her jaw. "Here comes one of my mistakes."

Roark was almost never seen with his wife, Lucy. They lived on a remote place near the edge of the Steinhatchee Wildlife Preserve where Roark could guide airplanes in at night with gasoline flares and unload them without troubling his neighbors. Roark never said exactly what he unloaded: if he talked about business, he pulled himself up to a full six feet and said, in a preachy tone, it was given to some people to have vices and given to some others to service those vices and without the Roark Drawdys of this world, who did not themselves indulge, Alligood County would be in a sorry state. If you let him go on, he would conjure visions of a population run amok without its vices. Merelene looked around at the inhabitants of Larup's and tried to imagine them with enough energy at the end of the day for vice.

She managed a sip of Coke and watched Roark carry on like a campaigning politician. She supposed he had to keep his alliances in order. Now he was talking to two young men covered with sweat and chaff who had parked a hay truck under the trees outside. "Harry, you still at the university?" One of them swirled his beer and said, "Not in the summertime, Roark. School's out in the summertime."

Roark could never see when he wasn't invited. "You still studying computers."

The boy nodded, swirling his beer and waiting to be left alone. Roark regarded the room. "Harry, when you learn how to program that computer of yours, I want you to come on back here and work for me. I ought to be about ready to *computerize* by then." He laughed big at himself and several heads at the bar made slow sorry arcs.

He gave the young man, Harry, a slap on the shoulder, and decided to notice Merelene and Louise. He did a dramatic double take, then sidled over and rested his hand on Louise's shoulder. "My two favorite ladies. How y'all today?" Merelene's eyes locked on Louise's sending a message: Ignore him. But something ignited in Louise's eyes; maybe a piece of the craziness people talked about. She tabled her beer glass hard and brushed Roark's hand from her shoulder the way a person would slap at a stinging bug. "Roark, if I'm your favorite lady, there must be something wrong with me." She looked at Merelene. "I can't speak for nobody else here." Roark grabbed at his stung hand and rocked back on his heels. Several of the men at the bar swiveled around and dangled their boots into the room. Merelene felt the color crawling up her neck. She held her eyes, saying ignore him, on Louise's face. Finally Roark did a comical backpedal toward the bar, as though to say, "Well, excuse me for living."

Merelene leaned across to Louise. The men were turning back to their drinks; talk was starting again, punctuated by a few barks of surprised laughter. "Louise, what's got into you?"

Louise chewed angrily, "Well, just a lot of things. I don't like him to take that familiar tone with me."

Louise glared out at the bright afternoon, the sandy dike with the asphalt road on it. Merelene waited. She'd heard rumors about Roark and Louise. Finally Louise looked back from the road. She pushed her half-eaten sandwich away and shook out another cigarette. "You sure you don't want one of these?" Merelene looked at the fetching red pack and shook her head.

"He came by last night." Louise's voice was low. Merelene leaned forward to the words. "Why?" The question was out of her mouth before she realized her stupidity.

Louise gave her a disappointed look. "I didn't let him in. I nearbout had to rassle him on the front porch. And I'm getting a little old for that."

"What did he say?"

"After I wouldn't let him in, he stayed out in the yard, leaning against his truck talking loud about what he needed and drinking from a paper sack. It woke Roland up and he poked his head out behind me and yelled, "Arrest that man," or some such. I can't remember it exactly. Roark jumped when he saw him. I think he thought it was Mayfield for a minute. He said, "Well, look here what we got. I thought that boy was had up and sent to the state home.""

"Well, I didn't know what to say then, so I said, 'He was but now he's back for a visit.' "

Louise looked over at Roark, who was rubbing his back on the bar, his elbows behind him, a long-neck beer dangling from his right hand. "That's when he said, 'I know somebody else that's visiting this sorry place.'

"He said Mayfield was back, your old Mayfield Durham, and that he's got plenty of plans for this little town. He's playing it close to his chest. A bunch of bullskate like that. I just told him to take it on down the road, I wasn't interested. But I knew you'd want to know."

Merelene nodded. Yes, she wanted to know. She said, "If he told you, he's told everybody else in town."

Louise swallowed and said, "About an hour later, I'm settling again and I got Roland down in the other room, and I hear another car roll in the yard. Well, this time amo get the gun . . ." Louise looked at Merelene and it was like the looks she had known from the old times that came from doctors; the looks that asked, Do you want to know? Can you take what's about to come? So Merelene nodded her head and drew back and waited inside the armor of years.

Louise took the nod and went on: "Somebody knocked very polite and soft. I went to the closet for Pete's old twelve-gauge pump and jacked a round into the chamber. I pulled the curtains aside a little and it was Mayfield. He was standing on the stoop and when he saw the gun he looked at me and smiled and I tell you I just knew I didn't need no shotgun. So I propped it by the door and opened a crack and he said, 'Hello, Louise. I hate to bother you this time of night.'

"Well, I thought about that. It was bother. But the look in his face—it's hard to describe, Merelene—he didn't want to bother anybody. He said, 'I'd like to see the boy, if that's all right with you.'

"I hardened up at that. I said, 'His mommer don't want him seen.' And then he said the strangest thing."

Merelene closed her eyes and waited. But Louise didn't speak again until she opened them. "What did he say?"

"He said, 'She told me to look at his grown-up face. So, I came by to do that. It's all I want to do, just look at him a minute. Then I'll be out of your hair.'

"And I forgot one thing. He called you his wife. He said, 'My wife told me to see his grown-up face.'

"I didn't know what to make of it. I thought for a while before I let him in. All he did was he walked to the little office room where I put Roland's cot and he stood there and he looked. I asked him if he wanted me to turn on a light and that was the only time I was worried. He almost seemed angry. He said, 'No, no, no. Don't wake him.'

"So he stood there and watched Roland in the dark and after a while it seemed like Roland was waking up, like he knew somebody was there. He started mumbling like he does in his sleep and Mayfield left real quick.

"When he was out on the stoop again, he tried to give me some money for my trouble. That's what he said, 'For your trouble.' I told him it wasn't trouble and he ort to know better. He said he was sorry. I was right and he was sorry. He said he just got used to paying for things. Most people seemed to want him to. Then he shook my hand, very formal and left. Just walked to his car and got in and drove off as quiet as he come."

Merelene stared at Louise; there must be more. And Louise stared back, her eyes saying, no more. Merelene thought: Louise, do you know what you've told me? Louise whispered, "Did I do wrong letting him in?" Before Merelene could think an answer, Roark launched himself from the bar with the beer swinging in his hand.

He took a chair at the table next to them, and pushed back in it with his long legs spread wide. He threw his arms back behind his head, stretching broadly, and sighed, "Hidey-tidey-tidey," addressing his exasperation to Larup's at large. A few heads came up. He stared straight at Merelene while he spoke to the young man who had come in the hay truck. "Harry," he said, "you gone come out and computerize me, out to my place like I asked you to?" The boy got up to pay his bill. "Roark, you can operate that asphalt pasture of yours without me and my computer." It brought a dark look to Roark's face, and more of the barking laughter from the bar.

Sprawled in his chair, his hands clasped behind his head, Roark stared at Merelene. It was like the too casual aiming of a gun. His voice was high when he said, "*Miss* Merelene, I heard you and the lawyer and that idiot boy was out my way. Out to Delvin Sweet's little strip. I told old Del he better not let that place get popular with the sporting crowd. That place is business with me."

She looked him in the eye and said, "Why are you telling me, Roark? I'd of thought you'd keep it to yourself."

Roark didn't blink. "My life is an open book, *Miss* Merelene. You know that."

She said, "Enos Sawyer's life is none of your business, nor any of mine except when I'm sitting at that desk in his office."

He smiled big and mean at her. "That ain't what Mayfield tells me."

The bar took a bite of air and held it. "No ma'am, that ain't what *he* says."

Merelene knew her face was as red as Louise's dress, but still the words came to her calm, and correct. If this was the worst he could do, it wasn't much. "Roark, don't you ever get tired of being the Mayfield Message Service?"

The grin ceased, and his face went slack with hate.

She got up to pay her bill. Even before she spoke, she could hear her words ringing down the grapevine, the long-distance line that started with these sunburned ears at the bar.

"The next time you meet Mayfield, ask him to come by and see me."

Seventeen

"I went to see my secret today."

She stared at him. He had come in late and angry and had passed her desk without the usual touch for her shoulder. He had ruffled papers furiously for a moment in his office, and then come out again.

"Del Sweet was out there drunk on his behind. He had a visit from Roark Drawdy. Roark told him to quit on my little project: said it ain't good for business." He watched her, waiting for a response in the key of his own indignation. She could not supply it. She didn't care about the airplane, except to fear it a little.

"What exactly does Roark Drawdy have to do with your airplane?"

The lawyer frowned as though it were a slow question. "Roark Drawdy owns that pasture and nearbout owns Dell Sweet. Sweet keeps it for him in what shape it needs to be in for his uses."

"His uses?"

"You know what I mean."

The lawyer was uneasy about this. He was an officer of the court in a county whose illegal income exceeded its receipts for tobacco, corn and peanuts. He turned his head like all the rest. You simply could not have a new idea about something like Roark's business. You grew up with your daddy's attitude toward Roark's daddy and you knew it went back to the generation of grandfathers. She didn't know what, other than Roland, the town would not allow. It had always allowed Roark Drawdy.

She said, "Can't you find another place to put that thing?"

"I could, if I wanted everybody to know about it."

She knew better than to ask why the airplane was secret. It was hard to change in Swinford. She looked down at her desk.

"Besides," he said, in a high fidgety tone that was not like him, "it's not just Delvin Sweet. He'll finish his work and to hell with Roark. That airplane smells like money to him, and I can make it smell good quicker than Roark can make it smell bad. At least I think I can. Roark is mostly bluff anyway, when it comes down to cases." He paused, watching her. She nodded to make him go on.

"Delvin told me that I'd been talking about Roark's business too much. I said, 'What to hell, Delvin? What you mean, *talking*?' Then he says, 'Well maybe not you.' I asked him what in hell he meant by that. I was getting a little heated. He tells me you and Louise Bates had it out with Roark down at Larup's. I said . . ."

"*Not* had it out. That's silly. We just . . ."

She quit talking because he was thinking and not listening. He clawed a cigar out of his vest pocket, and patted himself for his silver scissors. He trimmed the end of the cigar, regarding her with the expression he used on unreliable clients.

She said, "Roark was doing what he always does. He got personal with Louise and she answered him back. So he got mean. Said you and your airplane were damaging business. That's all."

"No, it's not."

"Well, the only other thing was some boy driving a hay truck. He said something about Roark and his asphalt pasture. Everybody laughed."

"And?"

He seemed to think he had caught her out.

"And Roark told me Mayfield was back which stopped a few hearts, I guess. I said right back to tell Mayfield to come see me. I wasn't going to have Roark Drawdy announcing things about me."

The lawyer's lip curled around his cigar. "About you?"

"Yes," she said, "about me. Mayfield *is* about me. He's about ten years of me at least."

His legal eyes, sharp and bright, bored at her. She softened, weary, not liking the way this was going. "Isn't he? Enos, tell me Mayfield is not about me."

He blew a plume of smoke, a stream of resignation which seemed to put the past visible there in the air between them. "Yes, I suppose he is. And did your heart stop?"

She looked away at the front window, at the Confederate boy on the pedestal, and after a space, it was as good as an answer. And before she knew what she was doing, she had gathered up her purse and keys and was past his quizzing face and out the door without looking back.

She had to ask directions twice before she found Delvin Sweet. A man at a one-pump Shell station came out to her with "Mickey" stitched in red thread on his pocket flap. He leaned on her windowsill. Yes, he knew about a landing strip like the one she was describing, but didn't think anybody used it anymore, didn't know exactly how to get her there. She followed his directions to the place where the lawyer had turned on Wednesday morning, but after a few miles, she was lost again.

A boy on a John Deere tractor pulling a sprayer tank

got down and came to her window in the smell of malathion and the whoop and thrash of the agitator in the tank
and frowned and rubbed his pimpled forehead, pointing
back the way she had come. He swerved his hand left and
then right in the air and said, "You cain't miss it."

She was sweating and tired from wrestling the wheel
over roots and holes when she finally found the track,
with the lawyer's tire marks still on it, that led to the rust-
streaked tin roof and the red metal of the airplane. Delvin
Sweet was having an early lunch in the shade of one red
wing. She stopped where the lawyer had parked and
called out her window: "Where's your dog?"

Del Sweet looked around and puckered his lips and
whistled a dry note or two. The fice came running from
the tree line.

Still in the car, Merelene said, "Could you put her away
so we can talk."

He set a wax paper bundle carefully on the ground and
shooed the dog away from it. He stood up slowly, slapping
dirt from his bottom. "I can put her away, but I done told
you she wouldn't hurt you."

Merelene said, "I never told you, but that's one I heard
before."

Del Sweet laughed and slapped his leg, "Come up here,
Pissant." The dog followed him, watching her as it ran to
the door of the shed. He turned the peg that closed the
door and said, "Now what can I do for you? You want
some of my lunch?"

Merelene got out of the car and plucked her skirt from
the backs of her legs. The heat was already coming on at
ten-thirty. Del Sweet went back to the wax paper bundle
in the shade of the red wing. She stood above him watching his jaws grind a fried chicken leg. "It looks good," she
said, "but I won't have any, thanks." She smoothed the
cotton across her stomach.

Del Sweet said, "You come out here to check on my progress?" He didn't look up at her, so she squatted.

"No, I came to ask you how to find Roark Drawdy." She laughed nervously. "I lived in this town all my life and I don't know exactly how to find him."

"Not many do," he said. "He likes it that way."

"Well," she said, "like it or not, I've got to talk to him." Now he did look at her, his jaw ceasing so he could swallow. "Lawyer told you what Roark said to me?"

"He told me."

He shrugged, acting small. "I ain't nothing but a dime-a-dozen aircraft mechanic. I don't know nothing bout any of this."

She smiled at him. "The lawyer says you're the best. Now that I've told you, you'll probably raise your prices."

"I know what the lawyer thinks. It ain't what *he* thinks I'm worried about."

She put her hand on his shoulder. "Me talking to Roark won't give anybody anything to think about."

A deer crossed the road in front of her not long after she entered the Steinhatchee Game Preserve. One bound over the fence, two heart-stopping leaps, one for each traffic lane, and a fourth to clear the fence on the other side—and nothing but a black hoof streak on the asphalt and a little fuzz of floating hair to mark the passage. She stopped on the lonely two-lane to catch her breath and watch the leaves quivering at the place where the animal had reentered the forest. Del Sweet's map, crudely scratched on a piece of wax paper, lay in her lap. It told her to turn on a road marked only by a number embossed on a tin plate nailed to a fence post.

It was an old logging road, set on the right-of-way of the narrow-gauge track that had been built in the 1870s when virgin trees had been cut by Yankee predators. As she went slowly, the deep secret forest odor, of pine resin and cinnamon insects and leaf marl and swamp ammonia, invaded her windows. It brought the sweat of fear to her armpits. These were the deepest and the oldest woods and some of their stories were grim. There was the skeleton found chained by the wrists to a tree. Its owner, a big man the pathologists said, had tried to use the chain as a saw. He had cut the tree half through before what the newspapers called "exposure" had come for him. Shotgunned lovers had been found in a car off one these lonely roads. And there were the game wardens who had looked too hard for poachers. Swinford knew the stories, and the stories made people watch their neighbors.

The wax map told her that her next turn was an unmarked road, a mile and a half from the logging track. She'd have to go by her odometer. From this intersection, Del Sweet had said it was only a few hundred yards to Roark's house. When Merelene found the turn, she stopped again and let the hot rush of the forest into the car. The heat fell from the treetops into the wet shade and the insects sawed a rhythm that mixed with the sound of her idling engine. It had rained here the night before and there were no fresh tire tracks leading in. She peered down the cypress and pine hollow for a place to turn around. She'd have to back out if there was nothing at the end, or if there was no end.

She was afraid she would quit, so she gave herself courage by counting all the markers in her passage to this place. She recalled rushing past the lawyer and his indignation and driving out of town as fast as she could—feeling good for the first time in weeks, feeling her life solid in her own hands. She remembered the gas station man, the boy on the tractor and Delvin Sweet. She had to find Roark.

The house was only a hundred yards or so down the narrow lane. It rose to the cypress tops three stories, a complete surprise. Merelene had expected an old cracker

house, the usual chaos of ells and wings and galleries, but
this was a new cedar house with balconies and solar heat-
ing units and a big fanlight of stained glass in the cupola
that crowned its third level.

A carpet of mulched pine bark led to a front porch fes-
tooned with potted ferns and covered in green Astroturf.
The house was quiet, all the windows shut tight. Maybe
that was music behind the humming of the central air, a
whiny country tune. Merelene rang the doorbell, a ten-
note church bell model, and then tried the brass knocker,
rapping until the echo came back to her from the cave of
trees.

A new car was parked in the side yard, a big maroon
Buick with gleaming wire wheels and the double antennae
that CBers favored. It hadn't been driven in days. Rain-
spattered sand still clung to its tires. With a trespasser's
tingle at the base of her neck, Merelene walked to the back
of the house, noticing all its signs of newness, the spar-
kling nailheads bedded in the cedar siding, the bright aluminum flashing and the dirt daubers looking for the places
to put their first nests. It had been a lot of trouble to truck
all this into the woods.

Lucy Drawdy was sitting on a blanket in the freshly
sodded backyard. She was holding a cigarette in one hand
and a drink in the other and playing a radio. Her yellow
bikini bathing suit was just inches decent, although this
far out she could lie naked and no one would know. Merelene waited for a space, sheepishly using her advantage:
Lucy had not noticed her yet.

Lucy raised her cigarette and puffed, then lifted her
glass with a tinkle of gold charms. She made a sour face at
the taste. Then she flipped a page of the magazine in her
lap. Young was what she looked; like a high school girl on
a picnic at the river. Her body was pale and would stay
that way in this shade, but her limbs were firm and

shapely and when she began to hum along with the radio, her voice was high and tinny and girlish and the words she sang were whiskey-soft at the edges.

Merelene didn't know what to do. She could walk up and let Lucy see her or call out or just wait until Lucy's radar picked her up. She decided to retrace her steps to the side of the house and announce herself.

"Hello the house!" she called out before rounding the corner again. Lucy was sitting in saucer-eyed surprise, holding the blanket to her chest when Merelene appeared. "It's only me," she called. "I hope I didn't scare you."

Lucy still held her glass out as though it were a weapon. "Scare me! My Jesus, I nearly inhaled this whiskey. Merelene, you ortn't sneak up on people like that."

"Well, if I'd of stood out at the car blowing the horn would you have heard me?" She didn't like the word, *sneak*.

"Yes, I would." Lucy reached over and turned the radio down.

"I'm sorry, Lucy. I guess you don't get that many visitors out here."

Lucy let go of the blanket and it fell down her ample front. Merelene couldn't help it. She stared. Lucy was what you'd call well-preserved. Merelene guessed she was about her own age, but she couldn't be sure because Lucy wasn't a local girl. Roark had imported her from Isle Hammock. Lucy spread the blanket again and crossed her legs. That was when Merelene noticed the magazine. A two-page color picture of a naked man was spread on the grass. Lucy sipped and raised the glass. "You want one of these. It's Mr. Jack's best."

"No thanks, Lucy. I can't stay. I'm just looking for Roark. I need to talk to him."

Lucy's brows narrowed, and it seemed to bring her little eyes closer together. She reached over and closed the mag-

azine, but there was a naked man on the front of it too.
Lucy sipped again and raised her chin in defiance. "Cute,
ain't he?" Merelene took a step closer. The man was wearing a black cowboy hat and still had his red stretch socks
on. He had yellow teeth and a Clark Gable mustache.
There was a tattoo on his left forearm, a naked woman
with a rattlesnake climbing one of her legs and an "oops!"
look on her face. He had the thick body of a laborer, leath-
ery red on his neck and arms and white as a fish belly
everywhere else. Well, almost everywhere else. She wondered what dive they had found him in and what they had
offered him to pose for a picture like this. She said, "I
suppose he's handsome in a certain way. Or was, before he
got that empty look in his eyes."

Lucy shrugged and scratched her arm with fuschia
nails. "Who cares about his eyes?" She stood up and
stretched her long white body and picked up the blanket.
"Come on in the house, Merelene. You ain't seen it yet."

Merelene followed, half polite, half curious. Had anybody seen it? She wondered what it was like for Lucy
living out here in Roark's big secret. When Lucy was in
town, she drove an old International Harvester pickup.
She did her shopping or got her hair done, or just drove
on through to somewhere else, stopping at the traffic light
with her thin white arm resting on the windowsill, smoking and looking straight ahead until the light changed.
People said her friends, if she had them, must be from
some other place.

The house was cool. Lucy took her in through the
kitchen and Merelene counted two of everything. There
were two toaster ovens and two blenders, two TVs and
two refrigerators, and everything looked brand-new. Appliances were stacked along the walls still in their boxes—
hair dryers and shower massages and vibrating foot baths.
Lucy ran her hands along the surfaces of counters and

cabinets as they went and rubbed her fingers together and squinted at their intersections.

Their feet were quiet on the carpet so thick it was like walking on the back of an enormous white rabbit. At the top of the stairs, Lucy stood at the fanlight and looked out over the treetops. "On a clear day," she said, "I can see all the way to Bronson. And you ort to see the sunrise from up here. That's why I had this colored glass put in; it's a sunrise." In the chill of the central air and the surprise and the embarrassment, Merelene did not know what to say. She heard herself repeating, "yes," and "oh," and "uh-huh" to Lucy's guided tour. "Yes I see" to the antique furniture Lucy had collected from auctions and distress sales in six counties and hauled back in Roark's old truck, and "yes" to the rooms piled to the ceilings with boxed appliances. One of the rooms on the top floor was Roark's "office." Pointing, Lucy said, "That's my Daddy's old rolltop." She let her restless fingers light on the golden oak writing surface. "Roark does his accounts up here."

"I thought he was only kidding," Merelene murmured.

"What's that?" Lucy turned on her, hands on bikinied hips.

Merelene pointed to a box in the corner of the room. "It says that's a computer, doesn't it?"

Lucy was still puzzled, but she couldn't keep the note of pride from her voice. "The way things is expanding, he's going to need it. Course, I don't know if he can learn to use it. She touched her own temple. "Roark ain't the smartest man in the world."

When they were back at the bottom and Lucy had darkened her glass with amber whiskey, Lucy sat down at the kitchen table, a beautiful old mahogany piece, and tilted her head to one side. "You know, Merelene, I always liked you."

Merelene smiled. "You don't even know me, Lucy."

Lucy looked a little hurt. "You don't have to know somebody to like them. People have auras. You can like someone from . . . afar." The way she said the word *afar*, sounded actressy. Loving from afar was something that happened a lot from noon to four on the TV. But there was something else, an invitation to honesty here among the goods.

"Well, then, thank you Lucy. It's nice to be liked. Even if it is from afar. There aren't that many people to be liked by in this place."

Lucy smiled, and then shivered in her two pieces of yellow jersey. She seemed younger than ever now. "You and me are alike, Merelene. More than you might think. People are scared of us. We got auras that scare them."

Merelene thought she heard the sound of an engine on the logging road. She said, "I don't know anything about auras, Lucy. If I got one, it's probably nothing a hot shower wouldn't cure."

"Well, then let me put it this way, Merelene. You scare them because of your bad luck and I scare them because I ain't from around here and I don't care what they think about me."

And Merelene thought: It's your husband that scares them. She said, "Is that Roark I hear?"

Lucy got up quickly and poured her whiskey into the sink. "It wouldn't be anybody else. But then, we want expecting *you* today either."

When they heard a car door slam, Lucy glanced at the sound and a little hurry came into her voice. "You never did tell me why you wanted to see Roark."

Merelene looked around. She could say she wanted a toaster oven. "I don't really want to see Roark, Lucy. I just want to find Mayfield and Roark can tell me where he is."

For some reason, Merelene had to reach across the table and put her hand on Lucy's, pale and chilly with gold charms. "You're very pretty, Lucy. You look the same as you did the day you came here." Lucy's smile was suddenly dazzling.

Roark insisted that she "come up to his office for a little talk." She followed his skinny shanks up the stairs, and stifled a laugh when he hurried ahead to the second landing and closed one of the rooms full of plunder.

Now they were seated across from each other in his little counting house, and he was propped back in a swivel chair at the old rolltop and twitching his green, snake-booted foot up and down as he rocked. He said, "To what do we owe the pleasure?" or some such television dialogue but she just looked at him. She wanted to see how long his eyes could meet hers. He did his best but it was nowhere near the county record. When he had stopped rocking and got the smirk off his face, she said, "Roark, we left a conversation unfinished at Larup's yesterday."

"Did we now, Miss Merelene?"

"You can stop calling me Miss Merelene, Roark. I'm way past the missy age, and you never meant any respect by it."

An expression of damage took up residence on Roark's face. "Now that ain't fair, Miss . . . It ain't fair, Merelene. I have always had you in my highest regard. Why Mayfield . . ." He stopped and his face colored a bit. She realized she had never seen him blush. Not even the day he had come down from the tower trussed and bundled and labeled a lunatic.

"What about Mayfield?" she asked, pushing herself forward in her chair.

He swept his arms out toward the four walls and looked around theatrically. His voice was slow, because she was slow, and he was instructing her. "Mayfield ain't here. You can see that. Just like that idiot boy of yours ain't here no more. Just like he's down at the state home and we all safe at last. Ain't nobody hiding anything. Not me, not you, not the lawyer, not Mafe. You see how it is don't you . . . *Mizriz* Durham?"

"Where is he?"

He shrugged, grinned, wiggled his foot.

"You won't tell me?"

"I would if I could. You know that."

"Let me ask you this, Roark. Did you give him *my* message? The one I mentioned at Larup's?"

The grin hadn't changed since high school when Roark had brought shine to school in a mayonnaise jar, calling it "product," or sold playing cards with dirty pictures on them. She said, "Did you tell him to come see me?"

He curled his lip up and closed one eye as though he were sighting a rifle. "Woman, I don't know what you're talking about."

On her way out, she used her toe to nudge the box that lay in the corner. "I see you meant it about the computer, Roark. You're not completely unreliable."

He rose and stretched. "It's for sale, Miss Merelene. If you see anything you want around here, you just say so. We'll work something out. Far as I can see, everything in this world is for sale some way or the other." He stepped over a little closer to her.

She touched the computer again with the toe of her shoe. "Do you think you can work that thing, Roark?"

"We'll see, won't we."

She smiled at him and then turned to the door. Over her shoulder she said, "A man who can fly can do just about anything."

She was turning her car around when Lucy came hurrying from the backyard balancing a replenished glass of whiskey. She tugged on the door handle, frowning until

Merelene leaned over and unlocked it. She slid across the seat, close, and tucked her bare white knees up under her chin. "I wish I could go with you."

"You're welcome." Merelene shoved the car into gear.

Lucy stared out at the cool cave of trees. "He's at the hunting camp. Do you know how to get there?"

"You mean Mayfield?" She felt her pulses jump.

Lucy took a long drink and then made the sour face and looked at the glass as though someone had put the wrong thing in it. "The hunting camp out the Caloosa Road. Do you know where that is?"

"I can find it," said Merelene. "You mean Mayfield's out there?"

Lucy slid across the seat, and spilled whiskey rose sharply to Merelene's nostrils. "Good luck," Lucy said. She closed the door and then patted the window twice, ringing her gold charms against the glass. Merelene looked at her through the window, nodded and mouthed, "thanks." In her rearview, Lucy was pale and naked but for two yellow stripes, lifting the glass to her mouth.

Eighteen

She knew the hunting camp by its reputation. Drinking camp was a better name for it. The local men hunted deer with dogs and trucks and radios, hollering and whooping across the citizens band and using the long straight secondary roads as their shooting lanes. She thought it was a trashy way to kill an animal (while you had it on the road, why not just smash it with a truck) and it was dangerous too. In season, every roadside was lined with fools hugging rifles whose foolish friends were out chasing a buck. The trouble was that the buck had to cross the road between two fools. Hardly a season passed without a wounding or a killing. When you added whiskey to the equipment they used, the foolishness become lunacy.

But now it was high summer and the camp would be empty, except maybe for the drinkers. A few of the local men used it for week-long binges and for a few, she supposed, it was legitimate therapy. They'd go out and soak themselves to the lip of death and then come home and sleep a week and then go back to the feed store or the farm for a year or two until the fit took them again. Women were not invited. By community consent, the camp was man's land. She shuddered to think what demons must have been loosed into its woods.

She had no trouble finding it. But going there had been forbidden since her girlhood. She found herself stopped in the middle of a sandy road with the last half mile still in front of her. She sat cursing herself for a superstitious fool and finally shoved her foot onto the gas pedal, roaring into a log-bordered yard in front of a little clapboard pavilion.

She got out and stood in the rattle of squirrels and the throb of insects. The camp was by the bank of Caloosa Creek, which became the Santa Fe River, a tributary of the Suwannee. There was a big barbecue pit and a fish-cleaning table and another covered table for eating. The house itself had a pump but no electricity and was walled halfway up, then screened to the joists. A few cots and chairs were scattered inside. She could see through the gray screening that no one was home.

She walked around it once, noticing fresh footprints and new fish scales and a place where someone had buried garbage. A sand path led down to the creek. She stood on the little bluff where the path plunged down through briars and palmetto scrub toward the creek and cupped her hands and called once, "Mayfield!" The squirrels ceased and there was a high trill of protest in the insect sound. She sensed him here. Was that the depression of a bare heel on the path? She called again, then followed her own voice down toward the cool breath of the creek.

He was standing on a rock fishing. He must have heard, but his back was to her and he let the hook and sinker swing out from the tip of a long cane pole to the deep channel like a man who owned the whole forest. Around him on the rocks were a bait can, his blue denim shirt, a sheath knife and a cheap straw hat. He was barefoot. "Mayfield?" she said, low and level, but he still didn't turn. His toes gripped the rock as he swung the line out toward a deep pool.

She said, "I've traveled all day to find you." Thinking: all the days, and what have I found?

He kept his back to her and spoke to the creek. "We've both traveled some, haven't we, Merelene?" He pulled the line in and touched a bare hook. He said to the creek, "Robbed me again, did you?"

"It's peaceful here," she said, remembering the anger of their last meeting. "Is that why you're here?"

"That's one reason." He let the cane pole rattle to the rocks and turned and sat down on his own bald limestone chair. His canvas trousers were rolled and his chest and feet were burned a shrimp red. His ankles and arms and neck were thin and traced with knotted arteries. She wanted to be closer to him to say what she had to say. She removed her shoes and tried to sight a path from rock to rock. The way out to him was slick and treacherous.

She twisted her skirt in a ball before her like a woman in a Bible illustration bringing in the sheaves or washing at the well or helping to pull the nets in from Galilee. She knew she was blushing and could not raise her eyes from the rocks for fear of falling. As she tightroped her way toward him, careful of the slippery lichens and moss, he watched her, smiling. "You still got pretty legs, Merelene." She stopped a few feet from him and sat down.

They sat facing each other for a space and then he extended his arms to the woods and creek. "Ain't nothing changed out here, Merelene. It's all the same here. Same fish, same water, same camp." He stared over her shoulder at the bluff, the trees that hid the falling-down building where the drinkers and hunters convened their crazy souls. He said, "I used to come out here to get clean."

"Did you wash yourself in whiskey?"

"Sometimes. And sometimes in fish scales and deer musk and war stories. Only I didn't tell my war stories. I ain't a hero. Just a grease monkey and something else you don't know about. The lawyer is a hero, but I ain't. Never wanted to be."

"What did you want, Mayfield. Did I ever know?"

"I wanted a whole life, Merelene. You don't know what happened to me before I came to this town. I seen a lot of things."

"You never told me."

"I wanted to. There was times I thought I was going to. But I didn't."

She remembered the night they had lain in bed, inches from each other becoming miles. The night he had scrubbed himself in the light above Roland's bed, the last time he had tried to sing his son back from the island where he was marooned. She knew he might have told her that night. She had felt him wrestling his secret in the dark. She might have reached over to him with the key of her fingers, her lips that could unlock the words.

"You were hero enough for me, Mayfield. You gave me children and made a decent living and everybody in this town loved you. It was a hero that saved Roark from planting himself headfirst in the ground."

He laughed. "I should have let him fly. Would have saved this town a lot of trouble."

She reached out toward him now and her hand hovered over his knee and he watched it. "I've been learning a lot about you lately from a friend of mine . . . and yours too?"

He raised his eyebrows and sighed and the thin sound floated to the creek and was lost in the noise of its heaving over rocks and roots. She looked at the shock of his black hair and his thin straight nose that time had cut to gauntness and his washed-blue eyes. "What friend?" he asked. "I got so many of them."

"Enos Sawyer," she said, watching him for a sign, some message about him and the lawyer. He kept the same smile on his face, but shaded a little to sadness.

"The good old lawyer," he said. He paused and she waited. He seemed to be trying to decide. "Yes ma'am, he's a good old friend of mine and a better one of yours."

Before she could speak, he raised his hand out toward her, calming, petting. "Don't worry. Don't worry. I know I ain't entitled."

She let her hand settle on his knee, and both of them watched. "I know what they did to you."

"Not all of it you don't."

"Do you want to tell me now? Right here? There's nobody but us." She looked around them at the trees, the quiet sky, the water. They were as far from trouble as you could get in this world.

She waited a long time for him, but he didn't speak, so she said, "There's things I've learned about myself, Mayfield. I wasn't perfect."

He looked up at her fiercely, at her hand caressing his knee. "Yes you were. You were."

"No, I wasn't. That's just a story two soldiers invented in Europe. About a town and a girl. I don't know why. Maybe it started out as a joke, a game. Maybe they needed it because somebody was going to die every day. But it wasn't true. This is just a poor little place, and she was just disobeying her daddy and staying out too late and burning up rationed gas when she picked you up hitchhiking. The story has to stop."

He shook his head, furiously, No, No, No.

She said, "Mayfield, if you can let me be an ordinary woman, and yourself be an ordinary man, then Roland can be our boy. Somebody who isn't perfect. Who doctors can't fix. Who has his ways and does . . . what he can."

His sorry eyes brimmed with his biggest NO. He shrugged her hand from his knee. The feel of her flesh leaving his made her sorry. It was her connection to that night years before, to the things she had not done. He stood up and looked around him, picked up the pole again

and flung the baitless hook into the water, his back to her.
She waited a long time, until his breathing eased and the
No was out of him.

"You always did like to fish," she said.

"And I never did catch anything."

"You never wanted to."

He winced as though she had found him out somehow.
Then he nodded his head. "Right again."

Then he said, "Why did you travel all day to find me out
here? I thought you'd just about finished with me."

She said, "I think it's time for you and Enos Sawyer to
get reacquainted. You knew each other once. I want you to
again. Will you come with me?"

"No," he said, tugging the hook a little.

She said, "What do we do then. The three of us?"
Thinking, the four of us.

He said, "I want my time with Roland. Like I told you
before."

She watched his back, sunburned and thin and vulnera-
ble against the violent green of the water oaks and wil-
lows. She said, "You had your time. There is no more time
with Roland. Roland doesn't know time. Or maybe he *is*
time. He floats in it. Maybe he's lucky. We have to go
through it, live in it and watch it change us. Kill us. Roland won't change till the day he drops dead and even that
won't be death." She offered him these things, things she
had won from confusion in long nights of worry and wonder about Roland. She had never said them to anyone. She
expected him to turn and see what she had said, agree with
her, acknowledge the philosophy of her midnights. He
only tugged the unbaited hook and watched the swift surface of the creek.

Finally, tired, sorry, at the end of what she could offer
him, she said, "I have told you doctors can't fix Roland. If
they could, I'd know it. I would have found some way
. . . without you and your money."

He spun around on her, the pole lashing the air.

"Where is he, Merelene? Where is he right now?"

"You know where he is."

He smiled. "Louise told you about my visit."

She only stared at his strange face, his eyes that looked past her to some plan he was making.

"I known she would. I don't mind. She's a good woman. Louise is."

She said, "Yes, she is. And Roland is a good boy, even when he's not asleep."

"I want to see him awake, Merelene. I want to wake him up. I've told you that."

She shook her head. He was taking her in circles. "Roland belongs to the State of Florida now as much as he belongs to me. They took him away because . . ." She was afraid to tell him the reasons. The Big Bath at Mary Heatherton's house. A town's resistance to mystery. Her own lack of resources. But he didn't let her finish.

"I know that. I found that out. Roark told me. That's why I came back when I did. That's only lawyers and money, a legal paper here and a few dollars there. I know lawyers, Merelene. I own a tribe of them. My life is a war of lawyers."

Her voice was flat, tired of circles and unbaited hooks. "Then come and talk to your old friend." Thinking: who you don't own.

"I'll come to the lawyer's fine house for a visit some time. When he invites me." He pulled his line out of the water and collected his gear and was hopping the rocks back toward the hunting camp. She caught up with him at the bottom of the little sand bluff. He had stopped to wait for her, annoyed, breathing hard. His face was a little bleached and he was rubbing his hurt left arm. He gestured toward the path. "Lead on Merelene, and I'll follow your lovely legs."

She climbed ahead of him feeling his eyes feeding. She

didn't mind. This deep in the woods, this many years from where they had started—in a woodsy place like this, by water—what did it matter that he played the fool?

When she was standing by her car with her shoes in her hand, she said, "I hate getting messages from you by Roark Drawdy. I never did understand why you wasted your time with him."

"Let's just say I deserved him. I'd say we deserved each other, but that'd be too hard on Roark."

She let him see the pain his words caused her, even now. He extended his hand toward her again: "Never mind that, Merelene. Forget I said it. I apologize for Roark." Then, he leaned toward her. "Let me give you a message." He touched his lips to hers gently and raised his hand to caress her cheek. She smelled fish and sunburned skin and the old unmistakable Mayfield musk in the air around her. She stepped back quickly from him, raising the back of her hand to her lips.

He smiled. "All right, all right. But it's a message. You read it." Standing back enough to give her back her breath, he said, "Tell the lawyer I'll come tomorrow dusk without an invitation. He ain't lawyering that late, is he?" She shook her head no.

"You remember that me and the boys used to go to his house to borry his dogs on Sundays sometimes?"

She nodded at the three gypsy ghosts in her memory. "I'll tell him tomorrow dusk."

Nineteen

Across the room from her the lawyer was on his second or third whiskey. He had offered her one, half in jest: You'll need it, Merelene. She had turned it down, but not angrily, saying, "Someday *you* won't need it."

Dark was coming to the windows when they heard tires crackle on the crushed oystershell drive. She felt her heart gather pace, and told it, slow down, but it was the heart that had always galloped at the mention of Mayfield's name, and it did not obey her.

Mayfield's footfall on the gallery was light and brisk, and then they heard a polite rapping. The lawyer called, "Come in!" and added, to his whiskey, "It's open." She expected Mayfield in boat shoes, and canvas trousers, his outfit from the hunting camp. Instead, he stood on the Persian rug in a pair of soft, shiny shoes of the sort she had seen in magazines. The rest of him was just as expensive, a dark gray business suit, a sky-blue shirt and wine-colored tie. She rose and then shied a glance at the lawyer, who was also struggling up. Mayfield touched his lips to her cheek before she could consent or protest, then stepped over to the lawyer. "Enos," he said. Their hands clasped, carrying the messages of years.

The lawyer said, "Mayfield. Welcome to my house. Will you join me in a libation?"

Mayfield declined with a quick shake of the head and then a careful glance at Merelene. He didn't sit. Softly, he said, "I been in your house before, Enos. You just don't remember."

The lawyer nodded, his voice courtly and careful. "I *do* remember. I say, Welcome back. Have a drink with me."

"A drink with my old friend Cap'n Sawyer?" Mayfield looked at her and smiled.

She nodded and smiled too, because he had used her words of invitation from the hunting camp.

"That's right," the lawyer said. "Merelene, will you do the honors?"

"Merelene told me out to the hunting camp she knows now what old friends we was."

The lawyer smiled and the recollections rolled across his eyes. "I told her some things. I figured she had a right. What do you think about that?"

"I think you know about *us*, but you don't know about me. Nobody does."

The lawyer lifted his glass again in a light and comradely way. "I'll drink to that too," he said.

"You better wait," Mayfield said. "You might not want to drink to some of it."

He sat down opposite the lawyer in an old wing-back and crossed his legs, revealing narrow ankles in silk socks and the unmarked sole of a new shoe. To save the lawyer having to do it, Merelene rose and burned the lights in the room. Their two faces changed in the light, taking on years and the gravity of things that had happened. "Thank you, Merelene," the lawyer said, and she nodded. Mayfield watched this transaction closely, as though it held some code. The lawyer said, "The way I see it, we start with the

question of custody. I haven't agreed to represent *anyone*
yet. I want that understood."

Mayfield smiled: "A lawyer always represents somebody. And he always represents himself."

The lawyer nodded solemnly, raising the amber glass to
Mayfield's words. "I have an interest here. I make no
claim of disinterestedness. I'm telling you I don't want the
job you offered me."

"What are you telling her?" Mayfield asked.

"I'd work for the woman if she wanted me to, but she
hasn't asked."

Mayfield looked at her again in the way he had the night
she had come home with the fringes of her nightgown
wet. The old beast, his jealousy, was in his eyes.

Suddenly she was talking. "There isn't any question of
custody. Roland is mine. We all know that. Let's talk about
. . . the rest of it." All this, the lawyer's house and
Mayfield's money, there in the cloth on his back, their past
together in the war, all were declarations; they were men,
but it was hers to see that things did not go wrong. No one
could have this moment for her. She knew it from the
childbed and the river.

Mayfield smiled, but it was an indecipherable smile, a
transient bit of mirth moving from his eye to the corner of
his mouth. Was he admiring her speech, or just conceiving
some mean joke? She felt her anger rise from cold depths.
"I don't think you want Roland. I think you just wrote
that letter to get my attention."

He only smiled.

"Well, you could have had it for the asking, as always.
You didn't have to skulk around like a crazy man in your
old clothes and pass rumors by the mouth of Roark
Drawdy. You could of driven your fancy car into my
driveway and knocked on my door in the daylight. Why
didn't you?" With the question aimed straight at him, she
waited. The lawyer, in the corner of her eye, was still.

Mayfield watched her and the smile was replaced by a stare of concentration. He winced and caught his left arm and rubbed it. "I told you why I came the way I did. I didn't want people to talk."

Suddenly, she remembered his chilly words in the grotto by the cave. *You are a respectable widow.*

He let go of his arm. "And I do want the boy. Ain't it clear why I want him? To take him someplace better. I can give him something now. Maybe an operation on his mind. I thought you might want it that way. You might if you think about it."

She tried not to see this as an insult. She tried to think of it as a man's logic. A young man abandoned home and family and went off to make a fortune and an older man came back to make things right. But she could only think: God, what is a man that he believes I want a mere term of responsibility with my own son.

"So you threaten me with the law to make me think."

He looked away at the window, the dark that was complete now.

She said, "You can give me the wherewithal to get him back and he'll thank you for it. That's what you can do. I don't know why you didn't long ago. Maybe you didn't want to believe there even was a Roland Durham."

He watched her with a hard concentration, then tilted his head to the side and looked at the window as though straining to hear something a long way off. His voice was soft and a little weary as though this were an explanation he had made to himself many times.

"There wasn't any wherewithal until two years ago when this bidnis of mine started flying. I'd of sent you what little money I had before that, but I didn't think you'd of wanted it from the likes of me."

"Wanting and needing are two different things," she said.

The lawyer cleared his throat. Over the rim of his amber glass, he said, "And the law is a third thing."

Mayfield turned on him. "The law is bought and sold ever day. I got six government agencies and all their lawyers chasing me and a tribe of my own lawyers throwing up fortifications as I go and the money keeps rolling in."

"And rolling out, I expect." The lawyer smiled and sipped.

She said, "Mayfield, it's not your money we are here to talk about."

He said, "All right then. Let's talk about my life. Let me tell you . . ." His voice fell in his throat suddenly to a place where it rattled a little. He looked hard at her and then swung his cold, angry eyes to the lawyer. ". . . *both* of you, where I been since you seen me last." He extended his left hand toward her, turned it over, offering it in the lamplight. "Do you remember what I used to do with this?" The hand hung before her eyes, pale, shaking a little. She blushed. She knew things the hand had done. She remembered it on her skin. She remembered it teaching Bull how to hold a shotgun, and plucking Roark out of the air, saving his worthless life. She remembered it touching Roland's face as he lay flaming in his bed, and then not touching him, unable to touch him any more. She remembered Mayfield coming home nights with grease on his hands, or cuts from the gill nets, and sitting long and turning them in the light. She nodded. Yes, I remember.

"There was times, Merelene," he said, still holding the hand out toward her, showing its pale shaking, "times when I would of cut this off if I had the courage. But I never did. I never had it." She watched the hand become a fist and his face clench with the effort of touching what he had always held back.

She could tell the lawyer didn't like this. He sat with his whiskey and his whimsy, his face tilted up, waiting to hear what he already knew, or maybe something he didn't.

Maybe he was remembering too. Mayfield working on his airplane once, just like Del Sweet was doing now. Mayfield at his back door one night and their talk in the light of the stoop while the rockets announced the Fourth of July. Mayfield saying, "Don't say you know me? Don't tell them we were together?" The plea there in his young eyes.

She said, "All right, Mayfield. Tell us. It's what you want that started all this."

"You know about us, don't you Merelene, the lawyer and me? You know about me fixing those airplanes and the fancy fools that flew them thinking I was magic, the man who could keep a pilot safe. He told you about that?"

She nodded. "He told me some of it."

"Well, after my friend the Cap'n here got shot down, I refused to work on airplanes. The Cap'n was off in the hospital and didn't know that part of it. I just wouldn't do it no more. Even though I known he was too much officer and too much gentleman to hold anything against a mere Mayfield Durham, I refused. But you don't refuse the Army Air Corps, Merelene. They called old Mayfield a hardhead. Some of them wanted to send me to the military jailhouse, but finally one of them officers got a better idea. A real dirty punishment for the shirker. He sent me to Graves Registration. Do you know what that is?"

"I know what a grave is, Mayfield. I've seen a few." She saw them now in rows in her mind, as she had seen them on the newsreels after the war.

He waved his hand at her. "This army they have today probably calls it a subdivision of marketing. I wouldn't be surprised. But in the Army of the United States of America, 1945, Graves Registration was the boys who go in after the battle and pick up the dead. They are the ones that send home your known and your unknown soldier. I went to work for the graves boys.

"Anybody can pick up the bodies and the pieces of bodies. And the anybodies who do it are usually the ones who can't do anything else. Or they're the ex-miracle workers like me. We had a lot of refusers in Graves Registration. It was dirty work, Merelene, it was the bottom, but I figured it was about what I was worth. Your friend the lawyer here was up at the top. He was in the air, and I was down in the bottom. From grease monkey to battlefield garbage man. Only those bodies on the battlefield ain't garbage. I learned that. When you see a thousand men lying where they took their last breath in this world, you know they are people. And some of them have to be people again.

"Not many, only a few. Mostly it's the sons of senators and tycoons who have to go on display in some funeral home. Most of the GIs just go home in a plain military coffin, a gunmetal box is all it is and they don't do a lot of work on them before they send them. They don't have time. Not in 1945. Not in the Hürtgen Forest. But a few of them get the special treatment. The sons of the politicians and the generals. They get rebuilt. And it was just my luck, just old Mayfield's dumb luck, to rise in the organization. Wherever I go, Merelene, I rise in the world. They thought they sent me to hell but it turned out to be a vocation. Do you know what that is, Merelene?"

Softly, she said, "It's what preachers get." The lawyer snorted but she didn't look at him.

"That's exactly right." He held up his left hand again, then he looked at the window, through it. She turned and saw that the lawyer was watching something just as far away.

"After a few months of picking up bodies, I started learning how to make faces. They'd send a photograph over from the States, or sometimes it was just a greasy mug shot from the service records, and we would go to work. We used special tools and putties and cement and sometimes I'd carve pieces out of soapstone or plaster, even wood, and cover them with paint and lacquer, and before you know it, Merelene, I had me another reputation. I was Sergeant Durham who could make a dead man look the bloom and breath of life.

"You don't get medals for that. When they send them home and put them in an open box and the people see them and they know it's their boy and not somebody else's —because that's what people are afraid of, that they got the wrong son, the wrong one in all that hurrying and mess—you don't get a medal. The colonel don't call you in and tell you, good job son. It don't work that way. The colonel is off fighting and making more work for you. But what you get if you're Mayfield Durham is a calling. You can make the dead look like the living. You can sell that, Merelene. It's something people want. I hated it and I loved it too. I hated it so much I came here and tried to live like a ordinary man. I even went back to grease-monkeying some of the time and pulling fish out of the water, but I was always hearing that calling. I'm still hearing it. It's what I'm doing now. I ain't no mortician anymore. I was for a while, but I've risen. I'm in cosmetics now, but it's the same field. I'm making dead faces live."

He watched her, still holding his hands stiff away from him. He turned them once more in the light and then put them in his pockets as though they were tired. He said, "Now you know about me. What I've always wanted you to know. And hated you to know."

She watched the hands buried in his pockets and then his face full of elation and sadness. All she could think was her question: "Why didn't you tell me before?"

He said, "Merelene, no woman wants to be touched with hands like these."

She felt the warm wrap of her own skin, and recalled his hands, hands that had caressed dead men's faces, on her those nights and years ago. She looked at the lawyer, who sat with his head tilted back regarding the air. He hadn't moved since Mayfield had begun his story.

She was about to speak, to answer, when Mayfield turned away and walked to the door, and she heard him on the gallery again and then a car door opening. She ran to the window. He was standing by the car, leaning down, and Roland was sitting patiently in the light looking up at him. Then Mayfield reached out his hand, and Roland took it and slid across the seat. The two of them walked toward the house in the pale porch light like two Mayfields, a young one and an older one. She had not heard the lawyer rise and make his way across the room. Now she felt him beside her at the window and, heard, "Great God, look at that," but it was only sound.

It was seeing the two men walking, past and future, that tranced her. Somehow, they were what she had wanted all these years, and what she had feared too. They stopped in the porch light and Mayfield straightened Roland's jacket and tugged his skewed necktie to the middle of his collar, and then raised his hand and rested it under Roland's chin, and lifted his face a little to let the light touch it. Then the two of them started again toward the front door.

Twenty

Mayfield guided Roland in with a hand on his shoulder, and they stopped for a second in the doorway. Mayfield pointed to a chair by the fireplace. "Go sit over there, Roland, son."

Roland looked at her, at the lawyer, at the room, his glossy eyes filming and filing them as they recorded everything, without judgment, and then he did as he was told. When he had seated himself, he plucked the tension from his trouser legs and said to her, "Daddy's home from the boat tonight."

Merelene said, "Yes, honey. He is."

The lawyer had regained his chair. He sat, white-faced and shocked. She rose and took his glass and poured him another whiskey. She knew he would not get up for it under Mayfield's eye. And she wanted to show them both something by this gesture. The lawyer took the glass from her hand with a flush of pleasure, and a nod, as though to say, of course you did, because you knew.

She sat down again, and smiling at Roland, said, "Why did you bring him here?"

Mayfield smiled calmly, pleased with himself, his body

relaxed. "Louise's girl let me have him for a hour or two. Louise was out. I told her it'd be all right. It is all right ain't it?"

He looked at the lawyer. "A father has a right to spend some time with his son, don't he?"

The lawyer smiled, and hefted the glass she had refilled for him. "Under some circumstances he does. When there's a legal agreement. Didn't those legal minds you bought tell you that, Mayfield?"

"I didn't talk about this to my lawyers, Enos. This is something Merelene told me to do."

"*I* told you?"

"Sure you did. That night I was over at your place"—he looked at the lawyer—"that night you come home in your nightgown, you tried to drag me in to see him. You said go look at his grown-up face. I'm looking at it now. I like it. It's a beautiful face. Why hell, I could put that face in a Kismet-Tique ad with a couple of New York models, the skinny ones with the 'who me?' look on their faces all made up to slay the world, and them hanging on his arms and old Roland dressed like I am now. He'd sell. He'd sell. I tell you. Pictures don't have to talk."

He turned to Roland. "Ain't that right, ole buddy?"

Roland said, "True and therefore correct."

Merelene said, "Mayfield, have you lost your mind? Are you crazy?"

He pushed back in his chair and folded his hands across his middle. "Half the world thinks so. The Securities and Exchange Commission does. So does the IRS. But I got an army of women walking the streets for me that don't think so. Folks that hear me talk about rising in the world and landing at the top of the pyramid, the people at the shopping malls and Holiday Inns don't think so. I tell you the truth, Merelene, I just don't think it's a very interesting question who's crazy and who ain't." He smiled and looked over at Roland, who did his best to imitate the smile on his father's face.

She said, "I thought you wanted to take him to doctors."

Roland said, "Dr. Ben Casey?"

"You told me it wasn't going to work, Merelene, and I believe you. You ought to know. You've studied on it. It's hard for me, but I can accept that. The next best thing is to put him into the world as he is and let the world change. He and I been talking, since I picked him up from Louise's. He makes some sense if you just listen to him, don't you, Roland?"

Roland smiled, nodded in an actorish way, his square jaw bitten down like Randolph Scott.

Her voice was small when she said, "I think I know something about the kind of sense he makes." She watched Roland, remembering the hours she had lain with him pressed to her heart, trying to pull from him the secrets of his language. She said, "And I don't like you talking in front of him like this."

"This is the world, Merelene."

That was when the lawyer put his whiskey on the table and stood up. It scared her to see him moving into the center of the room, the built-up heels of his shoes thumping the floor. He was still in his suit trousers and vest from the office, an old blue worsted, with the vest unbuttoned, its tails jumping as he walked and the heavy Cuban cigars pulling one side down. He was all angles and wrinkles and blotchy parchment skin stopping in front of Mayfield.

"Let me see now," he said, his face flushed, his voice coming from someplace she had never heard, slow and almost too low to hear. "Mayfield, you've brought the boy here." He rubbed his temple as though he were only thinking out loud, as though he were alone in the room.

Mayfield smiled, but drew his legs in and sat up in the chair and touched the old hurt left arm. He swept his

right hand at Roland there in the chair. "I brought him."
He held the smile.

The lawyer threw his head back and rubbed his chin,
and she could hear the burr of the beard that sometimes
scraped her face and her neck at night. "And you been
talking to him? The two of you been having some famous
conversations together. Is that right?"

Mayfield still smiled, willing to go along it seemed.

"And you want your time with him, like you told Merelene? You want him to go with you now, tonight? Is that
right?"

Mayfield knitted his brow and a wince crossed his face.
He reached for his left arm but his hand stopped halfway.
Carefully, he looked at Roland, at her and then at the lawyer. "Is this a courtroom?" He swung his right hand at the
old parlor, with its antique furnishings all glowing sepia
and cream and purple in the low lamplight. He managed a
thin smile. "Maybe I ort to go call one of my lawyers. Get
one to drop everthing and run over here and defend me. If
I need it. Do I need it?"

"No need for anybody to drop anything, Mayfield. I
was just wondering how far down the road you'd get with
Roland here before the conversations got kind of dull.
And what you'd do then."

Mayfield smiled but the smile was cold and the lawyer
rubbed his chin again and started walking in his scrape-
toe-and-jump fashion. He stopped at the fireplace where
the coals of one of his summertime fires were still smoking. "But never mind that," he said. "Never mind that."

He picked up a poker and stirred the ashes until a small
flame jumped. Then he turned, and his eyes lit as something occurred to him. "I was up and you were down? Is
that right, Mayfield?" His voice was still from that strange
quiet place.

Mayfield looked at him in pure puzzlement. "Say again,
please." He held a cupped hand behind one ear.

"What you said. I was up in the air and you were down on the ground with the dead men." The lawyer walked over and stood above Mayfield. "Like this," he said. "Like I am now. I'm up and you're down?"

Mayfield watched the lawyer from his chair. He was sitting and the lawyer slowly stretched and made himself as painfully straight as he could and still his dark eyes were just inches above Mayfield's pale blue ones.

After a while, Mayfield's face changed, and she knew he had the lawyer's message. He wasn't thinking about himself, she knew that much. He said, "For a while you was up and I was down. Maybe now it's different. I don't know."

"What was I doing all those years you were off making your fortune in powder and rouge?"

"I don't know," Mayfield said, "lawyering I guess."

"You were rebuilding people for a while, is that right? Making them beautiful, just like life? Almost real?" The lawyer's voice had risen a little now.

Mayfield nodded.

"Well, I was making too." The lawyer raised his knotted arms and flexed the muscles and smiled into Mayfield's face and then dropped his arms in a shrug. "Here you are." He leaned over and offered Mayfield his biceps. Mayfield lifted a hand, but then couldn't touch it. "What do you think?" the lawyer asked. Then more loudly, "What do you think of my project?"

Roland threw up his arms in imitation and flexed his muscles. The smile on his face was fixed, a rictus.

Mayfield looked down at his son and she could see in his face what it would be like down the road, when the conversations wore out. His eyes held the old disappointment.

The lawyer went back to the fire. He stood with his back to the little flame he had made and reached behind him with both hands for its warmth. Shrugged down to his real height, he looked tired now. He aimed his gaze at

Merelene for a moment as though trying to make up his mind. She knew he was asking her for something, maybe some permission. Her leave to do something. Maybe she gave a careful, almost imperceptible nod. He cleared his throat and the old courtroom music rumbled up. "Mayfield, what did you think I was doing yesterday when you were out at the hunting camp?"

Mayfield shook his head and stared at her. His eyes accused. She had invited him here: was this meeting a trap she had sprung? He said, "How do I know. I ain't a clairvoyant."

"I was talking to a couple of my fellow lawyers. Actually, they were looking for Merelene, but she was gone. She was out looking for you. These folks were from Jacksonville, a Mr. Davis, and a Mr. Trimble, both of them very seriously Esquire. They were on an errand from the branch office of the Internal Revenue Service. They said they hadn't been able to contact you for some time and they wondered if Mrs. Durham had seen you. I told them you hadn't been any of Mrs. Durham's business for a lot of years."

"Protect me, did you?"

"I don't know. That depends on what they wanted to talk to you about. Hell, maybe you got a big refund coming."

Mayfield looked at the windows and shrugged. "I pay people so I don't have to talk to Mr. Davis and Mr. What's-his-name. I pay a handsome wage so I don't have to mess with them."

"They seemed to think it was urgent that they see you. And they told me why it was urgent. Why time was such an element. They said you been paying some doctors too."

Merelene looked at the lawyer now, her eyes cautioning, wondering what this was. But he was boring hard at Mayfield.

Mayfield touched his left shoulder again, and then

looked at the lawyer and took his hand away from it. He smiled and shrugged. "I got my aches and pains, just like you do." He winked at Roland, who gazed back with interest. "Just like he does."

From the fireplace, the lawyer said. "Son, go sit with your mother."

Roland did as he was told.

The lawyer looked at her, and at Roland, his eyes bearing gift and challenge. Then, he turned to Mayfield, squaring himself up as best he could. "You know I want Merelene, don't you, Mayfield. You know we've been keeping some company now for a while. She hasn't said she'll change her name yet, but I believe she will." Mayfield raised his head quickly, and tilted it, concentrating as he had before, as though straining to hear a small sound far away.

She settled Roland on the sofa beside her and rested her hand on his knee. Quietly, she said, "I won't be deeded from one of you to the other like a goddamned cornfield."

Roland said, "Kellogg's cornflakes and milk."

The lawyer drew himself up in dignity: "I'm sorry if the words are clumsy. My intentions are not."

Mayfield lifted himself from the chair, she thought too carefully, and walked a circuit of the room. When he passed her, he did not look down. He seemed fascinated by the intersection of wall and ceiling. He stopped at the fireplace. His fingers touched an heirloom ivory fan, then strayed to a gilt picture frame, touched the canvas at the breast of the lawyer's great-grandmother, and then moved on to Old Patch, the one-eyed colonel. He picked up a piece of porphyry and put it down in a different place and then stepped back to marvel at the improvement. He turned to her and said, "You see what he's doing, don't you, Merelene?"

Holding Roland's hand now, she watched him, there at the fireplace, thinking: what you are doing too.

Mayfield's voice was angry and there was a rattle in it she had heard when he told her about the war. He said, "Look at all these things," pointing at the walls, the ancestral faces cracked and faded on warped canvas. "All these pictures and paintings of his people, all of them dead. All dead when they walked around this house. You want to *live* in this place?"

Before she could answer, he reached into his coat and flourished something, a paper, at her. He took three steps and stood before her, holding it out. "I got a picture too."

It was the four of them, an old faded black-and-white. Mayfield and Merelene and little Ethridge and Roland, aged five, standing on the riverbank. The trees on the far bank behind them were the horizon and the sun fanned on the gray water. They were all smiling, each holding a piece of the family secret—which was their happiness. She remembered the day it had been taken, only a year or so before Roland's accident.

Mayfield stabbed a finger at the picture and said, "That's where I want to be." He was showing her his own image, there beside her, years and miles and heartbreaks ago, and smiling. He tried for the same smile now, but in his eyes she could see all that had broken since that time, and all that couldn't be repaired and all that shadow and powder and rouge couldn't cover.

He pointed again at the lawyer's museum of ancestors. "You don't belong up there on that wall . . ." He leaned toward Roland. ". . . and he don't either. Do you, son?" Roland grinned his interest and said, "I got my pitcher."

"Where do I belong?" she asked him. "In there?" She pointed to the thing in his hand. "That day is dead, Mayfield."

"Is that night we climbed the fire tower dead, you remember that?"

They had made love in the abandoned ranger's tower with the moonlight raining down and the rusty girders speaking beneath them in the wind, and later they had thrown their clothes down and descended the ladder laughing, their naked bodies streaked with rust and sweat.

She stared at him while the lawyer froze on the edge of her vision. She couldn't answer yes and wed that night to death. The memory and a hundred others still fired her flesh late at night when she let them in.

"And what about those times at the spring? In our little place? What about them?"

She squeezed Roland's hand and tried to think only of the future, a long expanse of empty white time and herself its only author. She said, "The place is still there. You know that. You been back there, and I have too. But it's not the same." She remembered the two women she had been that night with him at the cave's mouth, the one lying with him in the old dance and the other standing up and pushing him away. He was trying to divide her again.

Mayfield shook his head violently and turned to the lawyer. "I want some time alone with my wife and son. Can you give me that?"

"I can when she asks for it," the lawyer said. And then his voice changed and the music from the instrument deep in his twisted chest was breaking. "It seems to me that she has a question of mine to answer."

There was the clearest plea in the music. Here were her two men, bare before her and before her son, the idiot boy.

She shook her head, and closed her eyes to both of them, to choice. And in the silence behind her eyes she felt them waiting and the moment stretching long and longer until it was that long white time she wanted and she was alone there in it with Roland, and then she felt his hand torn from hers.

"Come on, son." Mayfield was pulling Roland through the doorway and the lawyer was on his feet and moving after them. She extracted herself from the empty future and started running, passing the lawyer in the hallway.

When she made the porch, she saw Mayfield still in the pool of light from the house. He held Roland's hand but he stood exactly still, his right hand seizing his left shoulder. He turned back to look at her and his face owned a terrible panic, then a knowing smile.

She ran to them and tore Roland furiously away from him and then she saw Mayfield fall, gone before he hit the ground, all splayed and crooked, all his grace departed. Then Roland dropped, too, in his best imitation of his father.

Mayfield's face was ashes, but smiling, and the lawyer's yellow cat was standing by him. She had never seen human eyes so vacant as Mayfield's now, felt the flesh of a human hand so limp, so cool. She knew she must do something to save him. But first, she did the thing her heart spoke. She leaned to him, touching her lips to his, and called, "Mayfield?"

From the long, empty hollow of his throat there came nothing but a chill, and she called again. She rose to run toward the house, and saw there, halfway from the porch, the lawyer, standing in straight pride if not straight flesh, and watching her. She said, "Get . . ." He said, "I already did. They'll be here as soon as they can." And he bent his head and stumbled forward and when he did this, she saw that he would know what to do. Or that there was nothing. And she had seen something in his eyes that she had hoped never to see. He knelt and pressed his lips to Mayfield's, roughly, not as she had done, and began to breathe into him, making his chest rise and fall, ignoring her.

She leaned to Roland, still lying in solemn imitation of his father. "Please get up, honey," she said, and he did as he was told and then she saw that there were tears in his eyes.

Twenty-one

She held his hand. His pulse fluttered and lagged. She had heard the first bird speak its indignation to the dawn, and now light was plying the windows. His hand was cold and dry in hers despite her warming pressures.

His white face was peaceful on the pillow, and handsome. He did not seem aware of his predicament. There was only an occasional tremor, a misfire of the nerves, followed by a spell of ragged breathing and a sigh. It was all recorded in the machinery connected to him. She gazed at his face, thinking how this mishap had seemed to take years from him, remaking the face she had known when he was young. His crow-black hair flowed straight back from his forehead to the white pillow so that his widow's peak was as clearly drawn as by india ink on white paper. His large, wash-blue eyes, which had never owned much capacity for surprise, slept under lids as unlined as a child's. The skin was tight on the bridge of his nose, freckled and showing the configuration of bone beneath in a way that was noble, severe, a little cruel. His lips were full and slightly parted as though he were about to bring back a word from his dream.

She had spent a sleepless night in this county clinic, alone with the man she had slept with for ten years, and him as weightless as a shadow between the sheets, hardly there at all, and still beautiful. And maybe dying, using a heart that could give up any minute and her with nothing to do about it. She had not cried this whole night, and now she told herself she would not. She let go his hand and walked to the window. She could see now, across the small expanse of lawn to the county hardroad, a dusty cornfield and finally the piney woods and a ragged gray-green horizon. From the window, and the slow resolution of daylight, she looked back at him, at the hand she had been holding, limp on the cover. She would go take it up again soon, but not yet.

She circled the room to get her own blood flowing, and stopped at the closet where hung his fancy suit of clothes. His shoes with his socks rolled in them, his silk tie, with a little whorl where the knot had been: these were the costume of his tycoon life.

She stepped into the closet and pressed against his suit of clothes. A crisp, wine-red silk hanky decorated the coat, which was of a light summer material, dark gray with a thin black stripe. She ran her fingers down the lapels which gave back an odor of newness, of aftershave too much like perfume and of him—the old unmistakable smell, a perfume she had worn on her own skin.

She was standing in the closet with a rich man, playing the lapels of his coat like some vamp, a Bette Davis, who knew what she was leaning against. The cut of the jacket was smart; its creases fine without the vulgar sharpness of cheaper cloth. She closed her eyes and stood against him in the life they might have had together. What was she wearing in this story? A starkly white linen, or perhaps a raw silk suit, severe of cut, a Joan Crawford traveling outfit (for they were only passing through this little place), with wide lapels, large buttons of onyx. To soften it, a silk blouse, a floppy bow at the throat, bouncing as she walked gangplanks and hotel lobbies in her spectator pumps. What a couple they were! She leaned forward to place her cheek against the breast of his jacket, whispering, "Mayfield," and stumbled unsupported by the dream, into the closet. She stood tangled in his clothes. Why had he not taken her with him? She would leave this hollow man and walk to the bed and ask the real one. Why didn't you take me?

She stepped out into the white room where he was not available for questions. On the washstand by the door were his keys. Yesterday, she had gone, at Dr. Selfridge's instructions, with the keys they had found in his pocket to a suite in the General Baines Hotel in Live Oak. She had done as the doctor told her: Merelene, you'd best go get his things. He's going to be here for a while. Taking the role of messenger, she had drifted in his Mercedes on the hard-ribbed surfaces of county roads as though slipping through a dream.

On the top floor, in The General's Suite, she had found the fisherman's clothes he had worn those times in Swinford, stealing in and away like a ghost. She had found leather luggage with Italian writing on it and the strange names of airlines. She had even found his passport, in a drawer with his brushes, cigarette lighter, notepad, checkbook and shaving kit, and had turned the pages staring at border crossings, the impressions of stamps in languages she couldn't read.

She had packed the smallest of his leather bags with things he would need; the rest she had stored in the trunk of his car. She had checked him out of the hotel, using the American Express card she had taken from his wallet. She had expected to be challenged and wondered how much of their story she would have to tell to strangers before she could get done what was needed. But the clerk had not raised an eyebrow when she signed the bill.

After tipping the bellman three of Mayfield's dollars, she had eased the Mercedes away from the curb with the odd feeling that she had erased the traces of a fraud. As she drove, she remembered her moment of temptation, when she had lifted his diary from the nightstand by the bed. She could see by its dirtied edges, its fattened pages, that he wrote in it. Her fingers had ached to open it, her eyes to follow the scrawl inside to whatever revelations might be there. She had not read it. She had parked his car at the county clinic and brought the overnight bag to this room.

She could hear morning sounds from the clinic's small kitchen. Soon, there would be coffee. And after that, Dr. Selfridge on his rounds. If he made a special trip, she would know this was as serious as she feared, for Dr. Selfridge was notorious for understatement and arrivals in the nick of time. She wanted to be with Mayfield when he awoke. She remembered his fear of awakening in a strange place, with no one to give clues. She sat and took his right hand again, feeling her bones take up angrily the shape of her long night in this chair.

At the touch of her hand, his eyes opened. Shock, then anger, then a familiar confidence came to his face. She had damned his confidence many times, but couldn't now. It meant he was himself. She felt an upwelling of gladness at this, but dared only squeeze his hand to show it. He gave back a little pressure, but winced, and waited for the spasm to pass. Then he smiled at her, the old easy smile, a little blurred at the edges. She stroked his hand and smiled back. She knew her first words must be the right ones.

He said, "I been away."

"You have," she said, and thought, in more ways than one. "But now you're back and I'm glad to see you."

She stroked his hand until the warmth came back to it. He studied her as though she were his first discovery in a new world. Dr. Selfridge had told her how close he had been to the world that waited for them all; close enough to tell about it. His eyes watched her; they shifted from her face to the spot where her hand held his and her fingers moved in a slow, soothing circle, drawing the warmth back. He said, "My heart?" It hurt him to talk. She nodded, yes. He tried to lift his free hand to his chest but gave up halfway, raising his eyebrows as though to say, what next? She allowed herself a little laugh, a fragment of the hysteria she had suppressed through the long evening of his coming here strapped to a stretcher, his hand like meat in hers, his face ashes, his chest doing nothing she could see. Her laugh answered his lifted brow, and gave them complicity. She heard the jangling of change in a pocket in the hallway, and a low, musical voice, and knew that Dr. Selfridge would soon be at the door. It meant nothing good that he was seeing Mayfield first.

He was the doctor who had delivered the two children she had given Mayfield, who had told them about the disease that robbed Roland of his senses, who had given her pills to help her sleep and told her, chafing in the role of confidant, to forget about Mayfield Durham and get on with the business of her life.

She had fallen in love with Dr. Selfridge at that moment, and had loved him in a benign and distant way ever since. He was an old man and knew the weight of things. He had told her what Mayfield Durham was worth: nothing. Now he was coming down the hall jangling change to tell them what the scales still held.

Dr. Selfridge was tall with sharp angles buried in fleshy pouches, and pale so that he stood out among the men in this region like a fish among loaves. He was not tanned, not hard; he looked like the walking case of sleeplessness he was, ringed and ringed again under the eyes and wheezing from too many cigarettes and too much coffee. There were dark stains at the pockets of his seersucker trousers where his hands constantly jangled. He wore crepe-soled shoes that squeaked. There was usually a piece of toilet paper stuck to his face where he had cut himself shaving in some ill-lit bathroom at dawn. She let go of Mayfield's hand and walked to the door.

Dr. Selfridge gave her his hand in a companionable way and she noted its temperature, comparing it to Mayfield's. She said, "I wish I ever saw you when something good was happening." He pulled her roughly into the crook of his arm and into the circle of the tobacco and coffee and tired smell of him, and hugged her like a buddy. "Babies give good occasions, Merelene. They used to come jumping out of you like calves at a rodeo. That's what I remember." She blushed and slapped him on the paunch, and he laughed, rolling back on the squeaky soles of his Hush Puppies. She said, "You nasty old thing, tell me what's wrong with the man in the bed."

They turned to Mayfield, whose eyes were hooded, who knew their scene had been played for his benefit, to give him confidence. His eyes said, change the station.

Merelene stood back from the bed, giving Dr. Selfridge room to work. He looked at the chart, glanced at the machines by the bed, took Mayfield's pulse, felt his forehead, somewhat unnecessarily, mumbling, "Ain't nothing wrong with Mr. Mayfield Durham that a good kick in the ass wouldn't cure." He had perfected the art of rough optimism. She was not certain whether he lied or not. She knew the worst thing was that tilted look of concentration Mayfield had brought back from wherever he had been. She knew what it meant now.

Dr. Selfridge sat in the chair she had used, and scratched both his wrists vigorously, and watched Mayfield's face. It was closing up. She could see that he had spent time with doctors. "So, what do you think, Mayfield? You going to give down on us?" Mayfield made a sour smile, and tried to say what he was going to do, but winced and quit.

The doctor said, "Never you mind. We know you're still

the ass-kicker you always was." He looked over his shoulder at Merelene and winked, turning her into an actress again. She winked big and broad, stepping closer so that Mayfield could see. Dr. Selfridge stood up. Everything changed. "There's not much we can do but wait, and be sure that you rest, and feed you. I don't want you to get too drowsy, but I don't want you to hurt too much either. If you feel yourself wanting to sleep all the time, you let the nurse know, or if it hurts more than you like. We've got a little something to calm you down coming through that needle in your arm." Mayfield's eyes flicked at the needle with disdain. "It's just a matter of staying quiet and thinking good thoughts for the time being. All right?" Mayfield blinked. Merelene stepped closer still and said, "Yes," then her hand was in Dr. Selfridge's again and she was drawn out into the hallway.

They stood on the polished tiles and suddenly she was scared. Dr. Selfridge looked down at her, giving her hand a squeeze. "He isn't good, Merelene. This is not his first. I give him *some* chance of another one tonight or tomorrow."

She said, "Am I hurting him?"

He said, "It's hard to say what they need. Don't make him talk. Be with him when he wants you, and go when he doesn't. It's better for him to have what he wants now . . ." He looked over his shoulder at Mayfield's room, then took her shoulders in both his big hands, making her feel like a little girl. "He hasn't got more than a year or two at the outside. His heart is like paper. I'd rather you were in there with him than off somewhere hoping for the best. You see what I mean?" She nodded. Her mouth was dry. She wanted to press her face to the middle of Dr. Selfridge's blue shirt where a strong heart could be heard. Instead, she reached up and loosed his hands from her shoulders and smiled her strong and confident smile, stretching the bloodless skin of her cheeks un- til it hurt. "I see." She watched him roll like an old bear down the hall and turn at the nurse's station, his hands jangling the coins in his pockets.

Twenty-two

While she waited by Mayfield's bedside, watched his face grow daily more livid, and felt the warmth come to his hand, she worked for the lawyer as little as business would allow. She knew he expected little, in the way of work at least. What he required was some final declaration, though he had not said so, now that it seemed Mayfield would not die. She must declare herself; to love him was not enough. To love him and no other with her body was not enough. She must excise forever from her heart those chambers which held Mayfield—nothing less would be enough, and nothing could be more impossible.

Mr. Deloach had insisted that Roland come back to the Center. She had kept him seven days to cure a cold and that was enough. She had told him that Roland still had a sniffle, but that he was well enough to come back if Mr. Deloach was willing to risk the infection of an entire houseful of boys. The lawyer had driven Roland down to the Center for her.

She did not visit the lawyer at night, nor did they speak much in the daytime. Once, he drove her to the little field where his red metal secret was kept, but they didn't stay

long, only watched its progress under the greasy hands of
Delvin Sweet and then drove back home.

On the fifth day of Mayfield's heart attack, a letter came
from Roland. It had been dictated by him to a psychiatric
social worker who had included her own note at the bottom:

Dear Mrs. Durham,
   Roland is doing fine as I'm sure you can see from
what he says. He has put on a little weight, and is
tanned from working outside. We think he is adjusting
well.

It was signed, "Yours sincerely, Harriet Grissell." Roland's own words, if they were his, were no more revealing. She tried to read between the lines in this strange
woman's hand, but nothing was there. Roland said he
liked his boss at the nursery, Mr. Carswell, and had seen a
brand-new Buick car, and was watching *The Price Is Right*,
and would she send him some money for the canteen?

She took the letter to the hospital and sat for a long time
with it in her pocket and holding Mayfield's hand. Finally,
she took it out and read it to him without his consent, and
was finished before she realized she had no right to upset
him. He might expire before her eyes, in her arms if he
reached for her, and all because she had read him a letter
from a boy who babbled nonsense and expected no one's
attention but a dog's.

But she'd had to do it. She had the saving of his life in
mind. That day at the spring, he had told her he wanted
knowledge. If he wanted to know her, this was what he
must know. She loved this boy more than reason could
ever explain or cancel. She loved this nonsense letter, even
coming as it did through the mind and hand of a stranger.
That she cherished it was all there was to know about her.
Was he disappointed? He didn't say. He may not have lis-

tened. It was all over so fast and her own feelings had run
so high. She had walked out the door with the letter folded
in her pocket again, and with his cool good-bye kiss still
on her lips, before she had even known what she was doing.

Dr. Selfridge did not change his diagnosis. "Give him
your hand," he said, "it's better than anything I've got for
him." She had asked Mayfield who he wished to have noti-
fied of his illness. Surely there was someone, a woman
from one of those years he had been absent, the lawyers he
talked about? He asked her to say nothing to anyone. He
said the value of his properties would decline if she did.
He grew well enough to ask the nurses for a phone and
asked her to leave the room while he made business calls,
brief and secret.

A week passed and she received another letter from
Mrs. Grissell. She opened it, expecting more politeness
and Roland's mumbles, and was astonished to find a newspaper clipping inside: RETARDED MAN SAVES LIFE OF LOCAL
CHILD.

Roland had been working at his new job in the Center's
nursery, which sold plants at cut-rate prices to the citizens
of nearby Port St. Jude. A man had come to buy daylilies,
bringing with him his small daughter, a child of seven.
She had touched an electrical connection whose insulation
was frayed. Her heart had stopped.

The supervisor had stepped out to collect the potted
lilies. Only Roland heard the father's strangled cries. Roland took the girl in his arms and breathed life back into
her body. It did not take much breath; a young heart, low
voltage in the wires.

Sergeant Garland Talway of the Palm Beach County
Fire Department Rescue Squad credited the young man
with saving the child's life. "If you accept the father's account," Sergeant Talway said, "there were early signs of
the onset of morbidity." The father had done nothing

through it all but weep. To the departing stretcher where the little girl lay sucking her thumb and blinking, Roland had said (the article was very clear about it): "Code blue. I repeat. This is an emergency."

She put the article and a note of her own into an envelope and addressed it to Charley Patterson at *The County News Leader*. "Charley, this is news of my second son, Roland. Do you want to print it?"

As Mayfield grew stronger, he was more inclined to talk. Stilled by his illness, he found stories and thoughts he had misplaced. Gone was the strange concentration. The tilted head, the ear he had cocked to his own heart, had confirmed his fears and now he listened to her. Sitting by his bed, she was pleased but saddened. Why had they never talked, never like this in the bed they had shared? They had spoken only with their bodies and when need had waned, his before hers, nothing had taken its place that words could say.

The first hours of talking were not easy. She had started hard. One day, she asked him, "Mayfield, why did you come back?"

"I told you that, Merelene."

She waited, watching him. He was weary with the question, then his eyes, hooded by habit, slowly widened. She squeezed his hand and he looked her full in the face. "I came back," he said. "It was a start."

She said, "Yes?"

"I don't know it all, Merelene. A man don't know it all. If he knew it all before he started, he wouldn't start."

His left hand strayed to his heart; the effort cost him. He rested his palm flat on his bony chest. "This . . ." He patted himself. "This brought me back as much as anything. I didn't want to depart this vale before I had looked at some things. You and the boys, and what I was doing here, all those years ago when I was a young man and strong and in the bloom of youth. So I called Roark one day and he told me they were trying to take the boy. I couldn't let them do that to you." She knew he would go on now. She gave his hand the gentle pressure it needed.

"I looked at things. I saw the lawyer, and I saw Larup's and I saw Roark Drawdy, right after I came back. Oh, I was around a while before I saw you. They all seemed the same to me. Even with the passage of those years, they seemed the same. This place has been lost to the world, Merelene, do you know that? And maybe that's good. What I know of the world, some say it's a lot, *Fortune* says so; what I know tells me it has no mercy for what it misplaces. When I came back it was all the same, in a way, but you, I could see it the minute I walked into your house, what used to be our house, I could see it immediately: you were different, standing there in your wet nightgown which I known what it meant, and the boy asleep with the breath of disaster coming and going from his mouth. I could see it just like that; you were different. You had something I didn't have. All my toing and froing, and getting and spending could never give it to me, what you had. I could see it, and maybe you had it all along. Did you, Merelene, and I never known it?" He watched her now, from wide eyes, and what could she say?

She remembered him at the spring, saying Swinford was the same, needing to say it. She considered how people changed in a forgotten town like Swinford, a place where they could hide in their earliest selves if they chose to. She did not know whether to measure change by what she had lost or shed from her like the skin of a snake, or by what she had taken on with the years. Suddenly it seemed an important question, loss and gain. What did she have now that she hadn't owned sixteen years ago? She owed nobody money, owned a job, and some sticks of furniture in a falling-down house. A man wanted her and another wanted her back after throwing her away, and she shared one son with the army and another with the State of Florida. A woman lost her girlhood and gained a man. She lost her selfish sleep and gained the grace of children. Were these transactions in her favor? Now she possessed her independence, preserved by abandonment, enforced by her loneliness in this town, and its superstitious fear of Roland. And she loved the town, the woods and waters that fed and held it. Loving it, and yet living against it, had become her life. To refuse it somehow every day had become her meaning.

Mayfield was waiting for her answer. She knew what he wanted her to say, and it was part of the truth. "I had you. It was all I wanted for a very long time."

He smiled at this. She remembered this smile, of simple pleasure. She had seen it a few times, and would have seen it more, had it not been smiled in the dark. Maybe having it again was enough for his coming back.

His face clouded, letting go the smile. "The world is a cruel place, Merelene. I learned it was." He drummed his fingers lightly on his chest. "I have this heart to show for it. I came here to find out if there was decent things and goodness here. I thought I known them in you, and I run away because I couldn't live up to them, and I came back, before it was too late, didn't I, to see were they still in their place. Are they?"

He looked at her with pain and seriousness and wonder in his face, as though at some saintly vision. She blushed. What could she say to this? She, who only lived from day to day as best she could, trying to get by and let others do the same. She said, "I'll agree with one thing. The world I know would rather see a person confirmed in stupidity and vice, than suspect him of decency and never know for sure." She looked at the door of his hospital room, at the polished hallway where even now she could hear the dry rustle of whispering voices. "The world I know has to find out."

He nodded, his wasted head barely disturbing the starched white pillow. He seemed to listen to her as to an oracle. She was embarrassed. "Mayfield," she said, her hand giving his a hard squeeze, "I can't tell you the Big T truth. I don't know it."

"You do, Merelene, it's in you." He looked away from her, to the bare wall, then the window and she heard him mutter, "For the truth is not in them."

She let him rest for a space. She wanted knowledge too. Their marriage, she realized now, had foundered on the lack of it, but she knew she must try not to hurt him. She sensed him ready for anything, even to let this world go and learn the next one.

She told him about her life after he had gone, how it had been to go down and down and down, as in a dream, reaching for a bottom that was always further down, and never reaching it, and knowing from this that she could rise.

She told him about the life of a discarded woman in a small town. There were things that could still bring tears to her eyes when she spoke of them, and things she could not speak of at all. Times when strange men came to her door dressed for a night out and already drunk and told her they had her name and address from so-and-so down at Larup's or from Tom somebody on the other side of the river, and saying so, as though to know where she lived were enough, stuck a boot in the door so that she couldn't slam it, and be done with them. She had spit in a few faces, and had learned to keep half a broom handle by the door.

They were men she saw on the street in daylight, who did not meet her eye, or did with a great show of respect and a big wink. She hated them for believing what they believed, not about her, but about the world she shared with them, and she wondered, always wondered, with a grinding worry, what they had heard about her, and where they had heard it.

All this she told him, and he took it into his wide eyes, his head making its small dent in the starched pillow. She said what she said as she had to say it, with harsh language or in wonder, and he took it as he had to—as knowledge. For all she knew it cut him deeply. If it did, he did not show it. They were beyond the place of recrimination.

She told him about the boys, each a different story, each her heart's life and torment. She looked so closely at him when she began the story of Roland, told how she had managed through the years with a little boy who walked away followed by a dog, who never tired of the same toys because he did not grow older, who watched television as though in its lunacy were things only he could divine, whose pronouncements, occasional and oracular, were the words of the masters of ceremonies in the black box he stared at all day. Roland, she told him, was the only one of them who had truly received the world's mercy. He did not have to know, did not have to get older, did not have to worry. He took baths, but was never dirty. Her voice changed as she told him this; she did not know what Roland suffered in his new circumstances. She told him she was worried. He looked at her and said, "Your worries are over, Merelene. I have told you that. It's only money you need."

It was not only money. It was the reversal of a commitment to a state institution she needed. And, she realized as she sat looking into the eyes of a rich man, it was Roland's good name she wanted back. That comical thing, his good name. It was for his innocence, whatever it was and wherever in him it dwelt, that she feared.

She said, "Mayfield, I hope you didn't run away from me, and leave your sons and what we made with each just for the sake of money."

He colored a bit with this, and looked way, his eyes narrowing in a way they had not done this entire day. "Money is not evil, Merelene. Think of the times you could have put a little money between you and your trouble. I went away because I couldn't live up to what was here. You're a hard woman in your way, Merelene. Maybe that's what you can learn from me. Even when you were a little girl of seventeen and I was the old man of twenty-one—imagine it, me a man of twenty-one thinking I had seen and done it all. Even in those days, there was something very hard in you. I could not always give the best, and it frightened me. I was inventing myself every day to your specifications and failing, always falling short."

"Why didn't you tell me? I never thought you fell short, except in little things, things that didn't mean much at all. How could we have gone on years with this between us and you never said anything. I hate it that I didn't know you better."

"You see," he said. He seemed to grow smaller in the bed, his limbs floating on the white counterpane as though he might any moment rise into the air. "It's knowledge. Now you're beginning to see. Why didn't we know how to talk? Why does it come only now?"

She shook her head. Who knew the answer? She didn't. He had never given her the chance to change. This she would always hold against him.

There was a long space in which she felt almost comfortable with him, almost as though she fit again. He stared up into the room and his eyes didn't blink and his voice, when he spoke, was low and soft and scared. "There was one night, Merelene, when I wanted to talk to you. Something terrible happened and I had to talk to you. But I didn't. I don't know why I didn't. All I needed to do was reach across a foot of mattress ticking and you were there but I couldn't do it."

She felt her own fear taking her, and the mystery of their long, unbroken connection across the years. "What time was that, Mayfield? What night?"

"I don't know," he said, "a long time ago." She was

afraid he would stop. She held his hand hard and passed to
it her hope that he would go on. He was silent for a long
time, then he said, "It was just before . . . I left. Yes, I
did, I left. I might as well say it. Why is it still hard to say?
It was a month or a few weeks before I left. It was one
night very late. I was in his room, and I was talking to
him. I must have been crazy. I know I was crazy those
nights, maybe for a whole year, maybe for years after-
wards. But that night, I was talking to him, and trying to
get him to answer me, and lo, he did. He did answer me,
and I thought, Great God, glory and mercy be Thine, and
mine in Thy sight, because here they came, the words out
of his sleeping mouth. I don't remember what he said, and
then they stopped, and that was all and it was just one
more goddamned dirty trick on Mayfield Durham. And I
was in hell, Merelene. And I went to the room where you
were sleeping and I got down beside you and I wanted to
speak and I couldn't. I couldn't wake you up and say the
things in my crazy head. So I just lay there full of that
dirty trick until it was too much for me. Until it *was* me. I
was dirt, just dirt, and I had to get out of there. And I . . .
I . . ."

The tears rolled from his wounded blue eyes, and he lay
staring at the ceiling as she held his hand, stroking it,
sending him the messages of that night when he had not
touched her and she had not touched him.

Finally, she told him. "Mayfield, he said, 'Daddy's up
the tower.' " His hand tightened on hers with the old
strength for an instant, and the pain in his face was an-
cient, but then his grip eased and he smiled at her, and it
was a smile that lasted until she left him to sleep.

On the fifteenth day of his illness, a day when he seemed
better by the little bit she had come to expect every day, a
day when they talked as usual, and said useful things, a
day when she felt she could take away with her another

small piece of the puzzle, she got up to leave him, kissed him good-bye in the soft, sexless way she had learned with him, giving a kiss that was more like a word than anything else, a little bit of knowledge, and went out to the hall to tell the nurse when she would be back the next day.

She drove home thinking of him in a way not dark and fraught with anxious anger for the first time in sixteen years, thinking of all they had shared in these two weeks, which was, in many ways more than they had shared in ten years of married life, thinking of these things and of her plans for the future, of all the more she hoped to learn, she parked her car in the driveway and walked into the house to the ringing phone. Wearily, she picked it up expecting the world at the other end, the world of her work with the lawyer, and her obligations to this house and its upkeep, and all the trivial and usual that had been suspended since she had stood over Mayfield in the lawyer's dooryard at last knowing what he had meant when his tongue had slipped, calling her a respectable widow. It was Dr. Selfridge on the other end. Mayfield was dead.

He had died of his heart just after she had left, not alone, thank God, for the nurse, Marise Dowdy, had come to the sound of his thrashing in the bed. And had not died, she found she was relieved to know, with any prolonged agony of the flesh—who knew what it had taken for his spirit to be lifted from him? Dr. Selfridge told her Mayfield's last words. "I've got something to tell her."

Clinging with his last strength to Marise Dowdy's hand, he had spoken these words. So, Merelene knew he had still been struggling with it, the way she would always struggle until her own heart quit. She was sad, sad as she listened to the rest of what Dr. Selfridge said, sad that Mayfield had gone off again, without knowing.

Twenty-three

Mayfield was buried simply in the Warrington family plot. Merelene and the lawyer, and Dr. Selfridge, and the Reverend Tillman put him in the ground with little show of sorrow, and with this reading:

The slave does not continue in the house for ever; the son continues for ever. So if the Son makes you free, you will be free indeed . . . and you will know the truth, and the truth will make you free.

Afterward, she went home with the lawyer and sat in his front parlor and accepted a tall glass of ten-year-old bourbon. The lawyer didn't drink. She was not certain why he didn't. Perhaps this was the beginning of the new dispensation. She would have the grace to take a little of what gave him pleasure, and he would have the grace to take a little less of it. He would believe.

He sat watching her put the whiskey down in gulps and

said, "Easy now, Merelene. It's not water." She nodded her head at him, wide-eyed with the blasting chemicals in her brain, and kept taking the big gulps. She had tried so hard to listen these last days, had inclined her every fiber and bone to the mouth of Mayfield Durham, hoping for the truth, had lent every spark her brain possessed to the problem of him, and now she wanted her consciousness canceled for an unspecified time. How much time-out was in this glass she held?

When she had finished it, she took another, shorter one, and found the taste better the second time. The lawyer joined her, but poured himself a very meager portion. He had been watching her from the chair by the fire, from under his brows, but now he crossed the room, and sat by her on the old horsehair sofa and began to pet her. All he said was, "Go ahead."

She had no inkling what he meant. Go ahead? Then, as the last of the whiskey went to the root of her tongue, she gagged a little and felt the mighty upwelling of her sorrow. It came from the pit of her stomach, it forced its way downward and lodged in the dark, sorry bowl of her womb. It coursed in her like an impaling fire. She felt it force wide her knees and come forth screaming.

She writhed on the sofa beside him, only a little aware of his tender petting. She moved against him so hard that she feared they both might fall to the floor in the heap of uselessness she knew them to be. Her sorrow turned and turned in her guts stirring so cruelly that she was not aware of what she was saying until she heard the lawyer's answer. She was calling Mayfield's name, calling him here in this house where she had given herself to the man who sat beside her now. The lawyer's only answer was his plaintive "Go ahead. Cry to me."

She flung her arms around his neck and held him until she was certain Mayfield had come. She watched his poor soul circle above them, rising, always rising. She held to the lawyer, her anchor in this world, and after a space she felt her womb empty of fire, her knees no longer pinioned open, her breast loose from the fist of her grief, and she held to the lawyer now in sorrow for what she had let him see. Even as she sobbed and sobbed, released by the whiskey and purified of her last hope of Mayfield, she hoped that the lawyer held in his arms what he wanted.

She stayed in his house that night. He took her upstairs and laid her down in his bed, helping her out of the black dress she had bought for the burial. She was still drunk when he carefully pulled the black dress from her dangling limbs, and all she could say to him was, "Burn it."

"Yes," he replied, and she never saw the dress again.

As she was falling asleep, she said, "Is my car in the yard?"

"Yes," he told her.

"Shit," she said. "The whole town." She was ashamed for caring, but habits died hard. He petted her, using a terrible delicacy. He said, "Never mind. I'll take care of it."

He left her for a time. She supposed he had gone to take care of it, and went to sleep wondering how. She awoke in the night and threw her head to the side in time to keep the vomit from soiling the pillow. His hand, out of the dark, was on her face, petting her. She moved to it when the retching ceased and she knew she would not die. She fell asleep again, to the coarse chafing of a warm wet cloth on her face.

When next she awoke, morning was a gray wash at the window. He sat by her, his face a haggard blur. Her eyelids had stuck together with the matter of crying, and she reached up and used her fingers to open them. She saw him better, but still blurred by sleeplessness and his worry. "How are you?"

She nodded, yes.

"Want to clean up?"

She knew she was a rotten thing, burnt out inside, her mouth seared by whiskey and vomit, her eyes dulled by the glare of all they had seen these last hours. She made herself rise, conquering a wave of nausea and, as he supported her, walked to the bathroom. She lay only a little better in a warm bath. At the door, he asked, "Do you need me?" She wondered what he would have done had she said yes. She told him, with a slow shaking of the head, that she could manage.

When she was out again, and clean, and had washed the grim stare from her face, she heard him in the hallway with the jingle of silver on a tray. She could not move fast to cover her nakedness. To move fast would be to die here. She only stood by the bed, stark white and pulled by the gravity of illness toward the floor. He smiled as he struggled through the doorway with the tray. "Coffee?" he asked. He kept his eyes to her face.

She shook her head no. Her stomach would accept nothing.

He put the tray down. It was full morning at the window. She reached out to him with heavy arms, supporting herself by the bed at her thighs. He came to her and she enfolded him, and felt him grow hard against her. His fingers imprinted her bare back. She whispered in his ear, "Thank you for taking care of me."

He mumbled, "Yes."

"I knew you would." She was still in a kind of delirium; her voice sounded to her like a child's. She asked him to get in the bed with her and hold her.

"Are you sure?"

"I'm sure."

They lay in the narrow bed, and his hard question pressed at her thighs. She did not think she could answer it, at least not in the way she wanted to. Everything about him, the gentle petting he gave her, delicate as though he learned more and more of gentleness as he stroked her, contradicted the pressure at her thighs. Finally, she said, "Please, go ahead," hoping she could do what she wanted to do now. She moved to the farthest edge of the bed, taken by vertigo, fearing she might fall off, feeling the awful lurch in her stomach. Sweat broke on her brow, and she waited for the moment to pass. When she felt better, she indicated with her hands that she wanted him to lie on his back.

He lay as she directed him to. She found the place on him they had learned together, fitting the mirror to its image, and slowly, without heat, pierced herself. She wanted to move him in where the impaling fire had been. She wanted him to put out the last wisp of that other life. After a space, what she had hoped for came to them. He petted her and called her precious, thick in her, until they both grew fierce and forgot.

She stayed in his house three days, and in the evening of the third day, he asked her not to leave, ever. He said it would mean something to him if she did not go back to her own place, except to bring things she needed. He was not certain why. She honored his wish. The more she understood her life, the more she seemed to violate the town's sense of what was right.

She loved the lawyer many times after the first (and she did think of it as the first time now) without taking precautions against conception. Each time he released himself in her, shuddering and stiffening for long seconds, his face grim with the seriousness of it, she pressed as close to the point of him as she could; she had the mad thought that he could release himself directly into her womb, taking no chances. This was their new bond, and he knew it. As they lay together afterward, she tried to give back the sweetness he had given her during her long awful night.

* * *

One day he told her that Mayfield had left a will. He had written it in the hospital, by hand, and had designated it his only valid will. He had left instructions that it was to be given to Enos Sawyer, Esq., in the event of his death. The will, the lawyer told her, would almost certainly be contested by Mayfield's stockholders, and various corporate geniuses whose name was legion. In it, Mayfield left an empire to Roland Durham.

The lawyer explained to her Mayfield's trouble with the Securities and Exchange Commission and the IRS. "The empire," he said, "is not exactly founded upon the hard rock. Your former husband was a man of no little power of personality, but not sophisticated in the ways of commerce."

What it amounted to was this: Mayfield could get up in front of a roomful of people in a Holiday Inn somewhere at the junction of two interstate highways and persuade them to buy cosmetics franchises, but he couldn't keep ahead of the federal government. The government called him a fraud.

She asked him to tell her straight: was Mayfield a fraud? He looked at her straight and delivered himself of a legal opinion. "It's not that simple. It's a matter of interpretation. The law is a game and a man like Mayfield, with a lot of expensive help, might have played it successfully for years."

Trying to make it simpler for him, she asked, "Was he hurting anybody?"

"That," he said, frowning to a great legal depth, "I can't tell you. I haven't studied the thing sufficiently."

"Are you going to study it?"

"I guess I'll have to, won't I?"

"No."

"What do you mean, no?"

"Roland doesn't want the money. *Or* need it."

When he smiled at her, then shook his head, she knew it

was both too simple to accept, and exactly what he had hoped she would say.

"In any case," he told her, "that will's going to be in probate for months, maybe years. And I'm not enough lawyer to do much more than watch the show."

Twenty-four

One Sunday not long after Mayfield's passing, the lawyer sat across the breakfast table from her sporting more than his usual morning optimism. He had morning and afternoon and evening optimism, he told her, now that she stayed with him. They were eating eggs she had scrambled, and biscuits she had dropped and bacon and ham gravy left over from the night before, a big country breakfast, and he stuffed himself and beamed. He loved to have her cooking for him. Secretly, she knew he was just about as good a cook as she was, and she had plans to hand him a saucepan before too long, but for now, she was happy to oblige. She was putting Woman into this house with a vengeance, to show him that she could expel from its every corner all that sadness and doubt with which he had sheltered so many years. She couldn't do much with the lives that hung in frames on the walls, she told him; they had already been lived and were best forgotten about, but if she dusted Old Colonel Patch's picture once in a while, she was likely to blink both eyes at it and whisper, "See!"

This morning as he stoked the furnace with eggs and

biscuits and gravy and drank strong coffee, she said, "I don't want to camp out with no fat man."

He laughed and winked at her. "Don't worry, Merelene, I plan to get enough exercise upstairs to keep down the weight."

She called him a nasty old thing and he cackled like a sea gull.

When they had finished a second cup of coffee, watching the sun make solid its hold on the landscape, dispelling the dew, and chasing the birds and squirrels into shady places, he said, "Come on. Get a jacket."

She said, "A jacket? It's going to be hot in an hour and miserable in two."

"Never mind that, Merelene. Where we're going, the weather is cool."

She didn't ask him where they were going—underground, or to high ground, or into somebody's deep freeze. She knew better. He wanted to surprise her and she had to let him. It was a strain, indulging his little boy whims, but it came with the territory.

When they took the narrow little road which wound uphill to the pasture where Roark Drawdy landed his Colombian Airlines flights, she knew where they were going, and she tapped him on the thigh and when he looked over, shook her head emphatically. No.

He only smiled, but she could see he was worried. She knew how badly he wanted it, but somehow, just couldn't see herself thundering through the blue air (was it blue up there, or invisible like it was down here?) with him in a red airplane.

When they pulled up at the shed, Delvin Sweet emerged, and Pissant followed, her nose to the heels of Delvin's shoes. In the two or three visits they had made here since the first one, Merelene had mended her fences with Pissant, though she still couldn't bring herself to call the dog by name. Delvin Sweet was tired, she could see, and out of sorts; his face was pale and sweating, even in this still-cool morning. When they stood close to him, she could smell last night's good times, redistilled and powerful, coming from his pores. She stepped back and moved upwind, and reached down to the dog, who accepted her attentions.

"Delvin," the lawyer was saying, "I want you to make ready the chariot. I'm gone take Merelene up for a bracer." He was pulling on a leather glove and his hands were shaking.

Standing by, bent over the dog, she just shook her head again emphatically. No. She didn't care to argue with him in front of Mr. Delvin Sweet, whiskey factory, but she was not getting into that machine.

They stood watching as Delvin looked at some things under the removable metal plates that housed the engine, and as he walked around the plane releasing the knots in the nylon cords that held it to the big metal stakes driven into the earth. He jerked the two big cross sections of a cypress stump from in front of the wheels and turned to the lawyer. "Contact."

The lawyer laughed uproariously at this, and Merelene could not see for the life of her (which she hoped to preserve by remaining rooted where she was) what was so funny.

The lawyer turned to her with a look of supplication and she fought it with every hook and eye of her resistance. No.

He decided to resort to language. He stepped close to her, put his hands on her shoulders. But she stared past him, with the coldest look she could make, at Delvin Sweet, until he took her point and disappeared into the dark under the shed. Then she looked into the lawyer's eyes.

"Merelene, it would mean a lot to me. I ain't going to kill us, I promise."

"Enos, I'm afraid of that thing." She shuddered in his hands even in the warm morning air. "It's just that simple."

He wilted a little. He knew about fear.

They looked into each other's eyes for a space. He didn't know what to do. At last, he brightened. "Tell you what. You watch me this first time. If I come back more or less unscathed, then maybe you'll feel differently?"

She looked at him, nodding yes, then as he turned away, no, again. Yes, you go ahead; no, I will not feel differently.

He addressed himself to the wooden platform Del Sweet had used to work on the engine, pulling it around so that he could climb up to the place where he would sit. She watched him, thinking: God almighty, what arrogance! He has a hard time walking through a doorway with a tray of dishes in his hands and he is going to crawl into the middle of all this red metal and glass and rubber and gasoline and make it fly?

When he was in the seat, settling himself, strapping himself in, he put on a funny old leather helmet and a pair of goggles like the kind swimmers used for the English Channel. The glass in them was smoked, and she thought he looked like some strange subaqueous beast when he looked down at her and waved her back. She stepped away a few feet and immediately the blades of the propeller started to turn, slowly, then quickly, with a sound like rifle bullets ricocheting from rocks. When he had it going, with black, then hot, clear smoke belching from the exhaust pipes and its living body vibrating with the strain of holding down that engine, he sat and revved it like a kid at a traffic light. She could see him looking at the instruments and grinning like a fool. And she thought, arrogant fool.

He gestured her back with a gloved hand, then waved to her and then stared ahead. The flaps on the wings and in the tail moved up and down experimentally, and she noticed Delvin Sweet had come out of the shed to stand and watch, his face pure concentration now, as though *he* were flying this thing. He took a step forward and shouted something through cupped hands, but the lawyer did not hear him, did not even look down at them through the noise as solid as the earth where she stood. Finally, Delvin Sweet gave up and just waved one hand loosely at the big ensemble, man and machine, and stood there with his hands stiff at his sides, all pure concentration. Then the thing began to roll.

It moved at first as the propeller had moved, too slowly to be taken seriously, and then very fast, and as it turned to go the straightest way across the short, bumpy pasture, her face was spattered by grit and a wind snatched at her skirts and pressed them to her stomach and thighs.

She had never before considered the lay of the land as she did now. The pasture slanted westward, and in it there were little hillocks and sudden holes; how in the world was he going to bounce this thing into the air without turning it over or shaking it to pieces beneath him.

When the noise had abated, Delvin Sweet stepped close and answered her question. "He's gone taxi down that end and take off directly over our heads. *Then* you see something."

She waited to see something, terrified. A rock had made itself in her middle, in the same place where children were conceived and love was felt, and she knew, as she watched the little red plane swivel around at the far end of this pasture, that this was his homecoming.

Even before she heard the roar, she saw a gust of chaff blow backward from the redwings, and knew he had given it its head.

Delvin Sweet, standing in that pure concentration beside her, murmured to no one, "He's done put his foot in it now."

She did not know what he meant, did not care. The red

thing was hurtling toward them, getting bigger all the
time, its front end chewing the warm morning air, and all
the while she could see, just at the rim of the big silver
wheel which was the propeller, the leathered crown of the
lawyer's head. In thought, she saw him too, as the thing
rushed at her, pure terror and a wild grin competing for
his face.

The sound of the engine grew louder and then, it
seemed impossibly fast, the thing had separated from the
dusty field with a lurch and wobble and a slip to the side
and was bearing down on her and she felt she should
break for the tin shed and would have had she not felt the
tension go out of Delvin Sweet. The plane gained altitude
and cleft the air thirty feet above their heads with a roar
that furrowed the very earth between them, and she saw
in the last instant, as she turned and ran after it, the lawyer's gloved hand raised in the air. He waved as he powered over the treetops.

Twenty-five

They were married by Judge Harry Beldon, one of the lawyer's confreres, as he said it, in a fifteen-minute concession to propriety in the judge's chambers in Chiefland. Merelene could never again wholly embrace the institution of marriage. She had been ill-served by it. She could embrace the lawyer, and did, in front of Judge Beldon, and Dr. Selfridge who had stood up for the lawyer, and Louise Bates, almost unable to stand so copious were her tears.

The lawyer wore his best three-piece suit, the one he reserved for court appearances, and she "was resplendent," as *The County News Leader* later said, in an ivory linen suit whose jacket was boxy and white pumps, and carrying a bouquet of daisies. The lawyer had insisted that she wear his mother's pearls.

Dr. Selfridge rocked back and forth on his crepe soles, but did not jingle the change in his pockets until after the vows had been spoken. He was taking one of his rare days off, and let it be known that he was going to get a snootful for the first time in over two years; would anyone fill a snoot wit him? The lawyer assured him that as soon as the sufficient was taken care of, the necessary would begin.

Louise Bates, who connected drinking in all its forms
with her own early errors, blushed at this, but after the
ceremony, when they had "repaired," as the lawyer put it,
to his house, she took a cup with the rest of them. Merelene had set up a trestle table under the big live oak tree
in the dooryard, and they sat in the shade drinking cham-
pagne and eating pâté de foie gras and smoked salmon and
caviar on Norwegian flatbread. All of these things (which
were just seafood to Merelene), the lawyer had told her he
wanted, and so she had got them for him. And they were
fine. And it was a fine afternoon. The lawyer became
drunker than she had ever seen him before, and climbed
the tabletop where he stood, supported by Dr. Selfridge
on one side, and herself on the other, to declaim, "O, my
love is like a red, red rose," or as much of it as he could
recall in this condition, rolling his harsh music to the tops
of the live oaks where the first September breezes were
blowing. And Dr. Selfridge was moved a rare distance
from the practice of medicine, and gave a red-faced and
wheezy version of Frost's "Directive," a recitation which
ended with these beautiful words: "Here are your waters
and your watering place. Drink and be whole again beyond confusion." After much prompting, Louise sang
"Stand by Your Man." The lawyer called it the best a cap-
pella rendering he had ever heard, and a real cornpone
classic. Merelene was asked for something. But she had
only her own poetry, and it only came when it would.
And besides, she said, all of this is *for* me. And standing
there under the trees, before that big house which was
hers now too, and with these people she loved, she felt big
and full. Love was in her again.

The lawyer took a long nap that afternoon and woke up
shivering with what he called the fantods. In plainer
terms, she told him, it was a hangover. But she did not,
could not, scold him, not on this day. He lay with her in
the bed which was now theirs, sick and frightened, and

she was the only one who knew it would go away. It was a reprise of that time he had comforted her and she told him so. I will always love you for that, she told him. But she knew, she could see it in his face, that *love*, the word, meant nothing at a time like this. What he wanted was her cool fingers on his brow, the knowing that she would do for him as he had done for her.

Later, he came to her. Late at night, after she had moved to a bed in the guest room, he came cold sober to take her in his hands with a fierce hunger that frightened her awake. His breath in the darkness as fierce not with whiskey but with the heat of his love, and she could see nothing. She took him onto her, helping him find the places that fit, and they combined their flesh for the first time as man and wife. Lying in the darkness, they moved like some insane and transcending engine, until, for the first time, she could not find the place where was drawn the end of her and the beginning of him. And later, the words that fell deep with her into the well of her sleep, were these: He believes. At last, he believes. I have made him believe.

She walked to the sound of the saw. It was a high whine among the high pines. It was a sound she remembered from her childhood. The stone was quarried near Ocala, some of it, or shipped in by rail to Chiefland and carried here by truck to be cut and shaped by the hand of Billy Hinmuth. As a child, fishing this stretch of the river, she had seen the place where the white powder from the stone cutter's saw fell into the dark water on Billy's bank. It wandered downstream, thinning and slowly sinking, serpentine, until there was no trace. A little girl, she had stared at the rows of stones in Billy's place of business thinking it a graveyard, thinking of the souls slowly vanishing, thinking, I will thin and sink in the dark element and go forever from sight. Someday.

Standing now in Billy's yard, she watched the litter of half-carved stones, broken bits, mistakes, and a few displayed works, and thought, the child had not been far from right. Billy Hinmuth, cutting stone on the banks of the Suwannee River, his diamond saw a high keening in the high pines, was making philosophy out of rock.

She waited outside, watching the river and listening to the music in the trees, until the sound of the saw stopped and Billy walked out, covered with sweat and clapping white powder from his hands. He came smiling. "Morning, Miss Merelene."

She smiled back at him. He had not aged much since she had bought the stone for her father's grave. She said, "Billy, have you been expecting me?"

His face colored a little. He wiped his brow and grinned in a pained way. "I always known you to take care of the little things, Miss Merelene."

She nodded at this. It was not like her to leave last things undone. If a woman had to have a reputation, let it be this one.

"What can you show me?"

"I haven't got much in stock right now, Miss Merelene, but, you know, I can show you the books. You can sit in the office where it's cool and take your time and look through there and find just exactly what you want."

She looked into the dark cavern where the diamond saw blade was cooling. She wondered what color it was when it was hot and then it cooled. "Billy, bring me the book and I'll sit out by the water and look at it."

Billy nodded and turned, his overalls raining white flakes.

With the book in her hand, she sat turning pages of pen-and-ink drawings, hundreds there were, of stones and monuments and marble angels and catafalques and the words written on them, her mind in a dull worried heat, until the sound of the river and the smell of the river and the way it stretched its long neck down as far as she could see to the south; until these things came between her and the book and she stood and walked back up to the noise of Billy's saw. She waited again until he walked out, removing his goggles. She said, "Billy, I want a simple stone. I'll leave it up to you about the size. Not too big, and here's what you can write on it." She took a pen from her purse and in the margin of Billy's book, wrote: "Mayfield Durham, 1925–1973. By the rivers of Babylon, there he lay down."

Billy squinted at it, and looked up and produced the pained smile he had shown to thirty years of Swinford's grief. "I'll sure do it, Miss Merelene."

Twenty-six

Holding her handbag against her stomach, she stood in a copse of young pine trees watching figures swim in the smoked glass of a greenhouse. They moved as though in the waters of a dream. As the torso which she knew was Roland's passed from one pane to another and slowly stooped to unload its burden, she saw it warp and straighten, then warp again. Dr. Reid's voice on the telephone this morning had been straight. "I think he's ready for you to come for a visit." Roland, she said, had adapted well to Noble's Manor.

They had kept her away from him the first two weeks, saying that he needed time. The purse she held now to the hot bowl of her stomach held in all her longing to see, hold him. She knew she must soon move and she feared her legs would turn in revolt. Dr. Reid had left her where she was standing, saying, "Go ahead. He's inside. Take a break with him, but don't keep him from his work too long."

With a feeling of evisceration, she made herself go to the doorway, and stand on the threshold, shifting to the cover of a potted schefflera to watch him from concealment. He was with another, smaller boy, and the two, by the look of things, were transferring seedlings from small pots to larger ones. She focused immediately on Roland's hands. For the first time in her knowledge of him, it seemed they had found a definitive use. His hands were large, but soft. He had done little with them in his life but turn the knobs of a television and pet a dog. The last time she had seen them they had been stained by tobacco smoke. Now they seemed calm, strong, capable with the tender young plants. Occasionally, as she watched, he corrected the actions of the younger boy's hands. He lay an injured seedling in his palm and straightened it, mumbling something she could not hear. What he said did not matter. It was the way his hands healed, the way they taught the other boy's fingers; there was something in this that mattered very much. Standing in the doorway, she realized that in a small way, Dr. Reid had made Roland matter.

She felt that she had got what she had come for. There was no need to interrupt. She could never know if Roland was happy, or even that happiness mattered. She saw that he was absorbed, content here in this work. She continued to watch the lovely, sober rhythm of his movements until it became like a drug and she was soothed and no longer felt the hot constriction in her muscles. She thought she might turn to go, that this was too lovely to interrupt, when a young man appeared from the long run of the greenhouse carrying a tray of tomato seedlings. He could not have been more than twenty-five years old, and wore his hair in a long ponytail. His cutoff khaki trousers had a tangled fringe that shook at his thighs as he walked and a blue work shirt was knotted at his waist. His face was fiery red with his exertion and with a terrible affliction of risings. And yet he had a calm and happy way about him. He set the tray down beside Roland's kneeling figure and said, "Here's some more, Roland. You two can go ahead and do these."

Roland did not look up. The young man waited, wiping his brow on his blue sleeve. The smaller boy stopped working and looked at the young man standing over them. Finally, Roland raised his eyes from the plants. "That's a roger," he said. "Over and out."

The young man with the acne sores smiled, but briefly, and turned to go back in the direction from which he had come. Merelene stepped forward and called after his retreating figure, "Excuse me?"

He turned, smiling, a collection of dazzling white teeth in the angry swelling of his face. "Hello."

She said, "I'm Merelene Sawyer. Roland is . . ."

Roland was instantly next to her, a dog look of solemn adoration in his face. She took him in her arms and he pawed her with black potting soil and said, "Mudder!" She remembered the time they had greeted each other at the State Center. How he had sat in the bay window, composed as the painting of the young man in a city park, normal. Here, he looked agreeably strange, passionate about his plants, a little off-balance but enjoying himself. It was all better. Their embrace was an embarrassment to no one. The little boy watched with unabashed interest, still holding a tomato seedling. The young man with the red face smiled like Jesus Christ on the back of a revival fan. It was the most genuine smile Merelene had seen since Mayfield had awakened to her in the county clinic.

She held Roland at arm's length and looked at him. He *had* put on weight and the weight did him no harm that she could see. He was ruddy and clean of limb and fully fleshed. Roland never really smiled; the closest he came to it was to bare his teeth in a way that was solemn and a little unnerving. It was the look he gave her now. She showed him her brightest grin, the one she had always tried to teach him, but he did not make it back at her and she knew he never would. She turned to the one in charge. "May I take him for a short walk?"

The boy nodded, "Yes, ma'am."

She turned Roland by the shoulder and steered him ahead of her through the door. Once outside, there was no doubt where they would go. When they reached the riverbank, they stood side by side, and she felt her expensive new shoes sinking in the wet sand and did not care a whit. She said, "Look, Roland, there's . . ." but she could not finish, for she had nothing in her mind to show him. What was in her heart was the world: there, there is the world, Roland. It is ours again. He turned to her. She shook her head, never mind, but he was still at her with searching eyes. The sun was bright on the water, but clouds were churning up from the southeast in the great counterclockwise curve of the hurricane season. They were low-flying gray flannel airships, the exhalations of all the troubles of the Gulf Stream and the Windward Passage. Standing there on the bank in a light breeze with Roland content and solemn against her side, she heard an engine, a small, persistent sawing among the gray clouds. It made her think of the lawyer. For all she knew, it *was* him up there in the big blood-red project, cutting the seam he loved in all that dangerous air. And here she stood below, on the bank of the river, in the place where the furry gray edge of the blue wheel touched earth. In her hands she held the flesh of her flesh and of Mayfield's too. She had lost him to disease, and then to the State, and now she had bargained his father's life to those gray clouds, and had him back again.